LADY LIAR

A Series of Senseless Complications
Book Five

Kate Archer

ARE YOU SIGNED UP FOR DRAGONBLADE'S BLOG?

You'll get the latest news and information on exclusive giveaways, exclusive excerpts, coming releases, sales, free books, cover reveals and more.

Check out our complete list of authors, too!

No spam, no junk. That's a promise!

Sign Up Here

www.dragonbladepublishing.com

Dearest Reader;

Thank you for your support of a small press. At Dragonblade Publishing, we strive to bring you the highest quality Historical Romance from some of the best authors in the business. Without your support, there is no 'us', so we sincerely hope you adore these stories and find some new favorite authors along the way.

Happy Reading!

CEO, Dragonblade Publishing

Additional Dragonblade books by Author Kate Archer

A Series of Senseless Complications
Lady Ferocity (Book 1)
Lady Graceless (Book 2)
Lady Impatience (Book 3)
Lady Dramatic (Book 4)
Lady Liar (Book 5)

A Very Fine Muddle
Romance Me, Viscount (Book 1)
Be Daring, Duke (Book 2)
Stand With Me, Earl (Book 3)
Sweep Me Up, Baron (Book 4)
Write for Me, Marquess (Book 5)
Convince Me, Viscount (Book 6)

A Series of Worthy Young Ladies
The Meddler (Book 1)
The Sprinter (Book 2)
The Undaunted (Book 3)
The Champion (Book 4)
The Jilter (Book 5)
The Regal (Book 6)

The Dukes' Pact Series
The Viscount's Sinful Bargain (Book 1)
The Marquess' Daring Wager (Book 2)
The Lord's Desperate Pledge (Book 3)
The Baron's Dangerous Contract (Book 4)
The Peer's Roguish Word (Book 5)
The Earl's Iron Warrant (Book 6)

PROLOGUE

THROUGH THE TIME-HONORED tradition of marrying them off, The Duke of Pelham had begun his efforts at unloading his seven daughters some years ago. He'd launched four of them out of the house, which left three to go. It really did seem as if he'd climbed a mountain and was now poised to gently drift down the other side to a comfortable landing, ending in the long-anticipated empty house.

Certainly, it must be a gentle drift and a soft landing. After all, he'd earned it ten times over. Never had a group of girls made so much trouble on their way to an altar. Letting loose a Bengal tiger, setting a house on fire, necessitating a chase across half of England, a kidnapping of the three-legged dog variety, and sufficient tears to drown half of London—it was enough to wear out even the most stalwart gentleman.

Number five was poised to launch and his dear Verity was an original sort of girl. He'd thought she'd leave behind her penchant for claiming to know things she most definitely did not know. She had not. But then, a young lady occasionally spouting nonsense could not cause too much trouble. It seemed to him that spouting off nonsense was one of the primary activities of young people. Or as Verity might phrase it: "It is the usual case of things, or so I've been told." Nobody had the first idea who might be telling her all these random cases of things.

On the bright side, the girl was pretty as a picture. Of all of his daughters, Verity most obviously had her mother's looks, with her dark hair and dark hazel eyes. Any young buck encountering Verity would probably not hear half of what she said on account of it. At least, that was the hope.

Whatever the case might be, he would gird his loins and do his duty. As the season marched ever closer, there *was* one thing that put a spring in his step. He was on the precipice of doing battle with his sister, Lady Marchfield, once more.

He had high hopes, and had been watching the post, to hear that Lady Misery would try another gambit to get a butler into his house. He would be fascinated to discover how his trusty housekeeper got the fellow out again. It had been a battle of wills for four years now, and his household had emerged victorious in every single one of those years.

London was littered with the dashed hopes and broken dreams of the various butlers having had the temerity to step through his doors, but that could not be helped. A duke must have his amusements.

CHAPTER ONE

A Remote Estate in the Dales, 1807

LADY VERITY NICOLET, fifth daughter of the Duke of Pelham, had gone along over the years feeling as if her older sisters were a wall of soldiers ahead of her. She would not have to face the *ton*, or face the idea of finding a husband, while she had a slew of older sisters in the house.

Serenity had been her last bulwark of defense, and now she was gone to Lord Thorpe's house. It was Verity's moment, but she was terrified to have a moment. Her youngest sister, Valor, had almost convinced her to refuse to go. Valor did not want her to leave, and Verity did not want to leave either.

Well, she *did* want to leave. She did wish for a family of her own. She desperately wished for children, and her own household to manage as she saw fit, but how could it be possible? She had too much to hide.

It was all well and good to have Winsome challenging her on her every idea, but Winsome never got too far with it. Somehow, Verity had been able to hide what needed to be hidden about herself—she was the stupidest of the Nicolet sisters. And not just by a little bit either. The truth was, the rest of them were rather clever and she was very, very stupid.

Her terrible secret had been close-held for so long that it could never be admitted to now. She knew next to nothing, though her sisters knew all sorts of things. This circumstance was caused by her utter lack of intellect. She could not read because she could not learn how to do it. Because she could not read, she was stuck only knowing what happened to be said around her. It was not nearly enough.

That brief period when they'd had a governess, Miss Pynchon, had revealed it to that lady. Miss Pynchon had sat her down on a number of occasions and tried to get somewhere with it. She'd got nowhere with it. She'd accused Verity of being lazy, of not trying very hard, though that was not the truth.

Those days in study under Miss Pynchon had been painful and terrifying and Verity was only grateful that the lady had not been employed long. They would be meant to be reading something, and Verity would bend over her book like she *was* reading and turn pages when Winsome turned pages. But then when she was questioned on the material, she had nothing to say, but for attempting to parrot something Winsome had said. She'd become a master at phrasing something said in a slightly different way.

Unbeknownst to anybody, she'd kept those books of Miss Pynchon's under her bed, long after that lady had departed. Verity had stared at the pages by candlelight, trying to take in what they said. Trying to make sense of them. It was not as if she did not know her alphabet. She did. It was not as if she could not concentrate on a word and understand it. She could. Usually. Eventually. It was not as if she did not wish to be educated and know things. She desperately did.

But a whole page of writing would defy her. The words would jumble and make themselves into patterns and words that made no sense. Her sisters could read, the whole world could read, but her mind seemed to lack the patience and determination for it and just threw the letters up in the air.

As a way round the problem, she was in the habit of convincing Winsome to read aloud, using the ruse that her sister had the best speaking voice. Verity invariably encouraged Winsome to pick out a book full of facts so she could learn something, but Winsome was forever throwing them aside to pick up some dreadful gothic novel.

Verity kept her ears open to pick up whatever facts she could from wherever she could. In a pinch, if she was not entirely sure of the veracity of a particular fact or opinion, she tacked on a demure—she'd heard it said, or she had been told, or that was her understanding. That way, if she were proved wrong, she might shift the blame onto whatever anonymous person she'd heard it from.

If she'd heard it from anyone.

Sometimes what she said just came from her own guesses at what must be right. At other times, she said things that were ridiculous or outrageous and she knew it, but her rising panic over being found out clouded her mind. In those moments, it was as if a fog had settled over her thoughts and absolutely anything might be said before she could stop herself.

She was hungry for knowledge, she wanted to know things, but everything known in the world was secreted away in books, and books were beyond her reach. And what was she to do as a married lady when she got letters? Scrawly handwriting was even worse than a book. She had begun to think she would have to claim there was something wrong with her eyesight that no spectacles could rectify. There *was* something wrong with her eyesight, but only for words. She could see a far fence astride her horse, but words defied her.

They would set off for London on the morrow and then she would only have days before she must show herself in society. Just now, she bent over a bit of embroidery that she got nowhere with. She never did, as she found the close work of a pattern almost as frustrating as a book. Winsome read from a typically ghoulish novel, using inflections for the various voices in it. The heroine was beginning to suspect that everybody she'd been talking to in the old castle where she'd been employed was actually dead, but for the skulking earl. But maybe he was dead too! Maybe the heroine herself was dead and didn't know it. Or if still alive, maybe she would be dead soon!

Mrs. Right was keeping an eye on Valor, no doubt afraid the story would give her nightmares. She would probably be correct. Valor had matured over the years, somewhat, but she was still subject to nightmares.

Verity looked out the drawing room windows at the rolling hills of the Dales. The calm of it, the predictably changing seasons, and the quiet, all soothed her. Maybe it was not too late to refuse to go to Town?

But then, how would she ever have her own family if she did not?

Her father came into the drawing room, waving a letter. "It's finally come, Mrs. Right," he said. "The gauntlet has been thrown down once more and the game is afoot."

The only person in the wide world who ever dared throw a gauntlet in the duke's direction was Lady Marchfield, and the gauntlet she was in the habit of throwing was a butler. Every season, she moved a butler into the duke's residence on Grosvenor Square in her effort to make the Nicolet household more regulated. Every season, Mrs. Right hatched a scheme to get them out. For her father, it was one of the primary entertainments of the season and he would not put a stop to it for the world.

Mrs. Right folded her arms in preparation for battle. "What, pray, does Lady Marchfield threaten us with this time?" she asked.

"It seems this time, she makes it a mystery," the duke said, laughing. "Listen to this."

Roland—

I suppose you imagine me beaten and retreating from the field after last year's events. Nothing could be further from the truth. I have redoubled my efforts to mold your household into something resembling well-bred. (Despite what my lord says. His opinion is it is hopeless.)

I have been working on a particular idea since last season. Do not imagine you will come out of this victorious. As well, you can tell that uncouth housekeeper you continue to employ that she is about to get a dose of her own medicine.

Your disgusted sister

"Oh dear, she did say…" Winsome said.

"Said what?" the duke asked.

"Well, last year, we were talking of Mr. Cremble's departure. I said I supposed she would give up the whole idea of trying to make us have a butler in Town. And she said if I knew what she was thinking, it would send a chill down my spine."

"A spine chill—she *did* say that! Are you frightened, Mrs. Right?" Valor asked.

"Not a bit of it," Mrs. Right said. "Your aunt will not find a butler to defeat me anywhere in this wide world, you can be assured of that."

"He does sound scary, though," Valor said.

"That's because he does not sound like anything at all, Val," the duke said. "She means to frighten us with the mysteriousness of it."

"It's working," Valor said, pulling Sir Galahad onto her lap. The little pug was happy to be of service and licked her face. Verity got the idea that her youngest sister had traded in her raggedy stuffed rabbit, Mrs. Wendover, for the comfort of the little dog.

Verity did not mind too much that there was to be another butler adventure in the house. It would take some eyes off her, and that was just what she wished for.

"What about you, Verity?" the duke asked. "Are you all aflutter about what's coming our direction by way of another butler?"

Verity shook her head. "No, Papa. I am certain our Mrs. Right will see him out the door quick enough. At least, that is the usual case of things."

Everyone nodded in approval. While Verity often did not know if her pronouncing something the usual case of things was correct, this definitely *was* the usual case of things.

HENRY FOSTER, BARON Wembly, regarded his fellow intellectuals at a meeting of The Royal Society. There had been a time not so long ago that he had thrilled to attend such meetings. To be admitted into the society and surrounded by men who shared his interest in advancing scientific understanding had seemed the pinnacle of everything he could wish for.

The thrill had begun to wane just a little bit, though. At the end of each season, all these learned men, including himself, would retreat to their estates to spend the months in study. He was happy to do it. He was content enough to write letters requesting notes from various volumes he did not possess, answer requests of the same, pore through the volumes he owned, and spend a lot of time…thinking.

However, recently his thinking had begun to take a turn. All those months of study were done very solitary. The days were not too terrible, he occupied his time in his library and riding round the estate on various matters. In the house, there was the constant bustle of staff going here and there and doing this or that. The nights were rather too quiet, though.

Dining alone, surrounded by a butler and two footmen, was awkward. Did they watch him chew? Were they hoping he'd hurry up? He supposed a baron was not to care if his staff wished he'd hurry up, but he did care. There was something inherently uncomfortable about the whole thing. There were those lords of England who went along happily, never imagining that anybody beneath them had a stray thought they would not say aloud. Henry was all too uncomfortably aware of the fallacy of that, though. If he were his butler or one of his footmen, he would be hard-pressed not to toe-tap through those dreary dinners.

Afterward, he would be left in the drawing room, with one of them standing round in case he needed anything. He invariably sent them off early, as it was uncomfortable to sit alone with another person waiting to see if you would want anything. Sometimes, he heard the household staff's laughter drifting up from below stairs. They certainly had a better time during these nights at home.

He usually *was* at home at night, too. His neighborhood was rather thin of amusements as it only consisted of an elderly countess who lived in the glorious past of the 1750s and a viscount whose sole interest seemed to be shooting things.

His opinion on his predicament settled. He wanted a family. He wanted to hear talking and footsteps and laughter and doors slamming overhead. He wanted company in the evenings. It was time to wed. He was tired of being alone with his thoughts, however intellectual those thoughts might be.

He supposed his aunt would be delighted. She was his last living relative, but for a handful of more distant cousins. He stayed in her house in Town, as being preferable to renting his own house or a set at The Albany. Why not? She was a sharp old girl and they both appreciated the company.

Just now, various members wandered round The Royal Society's rooms for the annual reception that would kick off the season. Sir Richard had cornered a few gentlemen, including himself, to outline his observations of the behavior of the frogs in his pond, which he had gone to great lengths to study to the detriment of his clothes. In the interest of scientific progress and at great inconvenience to himself, Sir Richard had expanded his observations by traveling halfway across the country to study the frogs in Lord Hellburn's pond. As far as Henry could understand it, both gentlemen's frogs had acted as very usual frogs.

"My conclusion based on my observations," Sir Richard droned on, "is that, as a species, the common frog of England, or Rana temporaria as we would more properly name them, all share similar habits regardless of any environmental differences they might experience. Now what does this say about the more rare Northern Clade Pool Frog, or Pelophylax lessonae? That is not at all conclusive, but I assure you, my esteemed colleagues, I will be investigating exactly that in Norfolk over the next summer. The great question that hangs in the balance—do these two species of frogs maintain similar habits? The study of herpetofauna rather depends on our finding it out!"

Henry stared at the fellow. Did all frogs act like frogs? That's what they needed to find out? There were times when he really questioned some inquiries conducted by the society as being perhaps not critical to scientific advancement. This was the sort of thing that might be mocked by those who were not members of the society.

"I plan to present my findings next year," Sir Richard said. "Though, I did want my colleagues to have an early peek into my work. I will send all of you a copy of the paper I am developing."

Henry smiled. He was soon to be in receipt of a riveting paper on how frogs acted like frogs, regardless of which pond they resided in.

Please, God, let me find a wife.

VERITY WATCHED THE scenery go by, the farmland becoming less and the villages and small towns more frequent. The trip to London had been full of interest, though of a far different sort of interest than the Nicolet entourage had been used to. It seemed that they'd been so often to the various inns where they stopped over the years that the duke's habits had become a bit too well understood.

One of his favorite jests, asking for brocabbage pie or Grass-ington hambac, neither of which existed, did not cause the usual amusement. The duke liked to insist on the dishes as Yorkshire staples, the kitchens would go mad attempting to discover what they were, and then the duke would jocularly inform them that he'd made the whole thing up.

The duke had been foiled at that gambit several times. One innkeeper just answered flatly that they did not have those two items. When reminded that they were allegedly Yorkshire staples, he'd simply replied, "Then the Yorkshire lunatics can keep them to themselves. Your Grace."

At another inn, the woman who ran the kitchen operation had already proved herself immune to the duke's humor the year before by threatening to add some poisonous mushrooms to his brocabbage pie and pointing out she knew where to find those mushrooms. This time, she shouted loud enough for all to hear that she would "Grassington Hambac that duke all the way back to the Dales."

Another innkeeper took things a step further. That fellow joyously replied that they *did* have brocabbage pie. The family was then faced with a pie filled with dripping, boiled cabbage covered in black pepper that was just as terrible as anybody would imagine. The duke, not being at all offended to be the butt of a joke, laughed uproariously, and congratulated them all on the idea.

Verity got the feeling that they were a little let down over the duke's approval and had much rather he'd gone mad over it and never returned again. Of course, they did not know the duke as well as she did—there was nothing he liked more than a battle of wits, a cat and mouse game, and Verity was certain he'd come up with some new gambit to launch at them next year.

The duke's footmen had been foiled as well. They'd always been in the habit of drinking like young lords on a grand tour, singing into the early morning in the innyard, and then invariably depositing what they'd drank in that same yard. At one inn, they'd been relegated to wine that had been so heavily watered that they could not drink it fast enough to get drunk. At another, they were only given tea, that innkeeper explaining a local shortage of…everything else to drink.

Of the entire party, Sir Galahad seemed to enjoy the trip the most. He pushed his smushed pug nose out the window and took in the smells from the Dales to London. Verity did not know what was so interesting about cow manure or grass or goats or chickens, but Sir Galahad found the English countryside an olfactory feast and spent most of his time drooling.

Verity had been happy for the distractions, and she hoped the new butler would distract as well. Anything at all to keep people from examining her too closely. At least, examining what she said too closely. She worked with very little real information and anybody paying too close attention might notice it. She did not exactly know what sort or how much information a gentleman would expect her to have, but it certainly must be more than she'd acquired. All she could do about it was pretend to know things, else she looked a complete idiot.

As for the new butler, they were on the verge of discovering more about this man that Lady Marchfield had not revealed anything about. Other than he was meant to send a chill down their spines. The carriages had entered Grosvenor Square and slowed in front of the duke's house.

Much to Verity's surprise, Lady Marchfield stood at the doors with her arms crossed.

"Gracious," Verity said, "what does our aunt do here?"

Winsome peered out the window. "Nothing good, I am sure."

Valor did not look at all, but hugged Sir Galahad close. Verity wondered if they'd even be able to convince Valor to get out of the carriage.

Thomas opened the door, a look of trepidation on his features. "Chin up, Thomas," Winsome said. "Whatever awaits us, Mrs. Right will see that it's all to come right."

"Indeed I will," Mrs. Right said, patting Valor's hand.

"A very usual case," Verity muttered out of habit, climbing down to the pavement.

Their father had not been at all reluctant to get out of his own carriage. Loud enough for the neighbors to hear, he said, "What now, Lady Misery? What ill wind has blown you in to darken my door?"

"Dear Roland, you do jest," Lady Marchfield said with a smile. "Of course I would be here to greet my dearest brother. Serenity alerted me that you would arrive today and I would not miss it for the world."

Verity and her sisters stared at their aunt wide-eyed. Verity did not have the first idea of what her aunt was saying. Dear Roland? Her dearest brother? What was happening?

"What's the game, Misery?" the duke asked.

"Game? No game. Look, there are my darling nieces. Come, my loves, let us get you out of the chill air. Do come away from that… servant."

By servant, Verity supposed she meant Mrs. Right. But they did not look upon her as a servant. She was Mrs. Right! She was their stand-in mother, keeper of secrets, consoler of broken hearts, and the general of the duke's household. She cared for them when they were sick and brushed their hair at night and tucked them under their blankets. She soothed Valor when she'd had a nightmare. She kept the duke company with a brandy at night before retiring. She was not a servant. She was something else altogether.

"Come, girls, *and* Mrs. Right," the duke said. "Let us proceed in and leave the lunacy of Lady Misery on the pavement. Charlie? You and Thomas see the trunks and cases indoors and make sure that diabolical woman does not try to hide herself in one of them to get into my house! Stand aside, you deranged woman."

Lady Marchfield did step aside, though she looked suspicious-ly happy to do so.

As they stepped into the great hall, entirely distracted by Lady Marchfield's outlandish behavior, they were all but accosted by a man rushing at them.

He was a lumbering individual with facial features that re-minded Verity very much of a trout. His lips, rather than turn up, took a decided downturn and his eyes bulged as if he were a fish caught on a hook. His clothes were no less alarming—his coat was ill-fitting and underneath that coat was a simply bizarre waistcoat embroidered with little red, white, and blue flags. Flags with stars—not the Union Jack, which would have been odd enough.

He grasped the duke's hand and shook it heartily. Her father yanked his hand from the man.

"Duke!" the man said, "Mr. Morus Klonsume, Morry, to my friends. Pleased as Punch to make your acquaintance, been here for hours, had a look around. Took stock, as it were."

Lady Marchfield leaned through the front doors and said, "That's right, Roland. He's an American with exceedingly original ideas. Good luck!" With that, she set off and Verity could hear her laughing all the way to her carriage.

Verity looked to her father. What on earth were they to do with an American? Especially an American such as this?

"Whatever *your* name is," the duke said, "*my* name is Your Grace. Do not ever touch me again. This lady's name is Mrs. Right. She runs the place. Try not to get in her way."

"Hah!" Mr. Morus Klonsume said, seeming overjoyed with the information. "The English! Just as stiff as was said. Never fear, *Your Grace*, American ingenuity to the rescue. You've never seen the like and, if I may say so, I am quite the expert. Born and bred in the new world and took to it like a duck to water, you understand. The mind of Pliny the Elder and determination of General Washington! The Delaware? I can cross it! Prepare to have this house turned upside down, shaken around, and settled into a brave new modern world!"

"Mrs. Right," the duke said, ignoring the man, "for the love of all that's holy, send this individual below stairs," the duke said.

"Below stairs," Mr. Klonsume cried. "Know my way, been there already. Threw the cook for a loop, funny fellow. He says, do I want tea? I say, my good fellow, don't you know we threw it all into Boston Harbor? It was a good joke but I don't reckon the man knows his history very well—blank stare."

"I'll bet it was a blank stare," Mrs. Right said, grasping the fellow by his ill-fitting coat sleeve and pulling him away.

Verity took that moment to shoot up the stairs ahead of her sisters. Whatever was to happen this season, she was determined to secure the best room. Gracious, she had hoped the game of

Mrs. Right driving the latest butler from the house would prove a distraction but Mr. Klonsume was…well, she did not really know what he was.

All she could guess was that Mrs. Right and the footmen would have their hands full.

CHAPTER TWO

Henry had no plans to go out that evening and so he'd dined with his aunt in Berkeley Square. Now they had retired to the drawing room, he with his glass of port and she with her glass of sherry. Lady Pegatha Rysdale was nothing if not practical. The notion that he would sit alone in the dining room with a glass of port, and she would sit alone in the drawing room with a tea tray, was deemed absurd.

"So this is it?" Lady Pegatha said. "You've finally tired of living alone with your nose in a book?"

"Yes, I have finally tired of it. Naturally, I plan on continuing my current inquiries into the circulatory systems of slow-moving animals far into the future but—"

"It sounds fascinating," Lady Pegatha said drily.

"I know it is not of particular interest to you," Henry said, "nor would I expect a wife to take an interest in it."

"Yes, well, all I will say about it is you are a strapping specimen of a gentleman. I've seen you turn heads everywhere. You've just been too busy rushing to your little meetings to notice."

"They are not little meetings. They are Royal Society meetings."

"So I understand. Now, this wife to be, who is out there somewhere, what do you suppose she is like?"

Henry had certainly given that some thought. While he did

not imagine that his future lady would be interested in his research, he did imagine that she would have a certain intellectual bent. He'd been through the seasons in London enough times to be certain that must be the case. He had no use for shallow personalities that acted as if fan waving, clever repartee, and knocking down their fellow members of the fairer sex were hallmarks of intelligence. He had his fill of it last season, feeling very much like a stag on the run from leveled guns.

Lady Lilith, for one, had for some reason decided to set her cap on him. Their encounters were torturous, as her mode of flirting seemed to be noting another lady's dress and wondering if it were not déclassé, but then perhaps she ought not judge, she said. If she were not occupied with that unpleasant hobby, she was outlining what one could do if they wished to be a leader in society and dropping French phrases when English would do perfectly well. Comme c'est amusant, indeed.

Of course, he had encountered some deeply intelligent women too. A few he suspected of besting him in pure intellect. They had been, for one reason or the other, not right. They were already married, or his aunt's age, or there had been no other attraction there beyond the intellectual.

"I suppose I hope for my intellectual equal, even if our interests vary."

Lady Pegatha laughed. "Well then, I suppose you ought to secure the Dowager Lady Marie forthwith!"

"Very amusing," Henry said. Lady Marie was indeed remarkably intelligent. She was also seventy if she was a day. "I suppose it will not hurt if she is pretty, too."

"What about Lady Lilith? She will be in her second season this year and likely ready to settle. She seems to be reasonably intelligent."

Henry had no doubt she'd be interested in settling for him as she'd made clear. He did not think she really liked him but that she had other reasons for her interest, and he thought he understood those reasons.

He might only be a baron, but he was a very rich one. Through generations of good management of an extensive amount of land, coupled with conservative and judicious investments, he probably had a deal more at his disposal than lords with far loftier titles. Henry had the added benefit of not squandering what he had on stupid gambling. None of the men in his line had—it was almost a family tradition to avoid betting like a disease. Considering how some lords ruined themselves, perhaps it was a disease.

Henry had listened to Lady Lilith speculate ad nauseum about opportunities to "make one's mark," as she termed it. All of those opportunities, like the grandest house available for purchase, the newest fashions, and elaborate entertaining, all came with a price. As far as he could understand it, Lady Lilith wished to be a leading lady of the *ton* and would be happy to use his funds to get there. He, himself, was rather beside the point.

"I see you are not bowled over by the idea."

"Not particularly, no. I hold nothing against her, but I believe she is looking for a different type of gentleman."

"Very well. In any case, I will rouse myself and accompany you to Almack's on the morrow," Lady Pegatha said. "I would like to see what the field looks like this year and weigh in with my opinions."

Henry attempted to suppress a groan with middling success.

Lady Pegatha laughed hysterically. "You are pleased. No, do not thank me—I am delighted to do it!"

MRS. RIGHT HAD hauled Mr. Morus Klonsume down the stairs and into the servants' hall. They had passed by the cook, who'd narrowed his eyes at the man.

As well he should. What was she to do with this fellow?

"Sit," she said, pointing at a chair.

"Don't mind if I do," Mr. Klonsume said, throwing himself into it in the most ungraceful way possible. She was rather surprised the arms of the chair did not break under the force of it.

"Do not move," Mrs. Right said, turning to have a word with Cook.

As she passed through the doorway, he called after her. "I wouldn't argue against tea, assuming you've got any left after Boston. Hah! Tell him that joke again, maybe he's got it by now!"

Mrs. Right found Cook staring at her in horrified fascination. "I know, I know," she said. "I do not know how we are to rid the house of him, but god willing, something will come to me before the sun rises tomorrow."

"I'll do anything to help, Mrs. Right. Anything at all. Do you know how many times he's told me about the tea in Boston Harbor? Get that man out of the house."

She looked round the shelves in the kitchen. "I don't suppose you have any poison?"

"Mrs. Right?"

"Sorry, just throwing around ideas, early days," she said. "We'll think of something less risky. Hopefully. For now, do send in a tea tray while I attempt to discover more information about that person."

Cook had nodded and Mrs. Right made her way back to the butler. Mr. Klonsume was casually leaning back in his chair as if he were king of the hall. He looked exceedingly relaxed for a fellow arrived for his first day on the job. She was determined to find out more about this individual. That was the only way she could discover how to rid the house of him.

"The tea tray will be in shortly," she said.

"Hah! So there *was* some left after Boston Harbor! We called it a tea party, you know. Very funny."

"A gentle hint, Mr. Klonsume," Mrs. Right said, "it generally does no good to keep repeating the same joke, especially when it was not amusing the first time."

"Ah, Lady Marchfield said you'd be wound tight over my

arrival. Mrs. Right, you must not fear! Naturally, it can be startling to have a whirlwind of ingenuity whip into your house."

Mrs. Right stared at him. A whirlwind of ingenuity?

"But welcome the new ideas coming in! The Americans have arrived!"

Her eyes drifted round the room. Had he brought other Americans? "Where do you come from, precisely?" she asked.

"The great city of New York—what a town! By the by, I cannot help noticing that everywhere I look in *this* town, all I see is old. Does nobody build anything new here? Even the contents of this house are as old as the hills, it really is dreary. Lacking panache, if you will. Have you considered wallcoverings in the dining room? At my last house, we had a chartreuse and pink stripe—very striking."

Mrs. Right imagined a chartreuse and pink striped wallcovering *would* strike people. Rather hard, too. That was beside the point, though. There was something else she wished to know far more than Mr. Klonsume's taste or lack of it. "What caused you to leave that service in New York, then?"

Cook brought the tea tray in and Mr. Klonsume once more joked about Boston Harbor under his glare. Mrs. Right poured.

"A very sad case for my last employer," Mr. Klonsume said, adding half the sugar bowl into his cup. "But that's America for you! The land of opportunity. One minute you're up and the next you're down. Embezzlement, bad business."

"Do you mean to say, then, that your employer was an embezzler?" Mrs. Right thought this would go some way to accounting for the man's rather rough manners.

"It was a shock, I can tell you," Mr. Klonsume said. "The gentleman embezzled from his partner, and then one of the servants embezzled from the gentleman, and then another servant embezzled from the first servant. That's America— everybody's always climbing the ladder, no surprise that a fellow falls off it here and there."

Mrs. Right did not have the first idea if any of that could be true. Charlie and Thomas, having got the trunks into the hall, came in for their tea before the onerous job of getting it all upstairs. They both looked warily at Mr. Klonsume.

"There's my boys," Mr. Klonsume said. "Not quite as sturdy looking as what I'm used to. Jack and Richie could've lifted you both with their little fingers. Well, that's English food, is it not? It doesn't seem to grow very big people."

Now that Mr. Klonsume had thoroughly insulted Thomas and Charlie, Mrs. Right poured the footmen their tea. Thomas looked with incredulity into the near-empty sugar bowl. She said, "Mr. Klonsume was just telling me of his history in New York. Apparently, his house was chock full of criminals."

Thomas and Charlie did not look very surprised to hear it.

"Criminals? Now that's going far, Mrs. Right. I won't go into detail but rest assured, all three of those men had very pressing reasons to embezzle."

Pressing reasons to embezzle? That was comforting. Mrs. Right did not know what ship had delivered this person to their shores, but she was determined that another ship take him back again. She would not even mind if it sank. "Pray, Mr. Klonsume, you have still not accounted for arriving in England. Could you not find work in New York after the…embezzling…came to light?

"I *did* find work in New York, easy as you like. I saw an advertisement placed by an English viscount. That fellow looked for a valet while he was in our glorious town. We got on famously and so he brought me here with him. Funny fellow, drunk and looking like a tipped over statue more often than not—liked to have a valet that didn't frown over it."

"Why aren't you there, then?" Charlie asked. "With the drunk viscount."

Mr. Klonsume's brow wrinkled. "Very strange, that was. His father, he holds the purse strings, owns the house, an earl, wouldn't you know. All sorts of complaints."

Mrs. Right could just imagine what sorts of complaints.

"Anyway, the earl says I got to go, and my viscount was too drunk to stand up against him. There I was, far from home. But not at all put down, because I brought my American confidence with me. I see an advertisement for a butler for a duke's household and mind, I wasn't at all what the advertisement was calling for as it mentioned experience, English morals, and a stern taskmaster, but I answer all the same. I outline all my American ideas and wouldn't you know, Lady Marchfield was bowled over by them. Said she never heard anything like it in her life. Says she'll give me the job and here I am. Mind you, excited to try it out. Never been a butler before."

Mrs. Right could well imagine that Lady Marchfield was bowled over by this fellow's American ideas. But what did he just say? "You've never been a butler?" she asked.

"Never in my life!"

"What were you doing in New York before you became the drunken viscount's valet? At the embezzler's house?"

"Driving Mr. Wellby's carriage, then I get the job pouring my English viscount into his clothes, and here I am at the top of the heap—in charge of a duke's house. American ingenuity—it'll take a man to the pinnacles of achievement. Who knows, maybe I'm not even done climbing. Might do some grand thing for the nation and get myself knighted. Hah! Sir Morus—that would be tremendous! American confidence, after all."

Mrs. Right distractedly tapped her spoon on her saucer. American confidence, indeed. She would confidently march this fellow right out the door. As soon as she thought of an idea on how to do it.

BEFORE SETTING OFF to Almack's, Verity had spent quite an amount of time looking into the glass in her bedchamber. She wore a particularly pretty dress whose color Madame LaFray had named Prussian Blue. It was deep and rich, and the dressmaker claimed it would complement her coloring. She supposed she did look as well as she could do, and she supposed she would need to.

Verity well understood that her looks would have to carry her through. That, and being generally agreeable and using her well-practiced cover of pretending to understand a subject and judiciously adding to it by mentioning her understanding of the usual case.

None of it was very satisfactory, though. She would hide who she really was and then after the wedding—Surprise! You have married an empty-head of a lady who cannot read and does not know much. At least, much that she is sure of.

She thought there might be the slimmest chance that some gentleman would fall so violently in love with her that he would not care a whit about the deficiency. That was a very slim chance, though.

Whatever was to happen this evening, she would depend on her sisters to see her through. Serenity, who now lived just two doors down, had visited and told her that everybody was in Town and everybody would come to support her at Almack's.

Verity stood. Mrs. Right had left her to see to the downstairs over a quarter of an hour ago. Valor and Winsome had been driven out of her room, as she'd said she needed some moments to compose herself. But now it was time. She must face Almack's.

She went down the stairs to her father as he waited in the great hall. Mr. Klonsume rushed in out of nowhere. "Gad! There's a fine filly!" he said to her.

What on earth was she to say to such a thing?

"Klondike, or whatever your name is," the duke said, "do not ever make comment on my daughter's appearance again. Go away."

"Ah! English modesty. Right-O," Mr. Klonsume said. He did not look at all perturbed to have been dismissed so out of hand. He turned on his heel and whistled to himself as he made his way to the back of the house.

The duke helped her into the carriage and climbed in after her. "I suppose Mrs. Right faces her biggest challenge yet with that court jester."

"He is very strange, Papa."

"It would strike you, I suppose. You're accustomed to our rational English ways."

"Papa, I'm a bit frightened. I suppose that's a usual case?"

The duke regarded her. "I will assume you mean frightened of Almack's and not our American interloper."

Verity nodded. As always, her father was very perceptive.

"A very regular case, if your sisters are anything to go by. I always say the same thing—you are a duke's daughter. Fear nobody but the queen, and she won't be there."

Verity wondered if she ought to mention that she feared the gentlemen of the *ton* would not find her very interesting. After all, what did she know? However, it seemed a rather late date to mention she could not read. That, coupled with the idea that she would not wish to disappoint her father by revealing he'd sired a very stupid daughter, turned her away from the idea.

The carriage made its way down King Street and rolled to a stop. "Here we are, chin up, Verity. Remember, you can look down on all the world if you like it."

Verity appreciated the sentiment, but she knew very well that she had no right to look down on anybody. Rank could not confer intelligence. A tradesman's schoolboy could run rings around her in the knowledge department. She took a deep breath to steady herself.

As she had been forewarned by her sisters, the interior of Almack's was deceiving. Had it not been Almack's, it would not be thought very impressive. But, as Felicity said, once an institution reached a particular pinnacle of power, it no longer needed to try very hard. In fact, not bothering to try very hard was rather the point.

If that was true, then Almack's had certainly climbed the heights. The carpet was positively threadbare in places and the curtains had that telltale faded look that came from exposure to the sun for a few too many years.

"Ah, Countess," the duke said to a rather lovely lady in a midnight blue satin.

"There he is, the rascal of a duke with the never-ending supply of daughters," the lady said, laughing.

Verity thought the lady looked far less imposing when she laughed. And good gracious, the lady seemed rather fond of her father. So many people seemed to disapprove of him that it was rather gratifying.

"Number five," the duke said. "This one is Lady Verity. I'm launching them out of the house as fast as I can. Verity, this is the Countess of Westmoreland. She knows well enough that I've a flask of brandy in my coat and will not tell any tales about it."

"Why should I? I drank my fill of champagne before I arrived. In any case, I suppose a duke can do what he likes."

"That's the spirit!" the duke said.

"Lady Verity," the countess said, as Verity made her curtsy. "Charming. I do not imagine you will have any trouble in the launching out of the house your father is determined on."

Verity supposed this was a comment on her looks, and she was a little relieved about it as she was counting on them to see her through.

"Now, I will manage your card as it's your first time out. Do you have any particular preferences?"

Preferences? She knew nobody. The only preference she had at the moment was to dance with gentlemen who might approve of her. Such as she was. And not ask her any questions she would not know the answer to.

"Ah, never mind it, I see I have made you blush," the countess said. "Well, there are certainly plenty to pick from this evening. Lord Wembly has even decided to drag himself away from his intellectual pursuits to grace us with his presence. We did not see him at all last season, so I suppose we must feel the compliment."

A gentleman with intellectual pursuits? Verity felt a chill down her spine. The last gentleman in London she would wish to be introduced to was one who was taken up with intellectual pursuits.

She longed to beg the countess to find her a Corinthian who would not know a book if it hit him over the head. She stayed silent, though, as how would a request such as that possibly be phrased?

"Carry on, duke, and do not be too naughty about showing that flask," the countess said. "We should not like any other lords to pick up the habit." She tapped his arm in a mock warning and sailed off to greet some newer arrivals.

The duke put out his arm and led Verity into the ballroom, she all the while praying this Lord Wembly person would be entirely engaged for the evening. Whoever he was, he was not for her, and she most certainly was not for him.

She searched the ballroom. There they were—her family contingent, all gathered together. Felicity with Mr. Stratton, Grace with Lord Dashlend, Patience with Lord Stanford, and Serenity with Lord Thorpe. All together, waiting for her.

"There's my girls and my collection of sons-in-laws," the duke said jovially, leading her to them.

Verity felt as if she were heading toward her life raft in a vast ocean of uncertainty.

CHAPTER THREE

ENRY HAD LED Lady Pegatha into Almack's and then awaited the inevitable. The patronesses would have various suggestions for him regarding who he ought to dance with. He had not come at all last year, which they had noticed if their frowns were anything to go by. Therefore, he would make himself very agreeable.

The Countess of Westmoreland had just said, "Is your supper open, Lord Wembly? I have someone particular in mind."

"It remains free, Countess," he said.

"Excellent, I will put you down for Lady Verity Nicolet, the Duke of Pelham's daughter."

Lady Pegatha had not been able to conceal her mirth over it. "When will that duke ever run out of daughters, I wonder? Hold on to your sense of humor, Wembly—the duke is an absolute rascal of a fellow. Though, I've not seen him in an age, so perhaps he's settled."

This caused the Countess of Westmoreland to laugh into her handkerchief, so Henry must presume the duke had not settled. He'd not supposed that was the case, at least if the stories he'd heard over the seasons were true.

On the other hand, the duke had a reputation for producing very comely daughters.

He scanned the ballroom and found a battalion of the duke's family all gathered round a lady he had not yet met. She was positively lovely, with dark hair and dark eyes.

"Yes, that is her, she is pretty, is she not?" Rather than wait for Henry to answer, which would be in the affirmative, the countess went on. "Perhaps she would be just the thing to pull you away from your books."

"Ah, yes," Lady Pegatha said, "a pretty face is more pleasant to look at than dry words on a page."

"Just so," Lady Westmoreland said. She drifted away to locate her next victim.

"Goodness, that young lady really is very pretty," Lady Pegatha said. "She looks like her mother, who was quite the stunner. I remember when the duke stole that lady from under the nose of another lord. Apparently, he told her she might do any strange thing she liked, and she took him up on it. I once heard she'd insisted on being called Tulip after she'd delivered twins. It was said it did not last but was only an aberration from her ordeal, but the duke happily complied while it did."

"I suppose the duke and duchess must have got on well to have produced five daughters," Henry said.

"Seven. There are two more not even out yet."

Seven. What on earth did one do with seven daughters? "He does not seem too down at the mouth to have not produced a son, though. The title will go elsewhere, and he cannot be happy about that."

"I believe you are wrong, there," Lady Pegatha said. "The Duke of Pelham has the unique ability to be happy with whatever he's faced with. You should have seen him twenty years ago, when he was roundly denounced over setting Lady Vanderwake's curtains afire. He thought it all a good joke. Still does, I imagine. In any case, I do not believe he gives a toss for titles. That is why it amuses the duke to act in a very un-duke like fashion."

Henry was rather fascinated. Lady Verity, like Aunt Pegatha's memory of her mother, *was* a stunner. Her family, her father especially, were interesting.

He had, of course, heard some stories regarding the daughters over the years. The eldest had been involved in Lady Albright's tiger getting loose and mauling Stratton, whom she'd married. Lady Grace had somehow set one of Lady Montague's rooms on fire and then pulled Dashlend off the side of the house, injuring him severely. Then she married him. Lady Patience had some set-to at a masque that somehow led Lord Stanford to chase her across England. Then she married him. And the latest, Lady Serenity—nobody was really clear what happened there. Something about a three-legged dog being stolen that resulted in Thorpe punching his brother at The Albany. And then she married him.

He was most interested in discovering what Lady Verity would have to say for herself. Henry reminded himself to try to be interesting to the lady and not fall into talking about his research for The Royal Society. It had been so long since he'd immersed himself in polite society and he'd grown a bit too used to discussing all manner of things with his fellow society members that no lady could possibly have an interest in.

"Lord Wembly, Lady Pegatha," a lady's voice said.

He turned to find Lady Lilith. She was looking just the same as last year. He was certain she wore a new dress, not because he would remember any particular dress but because she would have insisted upon it. New or not, they all were similar and not really to his taste. They were too…something. His aunt called the style dazzle and dumbfound, and it was composed of too many accoutrements, as if the wearer wished to take attention away from their person. He did not know why Lady Lilith went for it, she was comely enough, but he suspected it was the ladder climber in her wishing to make an impression.

"Lady Lilith," he said with a short bow.

"Ah, there you are, Lilith," Lady Pegatha said. "I trust your trip into Town was pleasant?"

Lady Lilith sighed. "It never is, you know. My father likes to rush us in the most frightful manner."

As she spoke, she dangled her card very obviously. There was no way round it. "Might I put myself down?" he asked out of obligatory courtesy.

"If you insist," she said coquettishly.

As he was a man of science, he was a man of straightforward speech. He'd really like to point out that he did not "insist." However, a gentleman must sometimes swallow his opinions. He took her card.

"My supper is still open, Lord Wembly."

He got the hint, but happily, he could not agree to take the hint. "That is a disappointment on my side," he said. "Lady Westmoreland has engaged me to escort Lady Verity Nicolet into supper."

This seemed to strike Lady Lilith rather hard. "I see," she said with aspersion. "Goodness, another Nicolet."

"Yes, there are seven, you know," Lady Pegatha said with a snort.

Henry put himself down for the second set, ignoring that the first dance was open. If there was one thing a gentleman *could* do to express interest or lack of it, it was to choose a dance that did not say anything of a particular regard. He did not want to open the ball with Lady Lilith.

Lady Lilith noted it and sniffed.

He did not suppose he cared very much about her sniffing. The sooner the lady turned her sights elsewhere, the better. She wished to make herself into the first lady of London, but he had no wish to be the first gentleman. She'd be much better off setting her sights on another gentleman with a heavy purse who *did* have social aspirations.

Though he'd firmly decided to wed, and Lady Lilith was nothing if not willing, it could not be right. He could not envision her at home, in his house, on a usual day where nothing particular would happen.

No matter, he had decided what he would do, and he would seek out a lady he could imagine in his house, on a usual day.

VERITY FELT RATHER buoyed over her family coming out in force to surround her and support her at Almack's. They'd all gone out of their way to be encouraging. She was deemed pretty as a picture and assured her card would be filled to overflowing. Mr. Stratton, who she knew best of all her sisters' husbands, had counseled, "Remember, it is only a ball."

She would remember that. Mr. Stratton was always full of genial good sense. She might be encouraged by it too. She might not be in possession of a brilliant mind but there *were* some things she was good at, and dancing was one of them. As she'd gazed round the ballroom full of wonderful-looking people dressed impeccably, her eyes were arrested by one particular gentleman.

He was positively sublime. Tall, broad-shouldered, with very dark auburn hair and strong features. She did have a weakness for that shade of auburn, a brownish-red like the leaves of trees after they'd fully turned in autumn. She supposed his eyes might be a shade of green, though she could not tell it from this distance. He was a brick of a man. A man she might imagine dressed in the accoutrements of a warrior of old, daring anyone to challenge him. Really, his looks made her a bit swoony.

Felicity followed her gaze. "I see you examine Lord Wembly."

"Lord Wembly?" she asked. It could not be. Why was the most glorious man in the room to be the one who was consumed with intellectual pursuits? He did not even look as if that was how he spent his time. He looked as if he were forever on his horse or boxing or fencing.

"He is a baron and very rich, I am told," Felicity said. "I do not know him well, as he seems not to be out and about much. I understand he is very intellectual and involved with The Royal Society."

"I see," Verity said quietly.

"Goodness, perhaps he would be just the thing, Verity. You do so like to know lots of facts, and I imagine he must know piles of things."

Verity imagined he *did* know piles of things. Which was the problem.

Lady Westmoreland interrupted them. "All filled in, Lady Verity. I hope you come to approve of my selections," she said, handing over Verity's card.

"I am sure I will, Lady Westmoreland," Verity said. "I thank you for the courtesy."

"Charming girl," the countess said, drifting away. Verity glanced down at her card. Then she felt as if her heart had positively given up the ghost and ceased beating.

Lord Wembly. The handsome intellectual. For the dance before supper.

"Look at that," Felicity said, "the fates must be on your side. You can have extended conversation with Lord Wembly."

"Yes, look at that," Verity said wanly.

"There you are, Serenity," Lady Marchfield said, seeming to come out of nowhere. "You look lovely, my dear, just like your mother." She turned to the duke. "Roland? Might I be congratulated on your new butler? Mr. Klonsume is everything I would wish for you. Ah, those jests about Boston Harbor—one cannot hear them too many times."

The rest of his family turned toward the duke. None of them but for Serenity had set eyes on Mr. Klonsume, though they all were well-used to the butler game between the duke and his sister.

As he did not say anything at all to her teasing, she went on. "Yes," she said to the rest of the party, "Mr. Klonsume is an American and arrives with all the confident barbarism that land has to offer. What does he say? He has the wisdom of Pliny the Elder and determination of General Washington? Oh, and a soupçon of American bluster and imagined ingenuity ladled on top. Positively enchanting. Now come, Verity, I will introduce you to Lady Pembroke before the ball starts. She is the queen's Lady of the Wardrobe and an important person for you to know."

Before Verity could invent a way to avoid it, she was whisked away and introduced to the imposing Lady Pembroke. The lady had some very nice things to say about Serenity and her opinions about bees and the new idea of slatted skeps.

"Do you have an interest in bees yourself, Lady Verity?"

Verity searched her mind for anything Serenity might have said about bees. She could not recall much. "Oh, not as much as Serenity does, I'm afraid. They seem to prefer to die in the garden, I've heard say."

"Do they?" Lady Pembroke asked. "Well, I suppose the garden is as good a place as any. Lady Marchfield, good to see you again."

After Lady Pembroke left to greet an acquaintance, her aunt said, "Verity, I do not know where you come up with these things. I don't believe you've ever heard anybody say that bees like to die in a garden."

Verity shrugged. "That's where Serenity always finds them, though."

"Have a care about spouting off these ridiculous opinions and attempting to pass them off as facts. It will not get you far. You are grown now, and those sorts of childish habits must be left behind."

Verity did not answer her aunt, though Lady Marchfield's words terrified her. Her aunt did not understand that her niece said stupid things like that because she had nothing else to say. She was certain other people had read piles of information about bees from books, but all Verity had to go on was what she could remember Serenity saying about them.

She'd probably be better off saying nothing at all to anybody, though she did not know how it could be managed.

MRS. RIGHT NEVER did like to give Lady Marchfield credit of any sort, but she was hard-pressed not to on this particular occasion. Never in her wildest imagination had she thought that someone like Mr. Klonsume even existed. Or that Lady Marchfield would locate him.

According to Mr. Klonsume, he knew everything under the sun and everything in the duke's house could be improved. He kept talking about bringing in his modern ideas and American confidence. She did not know if they were modern, but they certainly were confidently bizarre.

Why was he so determined to put a striped wall covering in the duke's drawing room? Why did he keep talking about ears of corn as the side dish no table could be without? It had taken her some time to understand that this ear of corn was some vegetable she'd never laid eyes on, and not an exotic grain. And why on earth did he keep asking the footmen for their opinion on being bossed about by a King and Queen? Did he imagine the footmen were in regular correspondence with the palace?

In general, Mr. Klonsume had no notion about rank at all. He had actually asked if a title could be left in a will if a fellow did not like his eldest son. That drunken viscount he'd worked for had explained it could not be done, but Mr. Klonsume had wondered if that was only hopeful drunken imaginings.

He'd had to be told several times which rooms were for the servants' use and which were not. He'd sauntered into the drawing room while Winsome and Valor played Vingt-et-un and offered to teach them the American game, Twenty-one. When informed they were one and the same, he wondered aloud why the English went in for complicated names. Then he sat down.

He sat down. In the drawing room. Only Mrs. Right had the honor of sitting in the drawing room with the family. And that honor was on account of long service and the fact that she'd mothered the duke's girls all her life. This fellow just swanned in and sat himself down.

At that particular moment, Valor had hugged Sir Galahad.

Winsome chose to go in another direction. "Get out of my father's chair," she said to Mr. Klonsume in the threatening manner that only Winsome could muster.

Mr. Klonsume did so, and not particularly unhappily. It seemed he did best when someone hit him over the head with their meaning and he was near-impossible to offend. He claimed to be an expert at everything in the world, though subtlety must be left off that exhaustive list.

What was she to do to get rid of him? She'd briefly thought of drugging him with laudanum and leaving him down at the docks with the hopes he'd get pressed into service. What if he got away, though? He did not have the nice English manners she was used to. Had she left the last butler at the docks, he might have made his way back and delivered a stern lecture on her "outrageous behavior" and "lack of decency." An American might slit her throat for all she knew about it.

Maybe he could be framed for a crime and sent to Botany Bay? He'd fit right in at that foreign locale and might even be eaten by a crocodile. He could tell that reptile all about Boston Harbor as he disappeared into its gaping maw.

She realized her mind was going to very extreme ideas on account of the challenge Mr. Klonsume presented and how absolutely irksome he was. She'd lain awake the night before, wondering if she could put a pillow over his face—after all, she was still a strong and vital woman.

Mrs. Right well knew she had to get more practical. It might cheer her to think of putting a pillow over his face, but it really was impractical. Perhaps she might consider more straightfor-ward options.

That viscount Mr. Klonsume had worked for had seemed to enjoy his company, which could be accounted for by the idea that said viscount was drunk all the time. It had been the drunken viscount's father that had been against him. Perhaps master and servant might be reunited somehow?

She would look into it. She *had* to look into it, as she did not know what else to look into.

VERITY THOUGHT SHE had got through the dances with various gentlemen very creditably. She'd kept up her end of the conversations in a satisfactory and rational manner. She'd not felt the dreaded panic rise in her when she was asked about something and could not think how to answer. In those moments, she was likely to say something that made no sense, like bees preferring to die in a garden.

Lord Granger had mentioned he'd just purchased a spaniel puppy for his younger sister. Last season, Verity had extensive conversations with Lord Thorpe's brother, Lord Charles, on the subject of spaniels. During the dog walks between Serenity and Lord Thorpe round the square, she'd kept Lord Charles occupied with the topic. Now, she was able to mention that it was her understanding that spaniels could be depended upon to warn of fire. She really could not remember whether she'd posited that fact to Lord Charles or vice versa. Or if it was a fact at all. It did not seem to matter, though. Lord Granger had appeared very pleased to hear of it.

Sir Roger speculated that they were to have a warmer winter than they'd experienced the year before. Verity found this a particularly safe subject. While she did not know much about the weather, she did know one thing it was rather hopeless to predict it. She posited that much would depend on North Sea storms. Sir Roger said he had not known that was the case. She did not know either, but it might very well be true and how would anyone prove it was not?

Other gentlemen were even easier to manage, as they did not

talk of anything at all, really. They asked her things like: where she was from, and was this her first time in Town, and how was she enjoying it? All easy enough to answer without knowing anything in particular.

Now, though, she would face the real challenge. This was the high fence to clear on her ride across Almack's. The dance with Lord Wembly, the intellectual, and then the supper that would follow. She would not attend the supper long, Grace had alerted her to the fact that by the time supper rolled around, their father's flask, and his patience, were emptied. He would come to collect her before her second cup of tea. But nevertheless, they would dance and then walk into the supper room together.

"Lady Verity? Lord Wembly," he said with a bow. "Lady Westmoreland contracted me for this dance."

"Lord Wembly," she said. Now that he was up close, he made her even more nervous. His eyes were green, as she had suspected, and a rather dark shade. They were like moss in a shady forest. His complexion had a certain ruddiness to it that made him look as if he spent a deal of time out of doors. He was simply divine.

Why could he not be a Corinthian who had not opened a book since school and forgotten everything he'd read? He certainly looked like one. Why must he be a member of The Royal Society?

Verity was not altogether certain of what went on in that institution, but she did know that her father received a periodical from the society from time to time. She'd once asked Winsome to read one aloud, but they'd not got far with it. It was about, it said, the decomposition of muriatic acid. They did not find out much about that item's decomposition though, nor why it would be important to know. A few sentences in, Winsome named the whole thing too tedious to be borne and picked up a gothic novel.

Those few sentences Winsome *had* got through, though, gave Verity the idea that the society was a collection of exceedingly learned men who delved into obscure areas of knowledge.

She had not even had the chance to delve into not obscure areas of knowledge.

Lord Wembly led her to the floor. The Countess of Westmoreland had called a cotillion for the last set, and Verity found herself wildly relieved to note that her family had decided to follow her there. Serenity and Lord Thorpe, Patience and Lord Stanford, and Grace and Lord Dashlend hurriedly took the places of the three other couples to form their group. It was her understanding that it was not at all usual for husbands and wives to dance together at a ball, but her dear family did not care a whit for that when it came to supporting one another.

Patience gave her a wink and Verity did feel buoyed by it. The orchestra struck up for the Grand Rond.

CHAPTER FOUR

VERITY FOUND LORD Wembly exceedingly graceful for a man of his size and he led her with confidence. She was surrounded by her sisters and her brothers-in-law. Goodness, what had she worried about? This was very genial!

They took their turn at the figure, La Belle Poulé, and returned to their place. As the other couples took their turns, Lord Wembly said, "Do you enjoy Town so far, Lady Verity?"

A question she could answer without any difficulty and not at all intellectual. "Indeed, yes, though tonight is my first night out in society."

"I suppose you've accepted no end of invitations," he said. "I imagine a duke's door is battered by them."

"Oh, well, I have not actually had time to go through all of them. We only arrived recently. My aunt, Lady Marchfield, arranged our voucher and tickets for Almack's, but I cannot be certain what else is waiting."

"Lady Marchfield seems in very high spirits this evening."

Of course, her aunt did seem rather delighted with the world at this moment. Verity was not certain, though, if she ought to reveal the cause. A very off-putting American who'd named Verity a fine filly, among other outrages, had been moved into the house. Mrs. Right had not had a moment to get him out of it.

"Yes," she said, "my aunt is often in high spirits."

That was a very fanciful idea, but hopefully Lord Wembly

was not so acquainted with Lady Marchfield to know it.

"I have been through most of my invitations," Lord Wembly said. "I've accepted quite a few—Lady Remington's card party, Lady Jenner's musical evening, and Sir Jonathan's annual scavenger hunt for charity are all coming up soon."

Goodness, he was listing off everywhere he would be, which she imagined was very encouraging. Did it not hint that he wished her to know where he could be found?

But a card party? She was really not very good at cards. Vingt-et-un was all right, but she became entirely lost at whist. As for piquet, that might as well have been devised to torture people. The number of rules was maddening.

And then, Lady Jenner's musical evening must be out of the question. She did not play an instrument, and Patience had found out that all the young ladies were meant to demonstrate their talent. Patience and their father had to invent a sudden hand injury that prevented Patience from playing the crwth. Patience had claimed that obscure instrument was the only thing she played, betting that nobody would have ever heard of it. Lady Jenner, it turned out, had one. It had been a very close call, though these days Lord Stanford was well aware that his bride played not a note.

A scavenger hunt, though? She might be able to do that. She'd never participated in such a thing, but she imagined it would not be more complicated than the village's annual Harvest Festivity. The highlight of it was that Hunthouse apples would be hidden in all sorts of clever places by the vicar and his committee. Whoever gathered the most apples won a prize. Last year's prize had been a copy of selected sermons penned by Mr. Fordyce, which had been rather disappointing to everybody, but for the vicar and his committee of elderly ladies. The winner, young Harold Busterby, had not seemed at all impressed. Nevertheless, the running round looking for apples had been great fun.

"A scavenger hunt sounds exceedingly interesting. And it is for charity, you said?"

"Sir Jonathan raises funds for The Sewing Circle. It is a charitable concern training young women to be seamstresses who might otherwise…choose less ideal employment."

As Verity was not particularly naïve, she understood his hint. Young girls without means or protection were often forced to debase themselves to survive. It was a contemptible business and the shame of it, as far as Verity was concerned, landed squarely on the shoulders of the men who made it possible. "It sounds a very worthy cause."

"It is on Friday next."

"It sounds like just the sort of thing I would accept," Verity said. Gracious, this was going very well. Far better than she had feared.

Perhaps it did not signify that Lord Wembly was taken up with The Royal Society. Perhaps a person engaged in intellectual pursuits would rather leave behind thinking of them when he was engaged elsewhere. Perhaps all her worry over being discovered to be a dullard was never justified at all.

They executed the change and took their turn at Les Pantalons. Returning to their place, Verity said, "Do you have brothers and sisters in Town?"

Lord Wembly shook his head. "It is just me, I'm afraid." He glanced at their set, overflowing with sisters, and said, "You seem to have been lucky in that area. I understand there are seven of the duke's daughters."

Verity nodded. Her sisters. Another agreeable subject they might talk about. "It has been rather wonderful to be surrounded by so many genial sisters."

"My aunt, Lady Pegatha, I stay with her in Town, she says the duke is delighted to have so many daughters."

"I think that's right," Verity said. "I imagine people wonder why he is not sad over not having a direct heir, but that is not how my father is. He looks round at what he's got and finds it all very genial."

"A very intelligent way to live, I must think."

Thinking to steer Lord Wembly away from any talk of intelligence, which she absolutely did not want examined, she said, "Everybody is very happy with the way things are. Except Valor, of course. She is the youngest and does not like her sisters leaving. She did try to attempt to convince me to sit out the season."

"But you did not wish to?"

Somehow, she'd led herself right into a dangerous topic. She had debated that very thing, considering her deficiencies. "Well, in the end, I decided against it."

The dance came to a close and Lord Wembly led her to the dining room, her sisters all trailing behind her.

He led her to two open places and directed a footman to fetch them tea and cake. "I would ask you which you wished for—tea or lemonade—but this is your first time here. Nobody who tries the lemonade wishes to try it again, so I thought to save you from the experience."

Verity nodded, conscious of Patience on her other side. What would Patience make of Lord Wembly wishing to save her from an experience? Even if the experience was only sour lemonade? As well, the offerings at supper were another subject she knew something about, as her sisters had advertised their opinions loudly.

"Felicity says the lemonade, the whole supper really, verges on an insult, and that is probably the point. She says that if people not privileged enough to have been issued vouchers will spend vast amounts on their entertaining on a Wednesday night to pretend they do not care, the patronesses will spend nothing on it to point out that they should."

"I suspect you are right, though that sort of snobbery often strikes me as nonsensical. Perhaps those leading ladies of society would be better off improving their minds rather than proving a pointless point."

Improving their minds? What did he mean by it? Did he suppose everybody, meaning her, should be improving their minds?

She would improve it, if she could. What if he discovered she could not? Would he so offhandedly condemn her as he had the patronesses? He might well do. After all, it was not every gentleman bold enough to make such comment on the patronesses. Especially not when he was seated in those ladies' own palace of refinement.

He'd made the comment in such a decided manner. Almost derisive, really, as if he looked down upon the sort of pedestrian ideas the patronesses seemed to espouse.

Verity's nerves, which had gone a long way toward calm, began to climb again.

"Tell me, Lady Verity, what are your interests?" Lord Wembly asked.

Interests? Did he mean intellectual interests? What could she say? She could not think of a thing to say. Did she have interests? Verity's mind felt as if it were nearly collapsing in on her.

"Interests?" she said.

"Yes, well, I admit my own will not be fascinating to you. I am much taken up by The Royal Society. I imagine my research will not interest a lady." Lord Wembly laughed. "I am sure it will not. After all, what is a lady to make of my inquiries into the circulatory systems of slow-moving animals?"

Verity's mind was spinning and she felt her heart speed up. It was not a very foreign feeling either, as it came over her whenever someone talked about something she could not possibly know anything about. She always felt as if she should know something about it, and the details were hidden in a book somewhere. Everybody else would know something about it.

This overwhelming feeling had, in the past, caused her to say some of the stupidest things she'd ever said. It was a kind of panic that could not be reined in once it got going. Spinning, spinning, spinning, and then a dark blanket slowly fell over her rational thoughts, and she was not in control.

"On the contrary, Lord Wembly, I have looked into the same," she blurted out.

What did she just say? Why did she just say that? He looked startled. Of course he looked startled. What a thing to say!

"I admit to being taken aback, Lady Verity," he said. "I would not have guessed we had such a similar interest. Have you come to any conclusions on the subject?"

Conclusions! Of course she had no conclusions. She did not even understand the question.

"I believe the circulatory systems are at the bottom of why those animals move so slowly," she said, attempting a blithe tone.

What animals were they? What did their circulation have to do with it? She had no idea!

"There you are," the duke said from behind her chair.

Her father, thank the heavens, it was her father.

"You'll never guess. My brandy flask has mysteriously drained itself. Happens every time I am locked up in this celebration of how dull the English can be when we really try." Her father turned to Lord Wembly. "Wembly, is it? A baron, so I'm told."

"Yes, Your Grace," Lord Wembly said.

"Hah! Could be worse, nobody ever knows what to do with a baronet. Say, Wembly, I'm having a dinner on Friday, come along. You can bring your aunt too—I've not seen Lady Pegatha in an age. Well now, girl, can we be off before I either fall asleep or throw my empty flask at Lady Misery's head?"

That was quite a speech, and Lord Wembly did seem rather bowled over by it. However, Verity did not care a whit about that. She was rescued from being forced to expound any further on the circulatory systems of slow-moving animals.

What had she done? After she'd said that preposterous notion, she'd quickly concluded that she must never speak to Lord Wembly again. Now he was coming to dinner.

HENRY WAS BOTH charmed and confounded by Lady Verity

Nicolet. He'd been surreptitiously glancing at her all evening leading up to squiring her himself. She was painfully beautiful; an old master could not conjure a more lovely lady. And then, she seemed so genial. At least, he imagined so as she was very often smiling.

He'd seen other gentlemen's glances too and would not be the least surprised if she very speedily collected herself a pile of suitors. The diamond of the season, they'd all say.

She probably was the diamond of the season already, though he wished not so many gentlemen had seemed to notice it.

When they'd danced, her geniality was confirmed. His thoughts had raced far ahead of him. Would it not be the best course for his life to complete his studies of a day and then leave his library to find a beautiful and genial baroness waiting for him? He rather thought it was.

What confounded him was the conversation they'd had at supper. Even though he'd cautioned himself not to mention his research, he *had* mentioned it. Then she'd claimed to be looking into the very same question. He really did not believe it, though. When he asked her if she'd come to any conclusions, she'd just rearranged the words of the topic.

The carriage rattled along the streets to Berkeley Square while his Aunt Pegatha eyed him from the other side of the carriage. "I only say, she is very pretty," she said. "She is a duke's daughter, too. Quite a mad duke, but I do not get the idea it runs in the family, so no harm there. In any case, I find his brand of madness wildly entertaining. You could do worse."

Henry was well aware that his aunt spoke of Lady Verity. Even if the duke had not been mentioned, he would know it. "There was something odd that came up, though. I do not know what to make of it."

He gazed out the window and felt the sudden rap of a fan on his leg. "Gracious me, you are not to tell me something odd has happened and then not expound on it, you rascal."

Henry hardly knew how to explain it. He did not wish to

name Lady Verity a liar…but he was relatively certain she was a liar.

"Come now, what did you discover?" Lady Pegatha asked. "Is she a murderess? A spy for the French? An impostor of some sort?"

"Not that I know of. However, I mentioned my research, and yes, I am aware that I should not have, as it will bore a lady—"

"Good heavens, do not tell me she was not bored, that peculiar girl."

"Aunt, she claimed she was looking into the same question. I was startled, I can tell you, as I had not imagined any young lady was examining the circulatory systems of slow-moving animals—"

"Nor I."

"So I asked her if she'd come to any conclusions and she only rearranged the words. She said she believed the animals moved slow because of their circulatory system."

Lady Pegatha snorted. "Did she now?"

"Yes, she did. I do not like to say it, but…I really believe she was lying."

This caused his aunt to heave with laughter. When she caught her breath, she said, "That unconscionable little flirt. Oh goodness, I am amused."

Henry was taken aback. "Do you mean to say that was some sort of flirtatious gambit?"

"Of course I mean to say it, as I just did say it. She is young and inexperienced and thought she might be a looking glass reflecting your interests back on you. Hmm, I wonder how far she will take it."

"How far? I think she's gone quite far enough. How much further could she go?"

Lady Pegatha shrugged. "She is the Duke of Pelham's daughter, who knows how far she'll take it. It's bound to be amusing."

Henry leaned back. He was not altogether certain what he thought of it. On the one hand, it was gratifying to imagine that Lady Verity had attempted to flirt with him. On the other hand, it was really a very odd thing to claim.

Perhaps it had only been nerves. Perhaps his aunt was right—she was young and inexperienced and had attempted to impress him with an ill-advised gambit.

"By the by," he said, "the duke has invited us to dine on Friday. Actually, it might even have been an order as he did not actually ask. I suppose we will go?"

"Of course we will go, I would not miss out on it for the world. I would like to get a closer look at this lady who has caught your eye."

"I did not say she has caught my eye."

"Hasn't she?"

"Maybe. But what she said—"

"Wembly, I am certain you will hear nothing further about her supposed research. She probably died inside as soon as she said it. She'll not utter another word about it. It would behoove you to pretend you'd never heard it."

Henry nodded. His aunt was likely right. After all, what did he know of a lady's flirtations? Up until now, he'd been oblivious to the fairer sex, he'd been entirely taken up with his research and The Royal Society. He would not embarrass her by raising the subject. As one of his tutors used to say, sometimes it was better to allow an awkward moment to die a quiet death.

Yes, that was what he would do. He would forget he'd ever heard her invent such an absurd notion and it would die a quiet death. Perhaps it was even charming that positing such an absurdity was her bumbling attempt at a flirtation.

In the meantime, he would write Sir Jonathan to be certain that Lady Verity Nicolet had been sent an invitation to his charity scavenger hunt.

VERITY LAID HERSELF down on the sofa in the library and

dramatically laid a cold compress over her eyes. As anyone who has something terrible to hide would be well aware, her mind had spent hours the night before racing over how to avoid discovery. And finally, a solution had been found. Or at least, a place to start.

First, Winsome had been told of her aim, and then Serenity when she'd walked over from two doors down. Then Patience when she'd arrived. As of now, they all understood that Verity Nicolet was making serious inquiry into the circulatory systems of slow-moving animals.

She had, of course, had to explain herself as to why she would wish to make such an inquiry. Fortunately, her sisters seemed very understanding over the idea that she'd just blurted something out and now must cover her tracks. They saw the logic in sharing an interest with Lord Wembly, even if they did not entirely see the logic of it being about circulatory systems and slow-moving animals.

Patience had set off to Lackington & Allen to discover if there were any books on slow-moving animals, circulatory systems, or both.

Winsome located their father's collection of Royal Society papers to see if there was anything to be had in there. After all, Lord Wembly would read them and possibly contribute to them. It would be well to know what he knew.

Serenity scanned their father's library shelves for anything that might prove illuminating.

The plan, in its entirety, was that Verity would discover enough to back up her ridiculous claim of the evening before. Then, at some later date, she would pretend to lose interest in the subject and never mention it again.

As for Verity herself, she'd claimed a headache that made her eyes hurt so she could not participate in the investigations into the literature. She'd done so in the past from time to time to encourage Winsome to read to her and it had led her family to presume she was prone to headaches.

In the past, the strategy had never amounted to much, as

Winsome usually got bored with whatever subject Verity wished to know about and picked up a gothic novel instead. If it would be considered educated to know how many ways an innocent young lady could be in mortal danger in a damp castle, she would be a lauded intellectual by now!

This time, though, Winsome was wholly focused on the task at hand. Valor was a bit of another story. One could not very well tell her of a ruse and expect her to keep it a secret. She would try, usually, but she had far too many slip-ups. On top of that, Valor would hardly be approving of a scheme to impress a gentleman. She could barely contain her pique when their father had mentioned over breakfast that Lord Wembly was coming to dine on Friday.

For all Valor knew about it, Verity had all along been examining the question of circulatory systems in slow-moving animals and had simply decided to devote much more time to it.

The youngest Nicolet had speedily become bored with the subject and took Sir Galahad into the drawing room. She was teaching the little dog to play Vingt-et-un by laying the cards on the carpet and giving him the signal to tap his paw on the deck when he wanted another card. He was getting very good at it, since he got a little piece of biscuit every time he tapped. His biggest challenge these days was enthusiastically tapping too much and going over twenty-one.

"Oh, wait a minute," Winsome said, "here's a paper that mentions slow-moving animals."

Verity sat up, the cold compress sliding off her face. She quickly put it back on. "What does it say? What is it about?"

"Gracious, what a palaver. The title of it, if you can believe it, is an "Account of a Peculiarity in the Distribution of the Arteries sent to the Limbs of slow-moving Animals together with some other Facts." It is a letter written six years ago from a surgeon named Mr. Anthony Carlisle to an esquire named Mr. John Symmons."

"That is precisely the sort of thing I must find out about,"

Verity said. "What does it say about slow-moving animals?" She was not entirely certain if information on arteries was precisely what they looked for, but it was the closest thing they'd come upon so far.

There was a moment's silence and Verity peeked out from her cold compress. Winsome was reading and looking horrified while she was doing it. She laid the paper down and said, "I cannot even read it. It is too horrible. Especially not with Serenity in the room."

CHAPTER FIVE

W INSOME HAD PALED and set down the paper. She claimed she could not read the very thing Verity needed to know about. Winsome had to read it, as she herself *really* could not read it. How could it be too horrible to read? What was in it that would set off Serenity?

Serenity had whipped round from the shelves. "Why? What does it say? Was something done to the bees?"

"It's about slow-moving creatures, Serenity," Winsome said, attempting to ease her sister's worry. "Bees are fast-moving, one can hardly see them sometimes, they fly so fast."

"Oh, that's right," Serenity said.

They all knew well enough of Serenity's care of bees and her devastation when she found one dead in a garden, which she seemed to always be looking for. Of course, they'd only recently discovered that she'd kept all the dead bees she'd found in a wood box, and that Lord Thorpe had built a proper crypt for them in their garden at home. Verity and Winsome had privately agreed that Lord Thorpe must be off his head in love with Serenity to have done it.

"But then," Serenity said, clearly thinking things through, "do you say some slow-moving animal was hurt? I am not certain what constitutes a slow-moving animal. Is it a poor old animal who cannot move as fast as he once could? I should just die to know it! Our dear Nelson only has three legs and he's blind in one eye—he can be slow-moving and he's not even old!"

Serenity was already springing water out of her eyes, as was her nature. It was as if she had a well inside her eyeballs and could pump the water at will.

"Serenity," Winsome said, "Nothing has happened to Nelson. He is safe and sound at your house, lying around somewhere with Lord Thorpe's mastiff, like he always is. Why don't you go to the drawing room and see how Valor and Sir Galahad get on with their card game? Put all this science talk out of your mind and think no more about it."

Serenity nodded. "That would be best, I think. As she made her way to the door, she said, "Though I cannot help that my imagination is conjuring something very terrible."

"No, no," Winsome said soothingly, "it's not that bad. Really, it is not."

Serenity nodded and closed the door behind her. Verity stared at Winsome, entirely forgetting about her cold compress.

Winsome said, "It really *is* that bad."

"What? What could be bad in a dusty old paper from the Royal Society?"

Winsome picked up the paper. It says here that this John Symmons sent a Maucauco to this Mr. Carlisle for, well, for a…dissection."

"A monkey? For a dissection?" Verity said, hardly believing her own ears.

"Verity, you cannot wish to be like these people! They cut open a monkey!"

This was ghastly indeed.

"Does Lord Wembly cut up monkeys?"

"He did not say," Verity said. "I'm sure not. I'm sure he only reads about other people who did." At least she hoped that was true, as even that was horrifying. No wonder Lord Wembly looked so shocked when she posited that she was researching the matter. It was not preposterous enough to be conducting scientific experiments, but for a lady to be reading such horrors…

Winsome went on with reading the paper. Then she gasped. "You will not believe it—this Carlisle fellow sent the cut-up monkey *with* the paper to Mr. Symmons."

"No."

"Indeed, it says right here."

"What else?"

Winsome went on to read the entirety of the paper, occasionally gasping. It seemed the Maucauco was not the only victim of Mr. Carlisle's. There was also mention of an American sloth and a lion.

As if all that were not horrifying enough, the paper concluded with detailed drawings.

Verity fanned herself. Winsome had turned white.

"Serenity can never find out anything about this," Winsome said.

"Agreed," Verity said. She rather wished she herself had never found out anything about it.

"We should get rid of this paper and wipe it out of our memories."

Verity was not opposed to that idea. But then she said, "Wait, what were the conclusions, though? What was anybody supposed to know about…all this?"

"Nothing very important, I'm sure. The fellow just keeps pointing out that the circulatory systems are different."

All that, just to know that animals were different?

"Verity, you should give this up. I do not know what Lord Wembly has been up to, but even if he has not been…what Mr. Carlisle has been doing. You cannot pretend at an interest in this."

"I wish I did not have to, I really do," Verity said. "But I very stupidly backed myself into a corner and now I have no choice. I will just do it enough to prove that I do know something about it, then I will drop it and pick up another interest. Like netting a purse."

"You really like Lord Wembly that much?"

"I think so. I do not wish to appear foolish in his eyes."

Winsome sighed. "All right, lady scientist. You know we'll all back you up. But really, Verity, I've been telling you for years to stop inventing things."

"Well, it's too late now!" Verity said, feeling irked to have it pointed out.

Winsome ripped up the paper and threw the bits into the unlit fireplace. "What should we tell Patience when she gets back?"

"Um, maybe that we have uncovered enough of what…has gone on so far. Scientifically. Without mentioning the details."

"I never want to mention the details again. Or think about them."

Nor did Verity.

A half-hour later, Patience returned with a book of drawings titled *Interesting Creatures of the World*. "Look," she said, opening the book, "there is a whole section on sloths, which Mr. Lackington tells me are exceedingly slow-moving."

Patience was left wondering why her two sisters went white as dough and ran from the room.

LADY LILITH CRANDALL, daughter of the Earl of Berensby, was pensive as she regarded the pile of papers in front of her. None of them were very satisfactory. There were invitations, but she could not help noting that the stack was not as high as it might have been and there were certain invitations missing.

There were no dinner invitations, and she perfectly well knew why. It was thought that her father could not possibly reciprocate. Such were their circumstances that the earl had rented the first floor of a house on Berwick Street. It was near Mayfair, but it was not Mayfair. It was an embarrassingly unassuming street in an equally unassuming house, and they did not even rent the whole of it. It was humiliating!

Of course, she could not entirely condemn her father. Her grandfather had left the estate in a shambles and mortgaged up to its ears. Really, it was a miracle they still had it in their possession. Her father's life's work had been digging out of the hole and that had left him with a very limited purse to work with.

The earl had carefully weighed where to spend what he had at his disposal. Clothes were not too much stinted on, though a lot of what she wore last season had been recut and repurposed. They at least rented a rather fine carriage and horses as the earl could not bear to be seen going round in anything shabby. As well, they had secured entrance into Almack's through an old friend of her father's who had kindly paid for the vouchers. But the fact remained that nobody would ever come to call on her at this address. She would not wish them to, it was all so déclassé!

Her situation presented so many complications. Were she to leave her card at another lady's house, it must indicate her own address and at-home day. She never wished to be at home in this place and she never wished for another lady to venture here.

At her real home in the country, there was at least the illusion of wealth. Her grandfather had not been able to destroy the house or the furniture or portraits in it that had been in place for a hundred years. She had her own horse at home, but her mare could not be brought to Town as the stable fees would be an extra expense. Their everyday dinners at home were nothing elaborate, but on the rare occasions that they hosted, they could put on a show. The estate produced enough food and Cook was creative enough to cover the fact that great expense had not been gone to. Further, as the earl always said, if the wine was not of the first quality, most of their neighbors would not know it.

Here, in Town, she felt as if she were not fully clothed. London ripped away the façade that all was well.

She'd thought she might have wed last season, as did her father. The earl's disappointment was evident, though he tried to hide it as he was a kind man in his own way. Lilith had set her cap on Lord Wembly. She'd known his aunt long, as that lady's deceased lord had been a distant cousin of her father's and her estate was rather local to their neighborhood.

Lord Wembly's aunt, Lady Pegatha, owned an estate that had not been entailed and her lord had seen to it that she would inherit it. Lilith was in the same situation, but for the matter of the mortgages hanging over her head. Lady Pegatha had offered, from time to time, to teach her of the responsibilities that would be hers someday, but all Lilith wanted was a husband to take it off her shoulders and decide what ought to be done.

The idea of Lord Wembly had seemed entirely perfect. He was handsome and practically drowning in money. He could bail out the estate with little trouble. Together, they would make a dashing young couple and could take London by storm. They could be the leading couple of the town, the couple de pouvoir. She'd even hinted round at the idea, but he was entirely oblivious.

Why did he not see how wonderful that would be? No longer would she reside in Berwick Street, re-cutting dresses from last year and wearing paste because all the real jewelry had been sold off. Nobody would "forget" to include her in their invitations out of the humiliating idea that her family could not reciprocate. Or worse, that the earl might attempt it and would embarrass his guests with a paltry offering. No longer would she precariously float at the edges of society. She would be somebody of note, rather than some poor girl eking it out in rented rooms.

When she observed the likes of Lady Westmoreland or Lady Pembroke, it was not just their jewels and rich fabrics that caught her eye. It was their confidence. They stood on rock solid ground and feared nothing. How she longed for that.

Of course, Lord Wembly had been far too busy with his inquiries at The Royal Society to take much notice of her. Or of anybody else, it seemed. Who had suggested to him that he ought to look into the circulation of slow animals? That person, whoever it was, should be forced to explain himself. Certainly, it must have been a man recommending such a thing. A woman would not be so impractical.

After the season, she'd gone through all her father's periodicals to find something on the subject, thinking that might attract his notice. Well, she had found one, and what a palaver that had been. Why were these men sending each other monkeys and the like? She could not imagine, but she had gleaned enough of it to be able to speak intelligently on the subject if that became necessary.

She did not know how in the world she might work it into a conversation, though. What was she to say? That she had an interest in the subject?

Lilith flipped through the invitations once more. Plenty of routs, but no dinners as of yet. Also conspicuously missing was an invitation to Sir Jonathan's scavenger hunt for charity. She could guess why—Sir Jonathan would speculate that her father did not have any funds for the very high-priced tickets. Which he did not.

However, she was also aware that Lord Wembly was likely to attend. At least, she'd heard that he had attended in other years.

Perhaps she would just turn up? After all, Sir Jonathan was not likely to send her away if she simply arrived. If she were questioned, she might say she'd thought her father had sent in for tickets—an innocent mistake if he had not. Sir Jonathan would be all but forced to accept her presence, ticket or not. Sometimes, the *ton's* well-regulated manners could work in one's favor. It would be a daring thing to do, but what did she have to lose at this point? She would at least mull over the idea.

Lilith rang the bell to call for her lady's maid, who was in fact the landlord's daughter who lived above them. Clara was a rather unremarkable girl who could not handle a single piece of Lilith's clothing without pronouncing it too fancy, wondering how anybody could work in such finery, and who always seemed to smell of vinegar.

Still, chin up. Someday, Lilith would have a French maid. Perhaps she'd even have two French maids. She would have two very impertinent French maids. After all, was not the Marchioness of Ledderley always decrying how impertinent her French maid was and were there not knowing nods from other important ladies? She would have her own maid to complain about.

She supposed she did have her own maid to complain about even now, but descriptions of Clara being shocked at her finery were not as amusing as a French maid's impertinently clever bon mots.

Someday, she would be where she was meant to be. Someday, she would not fret over every guinea. She would be the feminine half of the couple de pouvoir.

MRS. RIGHT'S PLAN was slowly coming together. She knew that her talent for picking up disparate pieces of information and arranging them into some kind of helpful order was a skill not many had.

She might have outdone herself this time.

The information to be rearranged and massaged and taken advantage of to form an exit plan for Mr. Klonsume were:

First fact: the name of the drunken viscount Mr. Klonsume had once served, turned out to be Lord Watery. When she'd first heard the name, she'd found a certain irony to it, as it seemed the viscount had taken it to heart and watered himself until he was quite watery in both his eyes and mind. Lord Watery served at the Earl of Peddlington's convenience, that fellow being his father.

Second fact: Mr. Klonsume claimed he was a genius on every possible subject. Her poor footmen had been pontificated to ad nauseum on decorating, the fall of Rome, Napoleon, the Greek Gods, some fellow named Revere who liked to ride around at night shouting at people and was thought terrific, and of course, the doings at Boston Harbor. Mrs. Right was well-used to some blowhard in a tavern claiming to be the next Newton or Nelson, but those blowhards would give up the idea in the sober light of day.

Mr. Klonsume did not give up the idea, as it was not the fog of ale that caused his spouting off. He wholeheartedly believed in his superiority and had not the least skill in noticing he bored everyone to sleep. As far as that buffoon was concerned, his alleged American confidence and ingenuity would take him to ever greater heights. The sky was the limit for Mr. Klonsume. He had even, the night before and after a large glass of brandy, speculated that the queen would be well served to interview him regarding the current American styles of decorating. According to Mr. Klonsume, he could deliver the latest information, and his ideas were "innovative" and "modern."

Fact three: Mr. Klonsume was very mistaken regarding his expertise, especially when it came to understanding rank and how England worked, with everybody having their proper place given to them at birth. He seemed to believe that Americans were all equal to one another, which, if true, was rather hilarious—the place must be chaos. As for the queen requesting his expertise, not even the lowliest servant emptying chamber pots in the palace would ask Mr. Klonsume for his opinion on anything.

Fact four: Her dear Serenity lived only two doors down now, having wed Lord Thorpe. That girl was in and out of the house on the regular, chatting away on a myriad of subjects. Very naturally, one of those subjects was Lord Thorpe's brother, Lord Charles. Those two brothers had quite the set-to last season and Lord Charles had taken himself off to the continent until things cooled down between them. He had not, however, given up his set at The Albany.

Fact five: The season prior, Lord Thorpe had hired actors and a carriage to fool Valor into imagining she rescued Sir Galahad from an untimely death by drowning in the Thames. This was done to ease Nelson and Serenity out of the house by giving Valor a dog of her own she could direct her attention to. Mrs. Right had watched it play out, and what she'd taken away from it was that actors could be just as convincing off the stage as on.

Those five disparate facts, taken together, had been molded into a divine idea. Once she had access to the set at The Albany and could arrange things there, had special livery prepared, actors hired, and a carriage rented, she would be ready to set it in motion. The duke's household funds would easily cover the expenses as she'd been running a surplus for years. She'd always thought it wise to do so and save for any future calamity that came upon them. Should an emergency of the monetary variety strike, the duke would be pleasantly surprised to discover that it could easily be covered.

But first, the all-important letter to Mr. Klonsume would arrive.

The very idea of it did give her comfort, which was sorely needed just now. Mr. Klonsume was currently bent over the servants' table examining samples of wall coverings he'd had delivered. Though nobody had asked him to do it!

He was homing in on a print that appeared to depict the people and wildlife of the Far East as being just right for the duke's dining room.

"It really is majestic, if I do say so myself," Mr. Klonsume said. "Look at this, Mrs. Right, it's got maharajahs sitting under palms and monkeys hanging in the trees. The maharajahs are being fanned by young boys on account of the heat. Devilish hot there, is my understanding. Maharajahs. Very apt for a duke, is it not? If you think about it, he's an English maharajah. We don't go in for maharajahs in America, mind you—nobody is above anybody else. But then, it might be pleasant to be a maharajah."

Mrs. Right smiled at him. In not many more days, she would maharajah him right out of the house.

She would simply restrain herself from putting a pillow over his face in the meantime.

CHAPTER SIX

VERITY HAD BEEN exceedingly pleased to have an invitation delivered for Sir Jonathan's charity scavenger hunt. Her father claimed to never have laid eyes on the man, which might or might not be true, as the duke was not very good at remembering people. What she did know from her sisters, though, was no such invitation had arrived in prior years. Certainly, Lord Wembly had arranged it. The duke was agreeable to the scheme and had sent the funds for tickets.

She felt a little shiver whenever she thought of Lord Wembly. Especially if she could block out of her mind any thoughts about slow-moving animals who may have given their lives in the name of science. Or block out that he was an intellectual, while she could not even read. Or block out that if anything were to really develop between them, she must inform him of that fact. If she could block out all of that, thinking of him was positively lovely.

Her plan that at some future moment she would claim she'd lost interest in the subject of his research had not been fully rounded out as to when that moment would arrive. Verity had begun to believe that perhaps the time in question must be soon. Very soon. She really did not wish to think of the subject further. She was determined to communicate an understanding of the topic and then be done with it.

Now, it had finally come. The night Lord Wembly and Lady Pegatha would come to dine. She'd picked out her favorite dress, but for the one she had packed away to wear at her wedding. Should there be a wedding.

The one she wore this evening was a crème silk with matching crème roses round the neckline. Mrs. Right secured a modest necklace of rubies set in gold and fashioned in the shape of a rose round her neck and smoothed her hair into order. Winsome was going through her jewelry, examining the pieces. Valor laid on her bed with Sir Galahad, watching the proceeding.

"I don't see why he has to come to dinner," Valor said, pretending to talk to the little pug. Sir Galahad shook his head and sneezed by way of his opinion.

Verity was well-used to Valor's displeasure at the idea of a gentleman turning up to dine. Thinking to soothe her, she said, "Valor, the dinner is not really for Lord Wembly, he's only coming along. The real point is to honor Lady Pegatha, an old friend of our father's."

"I imagine you will like her, Val," Winsome said helpfully, "as you do always get on with an older lady."

"Oh, you mean like my very good friend, Lady Margaret?"

"Just so."

"Lady Margaret considers me her dearest friend," Valor said. "She admires my youth. Also, I wrote her about Sir Galahad, and she wrote me back about it. She reads my letters to Lord Harraby, and they agree that Sir Galahad sounded like the most tremendous dog in England."

"That was very kind," Verity said.

"No, she was not just being nice," Valor said with a note of irritation. "You see, I told her about teaching him how to play Vingt-et-un, and how I pick him up and put him in my bed at night because his legs are too short to manage it, and how he sometimes has sneezing fits on account of his flat nose, and how close he came to drowning in the Thames. Anybody would realize he was tremendous from all that."

"Yes, that's very true," Verity said. They all knew that Lord Thorpe had set the scene for Valor to rescue Sir Galahad from the clutches of an evil lord who would drown him for being the runt of the litter. Nobody would ever say a word to Valor about it being a carefully composed tableau, though. Her recitation of her courageous rescue had grown to include fetching her father's pistols and threatening the lord with imminent death. Fortunately, the only thing that had fetched the pistols was Valor's imagination.

"I suppose Lady Pegatha will be bowled over by Sir Galahad," Valor said.

"No doubt," Winsome said, picking up a pearl necklace.

"Put it back, Winny," Verity said, knowing all too well that Winsome would make off with it if she could.

"Positively bowled over," Valor said, scratching Sir Galahad's chin.

"Come now," Mrs. Right said, putting the last pin into Verity's hair, "your father will be bowled over by how late you are if you do not get going downstairs."

Verity hopped up and they made their way down to the drawing room. As it happened, they were a bit late. Lord Wembly and Lady Pegatha were already there. Gracious, she had not even heard a carriage arrive.

Lord Wembly was looking even more smashing than he had at Almack's. His clothes were tailored to perfection and his knot was of the neat and unfussy variety. He had a devil-may-care style, the sort that was perfect, though looking as if hardly a thought had gone into it. As well, there was something in seeing him standing in her own house that gave her a thrill. He was very tall and broad and almost made the drawing room seem smaller than it was. He was such a man!

"There they are, the last of my daughters I've not yet launched out of the house—Verity, Winsome, and Valor," the duke said jovially. "We only wait for Serenity and Thorpe—they are just two doors down, so we should not wait long."

Patience and Lord Stanford and Felicity and Mr. Stratton were already there. Verity knew that Grace and Lord Dashlend would not come, they were already engaged to dine with one of his relations and could not beg off.

Verity and Lord Wembly were looking at one another in some sort of dumbfounded stare. It was really very awkward, but she could not look away.

Valor went forward with Sir Galahad in her arms. She walked past Lord Wembly, knocking into his arm and giving him nary a glance. "Lady Pegatha," she said. "Allow me to introduce you to Sir Galahad."

"He is very charming," Lady Pegatha said.

"I know, everybody thinks so. He was almost drowned, but I saved him. If you want, you can play Vingt-et-un with him. He is very good, but getting too much in the habit of going over twenty-one on account of biscuits."

"Goodness," Lady Pegatha said. Verity could see very well that she was leery of playing cards with a pug.

Just then, Serenity and Lord Thorpe came in. "Are we late?" Serenity asked. "I am sorry if we are, but Nelson and Havoc were being so charming this evening. They've brought in a branch from the square and are rather delighted to steal it from one another."

"You see how it is, Wembly," the duke said, "get involved with this family and I guarantee you'll come out of it with a dog. Will it have the usual number of legs? Not guaranteed. But then, maybe it will look like that one," he said, pointing at Sir Galahad. "Never was there a dog who more looked like his face was stomped on by a horse's hoof."

"Papa!" Valor said, offended that anyone would point out Sir Galahad's rather flattened features.

"His eyes look as if they might fall out of his head and roll across the carpet," the duke said, laughing at his own joke. "Wouldn't be surprised if they did one of these days. Well, now, we're all here, let's get going and hope the butler who is currently haunting my rooms has managed something. Wembly, take Verity in, if you will.

Lord Wembly held out his arm. Verity laid her hand on it. So far, neither of them had said a word. It was as if they were both struck dumb in one another's presence. It began to make her nervous.

Her nerves were somewhat distracted by what they found waiting for them in the dining room. What on earth?

It seemed Mr. Klonsume had been so bold as to redecorate. At least, she must assume so as she could not imagine who else would have done it.

The duke had stopped in his tracks. Mr. Klonsume hurried forward. "Your Grace, welcome to East meets West, a triumph of ingenuity."

The triumph in question was an odd wallcovering that had been nailed to the far wall, depicting Indian men being fanned under palms. Most disturbing to Verity, there were monkeys in the trees, and she could not help thinking of the poor monkey she and Winsome had read about in the Royal Society paper.

"For the love of heaven," the duke said.

"You note the maharajahs," Mr. Klonsume said, somehow imagining that the duke's comment was in appreciation.

The duke turned to his guests. "Ignore the wall covering as best you can. Now, let's get on with it!" He took his seat and everybody followed suit.

Thomas had already arranged the place cards for Lady Pegatha to be on the duke's right and Verity would be seated next to Lord Wembly with Mr. Stratton on her other side. Felicity, being the oldest married lady, took the hostess' seat.

The duke motioned to Charlie to bring round the wine. He said, "As you see, Lady Pegatha, Wembly, we do not host large dinners here. We like for the table to be able to talk together, rather than having the din of thirty people all talking to their neighbors."

"Excellent notion, Your Grace," Lady Pegatha said.

"We have known each other an age," the duke said, "you'd better call me duke."

Lady Pegatha nodded graciously. Valor stared at her father

and said, "Papa?"

"Ah, yes, my youngest has got in the habit of saying something to kick us off. Hopefully it won't be as startling as last year's something."

Valor shook her head at him as if she had no idea what he was talking about. "Welcome, Lady Pegatha, who is the honored person at the dinner."

Verity suppressed a sigh.

"I always make a speech because I'm practicing to be my Papa's hostess forever," Valor said. "I will never leave him. If any of my sisters want to stay too, well, all I can say is that we would be very merry altogether. Also, we would not have to worry about a gentleman staying in our room all night. And staring at us while we sleep. Mr. Stratton."

"One time," Mr. Stratton muttered.

"We would be much happier all together and it's just too bad some of my sisters didn't think of that in time." Valor allowed her condemning gaze to touch on Mr. Stratton, Lord Stanford, and Lord Thorpe.

"We are all very happy, though, Val," Felicity said, laughing.

"You have to say that," Valor said, leveling her gaze at Mr. Stratton. "He's sitting right there. I only leave you with my hints for happiness, with our Papa, forever."

Valor curtsied.

"Well! Rousing speech, as always," the duke said.

"It must be hard to be the youngest of the sisters, losing them one by one," Lord Wembly said.

"It is," Valor answered. "Maybe you want to help me out!"

Lord Wembly did not answer and Verity felt as if she would like to sink through the floor. Valor had all but hinted that Lord Wembly had an interest in her, though Lord Wembly had not hinted it yet.

He would, though, would he not? They could not stop staring at one another in the drawing room. Certainly that meant something.

"Lord Wembly," Winsome said, "we could hardly drag Verity

out of the library today. She gets so engrossed with her learning. About the slow-moving animals."

Lady Pegatha's head snapped up from her soup. "Really?" she said, looking very surprised to hear it.

Lord Wembly had turned to Verity. This was the moment to prove she actually knew something about the lord's research, and then gracefully exit it, never to be spoken of again. "Indeed," she said, "I found Mr. Carlisle's observations regarding the circulatory system particularly illuminating."

"Oh, I see," Lord Wembly said. "Well, yes, of course, the dissection of the monkey did provide some valuable foundational information."

A loud clatter interrupted him. Serenity had dropped her spoon. "Dissection?" she cried. "Of a monkey?"

Lord Wembly looked entirely startled. "Uh…no, no, it was, hmm, what is it called? Ah, predictive research. Meaning, what would be the result if he had. Done anything. Which he did not."

Verity and Winsome stared at one another, as they both knew the truth of it. She must admit, Lord Wembly was very astute to so quickly recover what might have been a festival of tears. He was very kind to do it, too.

Serenity wiped a tear from her cheek. "Goodness, you frightened me."

Lord Thorpe stared grimly at Lord Wembly, no doubt displeased that his wife had been frightened.

"You see?" Valor said, apropos of nothing.

"So you are researching the matter, Lady Verity?" Lady Pegatha asked with a raised brow.

Here was her moment to back herself out of this ridiculous situation. Verity said, "I was, but I've decided to leave it behind. For now, at least."

"Ah, I see," Lady Pegatha said, "no doubt some other subject has captured your attention."

Verity nodded gratefully. "Indeed."

"What is it, pray?" Lady Pegatha asked.

What is it? It was nothing. Why was Lady Pegatha asking what it was? Why had she not thought she'd have to come up with some new interest? She'd briefly considered that she might say she was netting purses instead, but that was ridiculous. One did not replace scientific research with netting purses!

Verity felt her thoughts begin to spin. The prickly feeling she sometimes felt on her arms and face rushed over her.

"She won't say," Winsome said, attempting to throw her drowning sister a life ring, "but we're sure it's very…scientific."

"Oh, come now," Lady Pegatha said, "we must know."

Verity's thinking had gone blind, it was doing nothing at all. What interest, what interest, what interest?

"I hope it's more interesting than whatever that other thing was," Valor said.

Her other sisters were staring at her in alarm. Particularly Patience and Serenity, who knew very well that she'd invented the first interest and now she was to have a second. Even Felicity looked wide-eyed, as she had perhaps heard some of Verity's ideas in the past that were not quite right. Or true.

"Lady Verity?" Lord Wembly said, looking curiously at her.

Thomas had come round with a platter of whole broiled cod. She stared down at their dead glassy eyes and felt her own eyes go glassy.

"Well, as one might imagine, I'm looking into the ability of fish to see when out of water. Rather, if they can," she said.

What had she said? What had she done?

Again.

"Well now," the duke said, "that explains all that hanging around the lake in the Dales. My advice, keep it all to yourself for now, in these early stages. Wouldn't want to come to any wrong conclusions by rushing the thing."

Dear Papa. Of course he would come to the rescue. She *would* keep it to herself. Forever, if she could manage it.

HENRY WAS ENTIRELY confounded. What was he meant to think? Lady Verity was looking into the parameters of a fish's eyesight out of water? What on earth was he to make of it?

On the one hand, when Lady Verity had entered the drawing room, he'd had to steady himself a bit. She was so striking looking, and he was so attracted to her. She was perfection. He'd really been a little bit breathless.

He had expected that the duke's household would land on the eccentric side of things. After all, His Grace had been in Town for four prior seasons and word did get around. He was not even that surprised to encounter a youngest sister practically knocking him out of the way to show off her dog to his aunt.

He *was* rather surprised at the tacked-up wallcovering of some sort of Indian scene and the very odd American butler who'd seemed to be at the bottom of it.

All of that, though, would have been nothing. He knew very well that his Aunt Pegatha had been teasing when she'd inquired into Lady Verity's studies. His aunt could not resist it when Lady Winsome had claimed her sister had been in the library all day, deep in study.

The strange part was, she must have looked into it at least a little bit. She'd mentioned that letter between Carlisle and Symmons from years ago. It was what had piqued his interest in the subject of circulatory systems in the first place. *Had* she been investigating the matter? Or had she lied about it and then scrambled to find something on the subject?

And then she claimed she'd given it up to investigate if fish could see out of water. How would a lady go about doing those experiments?

Perhaps it was just an idea, and she would soon enough encounter the impracticalities of it.

Was she a lady interested in scientific pursuits, or was she a complete fibber, as his aunt believed?

The conversation had gone on to more usual topics, led by Lady Felicity and Mr. Stratton. Those two seemed determined to steer far away from any conversation around science.

Mr. Stratton said, "Wembly, I don't know how familiar you are with Dales ponies, but the duke's daughters all ride them—they are something to see."

He'd turned to Lady Verity. "Are you fond of riding?"

"Yes, goodness, we all are," Lady Verity said. "Except Valor."

"I'm fond of going slowly, that's all," Valor said.

"Perhaps we might meet in the park for a ride," he said, "assuming the duke's permission."

"I'll tell you what, Wembly," the duke said, "Verity and Winsome can ride with the grooms and I'll bring Valor and Mrs. Right in the carriage. How is Monday at four?"

"Excellent, yes," Henry said. Though, he had not the first idea of who Mrs. Right was.

"And Sir Galahad," Valor said.

"Why not?" the duke said. "Now, what say you, sons-in-laws of mine? Were you planning to warn Wembly about what he could expect in the drawing room? A game with tickets, perhaps?"

Henry did not know what game the duke referred to, but he was not encouraged by the three gentlemen's expressions.

"Fact or Fib!" Lady Valor shouted.

"Fact or Fib?" Henry asked.

"I'm afraid so," Lord Stanford said. "We'll bring the brandy and port in to make it easier."

Make it easier? Make what easier? He'd never heard of the game. Was it something peculiar to the Dales?

"Sorry," Mr. Stratton muttered.

Lord Thorpe shrugged. "It can't be helped."

Henry did not at all understand what they meant by it. The gentlemen were all looking very down about it, but then their wives seemed to think it terrific.

"You'll love it," Lady Winsome said.

"A very hopeful prediction," the duke said, laughing. "Well, let's get on with it. Klondoom, Klondike, whatever your name is, take the bottles and glasses into the drawing room. And Lady Pegatha, might I interest you in a sherry?"

"You find me very interested, indeed," Lady Pegatha said. "What a delightful idea."

"Lady Pegatha," Lady Valor said, "you can sit next to me and pet Sir Galahad. I always get along with old women. Ask anybody."

Henry's brows raised the slightest bit, not entirely certain how gratified his aunt would be to be named an old woman.

Thankfully, she laughed.

As the duke rose, his butler said, "A quick word to the party, Your Grace."

The butler was going to have a quick word with them? How extraordinary.

"I could not help earlier overhearing talk of a scientific nature," the butler said, soldiering on despite the duke's frown, "and, as an American, I thought I might weigh in. Our deceased and revered American citizen, Mr. Benjamin Franklin, invented electricity—"

The duke held his hand up. "He did not invent it, he noticed it, as anybody who's ever looked up in a thunderstorm has done since time began. What *I* notice is that you do not yet have those bottles and glasses in hand."

The butler looked entirely startled to be interrupted.

"And after those duties are accomplished," the duke said, "get that absurd wallcovering down."

"The maharajahs?" the butler asked, looking entirely perplexed over why anybody would wish to have them removed.

The duke did not bother to answer, and Henry supposed that was a duke's prerogative. He'd given an order and did not expect a debate about it.

As the duke led the party across the great hall, Lady Winsome hooked her thumb back at the butler. To Henry, she said quietly, "Another one of Lady Marchfield's butlers. He won't be here long. Mrs. Right will get rid of him."

CHAPTER SEVEN

HENRY HARDLY KNEW what to do with Lady Winsome's statement. Lady Marchfield was lending the duke a butler, but he was to be got rid of? Where did Lady Marchfield even find an American butler? And again, another mention of this mysterious Mrs. Right. Could it be possible that the duke kept a mistress? Was she above stairs somewhere, considered inappropriate company for Lady Pegatha?

It sounded deranged, but considering all he'd experienced so far, he could not rule anything out of bounds.

But no, surely not. Whatever the duke was, he did seem to have a care for his daughters. He would hardly have a mistress living in the house. Who was she, though?

Lady Winsome and Lady Valor had pulled all the chairs round in a circle and laid piles of blue and yellow tickets on an ottoman.

The footman came round with the bottles of port and brandy. Apparently, they had left the butler behind to take down the wallcovering and think of Mr. Benjamin Franklin.

One of the footmen poured Henry a glass of port. Lord Stanford said, "Better give him more, Charlie, first time at Fact or Fib, you know."

The footman nodded knowingly and filled his glass nearly to the top. Henry was becoming very wary of what would come next. His aunt looked a little wary herself, as Lady Valor had just thrown her pug into the lady's lap.

"Now, the game is simple," Lady Valor said. "We'll ask you a question and then if you tell the truth, you get a yellow ticket, and if you fib, you get a blue ticket. Two yellows wins, but a blue cancels a yellow. I always go first."

Henry was seated next to Lady Verity. He leaned over and said quietly, "How do they know whether anyone has told the truth?"

"They just decide," Lady Verity whispered.

Henry took a long draught of port. They just decide.

"Lady Pegatha," Lady Valor said, "Do you think there could be any other dog in the whole world who is as tremendous as Sir Galahad?"

As a further prompting, Lady Valor held up the dog to Lady Pegatha's face.

"Gracious, well, if there is, I don't know about it," Lady Pegatha said.

"Fact!" Lady Valor said. "I know it's a fact because Lady Margaret thinks the very same thing." She hopped up, threw a yellow ticket in Lady Pegatha's direction and took her dog back. "I'm going to bed now. I've matured and don't always wait to have an overtired outburst. I feel it creeping up on me, is what I say." She turned to Lady Verity and said, "Try not to get married while I'm gone."

With that, Lady Valor made a little curtsy and left with her dog hanging in her arms.

That was an odd display, but the game did not seem insurmountable. Henry did not quite know what he'd expected, but it appeared as if it would not be as bad as he imagined. He was happy enough to give his opinion on the household dog, or whatever other subject came up.

"Lord Wembly," Lady Winsome said, "what was the first thing you noticed about our Verity?"

Henry felt rather frozen. What a question. It did not help that his aunt had outright snorted. "Oh, as to that, well, I would say, if pressed, I suppose it must be her mind." He'd imagined that would be a safe answer, but began to doubt himself, considering the dark looks coming from the duke's daughters. Stanford sighed next to him.

"Fib!" Lady Winsome cried. "It is her eyes, everybody knows it. Papa says they are like our mother's."

"That's true," the duke said.

Henry had a blue ticket thrown in his lap. What he was supposed to do with it, he did not know. Of course, the correct answer probably would have been her eyes, if not her complexion or hair or lips or charming little nose. But he could hardly be expected to say so!

"I'll go," Patience said. "Verity, what did *you* first notice about Lord Wembly?"

Henry dared not look at her, though she was just to his left.

"His hair," Lady Verity said. "It is a particular shade of auburn."

His hair? It was his worst feature! But then, what one first notices about a person is not always what they find most genial. It could be she was very against the color and struck by it in that way.

The sisters looked at one another, as if they could not decide. Then Lady Felicity subtly nodded, and they all cried, "Fact!"

Lady Verity was handed a yellow ticket.

As Lady Winsome turned her sights on Lady Pegatha, Henry leaned to the left and whispered, "My hair. Is it bad?"

"No," she whispered back and then turned away in her chair.

So. His hair color was not bad. Surprising.

THE FOLLOWING DAY, Verity had been about as relaxed as a cat caught in a downpour. All day long, she'd attempted to settle on something or somewhere or some attitude. She was all mixed up!

Winsome had followed her around saying things like: "Verity, why on earth did you say you were trying to find out if fish can see when they are on land? What are you to do about it? Why does it even matter, what good could it do them since they cannot breathe on land?"

Of course, she very well knew it was ridiculous. She'd felt cornered, as if she had to say something, and then there were those broiled cod staring up at her and it had come out.

That was not the least of it, either. When Lord Wembly had been asked what he'd first noticed about her, he'd said her mind. Her mind, her intelligence—it was the exact worst thing about her! She was an idiot who could not even read, and he admired her mind? Why had she ever pretended she was at all interested in the circulatory systems of slow-moving animals? It was the same old problem that had haunted her forever—she panicked because she was certain somebody was on the verge of discovering how stupid she was.

What was she to do about it? It was as if all her worst fears were coming true. She had held on to the shred of hope that a gentleman she admired might admire her too because he was attracted to her looks. Even if she were not the prettiest lady in Town, Mrs. Right often said there was a lid to every teapot. If she could be a lid, perhaps the teapot would not notice her less than middling intellect.

Baron Wembly was not the sort of gentleman who would remain blind to a middling intellect. Or appreciate it.

As she had a hundred times before, Verity searched her mind for some way to become smarter. Why could everybody else read while she could not? Was there some trick to it that she was missing? She could not ask anybody without giving herself away, so she had never asked anybody.

This afternoon, they were to ride in the park. That, at least, she was competent at. But would he ask her anything about the fish? She did not know the first thing about fish, other than she was not opposed to broiled cod.

She probably should have taken Valor's advice and sat the season out.

But she had not, and Lord Wembly was glorious. She could not give up thinking about him. Even if it turned out to be hopeless.

"What did he whisper to you, Verity?" Winsome asked. "When you said the first thing you noticed was his hair. He whispered something."

"Oh, he asked if it was bad. I said no," Verity said.

"That's a bright spot, then," Winsome said.

Winsome was right, that was a bright spot. Verity had been a bit thrown off by the question—who could think that glorious auburn hair was bad? Perhaps he just wanted to be sure she approved of it. That really would be a bright spot.

"I know what you should do, Verity," Winsome said. "About that ridiculous fish idea, why don't you just say it was an *idea* but you haven't done anything to look into it. That way, you won't be tempted to make up any outrageous stories about it."

Verity supposed she should be affronted that Winsome had mentioned her outrageous stories. But then, Winsome, of all her sisters, knew her the best. It was one of the reasons Winsome was always challenging what she said. Winsome did not know the real reason for what she did, though.

It was all becoming too much. Who she was, what she was, had always weighed heavily on her. When she was younger, she could go for hours without thinking about it. Now it was on her mind every second of every day. When she was younger, she used to fool herself with the idea that her mind would catch up to everybody else's and she'd learn to read.

Maybe it would be easier if people just knew. They could condemn her or feel sorry for her or however they wanted to feel. They could accept her or not, whichever they wished. She felt a tear roll down her cheek and swiped at it, turning away from Winsome.

"Are you crying? You never cry. What's happened? Keep

going with the fish story if you like—it was just a suggestion."

"Winsome," she said very quietly. "I have a secret. A terrible secret."

Winsome laughed. "Whatever the secret, I doubt it's very terrible."

Verity was silent for some moments as Winsome stared at her. She took a breath in and said, "I cannot read. I've tried and tried but I cannot do it. I've hidden it all these years—I am exceedingly stupid. Lord Wembly is going to find it out and want nothing to do with me."

Mrs. Right had just left Verity and Winsome sobbing together in the library. They would not say what it was about, only that it was a secret between sisters.

She was inclined to think it had something to do with Lord Wembly. She was inclined to think it because of how many other times they were in Town and one of her girls had been weeping and it had been because of the gentleman she admired.

If that baron had done a single thing to upset her girl, he would hear about it. Or if not hear about it, then suffer some anonymous consequences over it. Lord Wembly ought to be very wary of the prospect. Had she not proved last season that she could be as sly and skilled as any housebreaker, slipping through the darkness with impunity to wreak vengeance?

Upon reflection, it had turned out to be not at all necessary to meddle with the springs on Lord Thorpe's carriage. As well, it had caused a delay in that couple's setting off for their wedding trip when the carriage collapsed in front of their house. So that had been regrettable. Fortunately, that was all water under the bridge now.

Mrs. Right made her way down to the kitchens to arrange for a tea tray to be sent up to her weeping girls. At least Valor was not involved in the palaver. She'd taken Sir Galahad over to Serenity's house two doors down to play with Nelson and Havoc. Mrs. Right just hoped that Havoc, that great beast of a mastiff, did not swallow Sir Galahad whole. He was a cheerful little pug, but not very fast on his feet, as the legs attached to those appendages were exceedingly short.

She turned the corner and found Thomas and Charlie staring at Mr. Klonsume, who was waving a letter. Considering the expression on his face, she had a good guess at what letter it was. She'd not imagined it would come today. She had thought the post would bring it tomorrow. The all-important letter that was to kick off the proceedings of getting Mr. Klonsume out of the house had arrived.

"Mrs. Right," the butler said, "you arrive at a propitious moment in my career. Gad, if my friends in America could see how far I've risen!"

"What's happened, Mr. Klonsume?" she asked. Though, she knew perfectly well what had happened. Or at least, what Mr. Klonsume would believe had happened.

"Here," he said, shoving the letter at her, read it for yourself."

Mrs. Right nodded. She hardly needed to read it, as she had written it. She'd borrowed some paper from the duke, resplendent with his crest and knowing full well that Mr. Klonsume would not recognize it, as crests and titles seemed to go right over his head. In as manly a hand as she could muster, she'd written as Lord Watery. She'd done her best to sound like a drunken viscount.

Klonsume—

Dastardly of my father to send you off like that. Heard you were found a place through Lady Marchfield (stern old girl). Chin up, old fellow, I write with very good news.

It seems Buckingham has got a scheme going called "Operation Flattery." Something about increasing trade with the Americans and smoothing over any irritations of the shipping variety. They intend on knighting a pile of you fellows to show their friendliness and drum up some goodwill. I slipped you on the list—made up a whole palaver about you inventing a piece of factory machinery, if you can believe it! Going to revolution-ize something or other. (I think I said gun manufacturing but who knows—I was entirely under the table.)

Promised my father I'd ease up on the brandy if he put your name forward. (I won't but what can he do about it now?) Things are moving fast—the Lord Chamberlain will send a carriage for you on the morrow. They will take you to a set at The Albany and there will be further instructions there about what's next. That's all I know about it.

Oh, except that Lady Marchfield will be apprised of the thing and escort you to the ceremony. I'd do it, but would probably be in my cups and the queen don't like that sort of thing. My father would do it, but he doesn't particularly ap-prove of you. (Or believe you invented anything, hah!)

Anyway, this eases my mind about my earl throwing you to the streets. Very shortly, you'll be Sir Morus Klonsume! You always said, well, I don't remember exactly what you said, something about American confidence.

Cheers, old boy.

Watery.

Mrs. Right laid down the letter after pretending to read through it. She'd worked very hard to put just the right expression on as she took in this astonishing news.

"What did I tell you, Mrs. Right?" Mr. Klonsume asked. "What did I tell you all along?"

She did not answer, as the butler had told her no end of non-sense and she would not know where to start. Thomas had turned away and Charlie pressed his lips together in an effort not to laugh. Both those boys would have instantly recognized the duke's crest. Not the Maharajah of-I-know-everything, though.

Mr. Klonsume glanced down at his ridiculous waistcoat, embroidered with American flags. "I'll need something new," he said thoughtfully. "A waistcoat with our two nations' flags on it—a merging together of two fine peoples represented by an American knight. Oh, now I did not think, will I get a crest? That should go on the waistcoat too."

"I'd be surprised if you did not, Mr. Klonsume," Mrs. Right said.

He nodded. "Yes, of course I will get one. One cannot be a knight without a crest, I reckon. With any luck, I can put in a request about the design of the thing. A lion must represent my courageous nature. And then, I wouldn't mind a phoenix on my crest. I've risen from the ashes more than once in my time and now I am poised to fly to ever greater heights!"

"It certainly is surprising how life can suddenly take a turn," Mrs. Right said pleasantly.

This was a bit much for Thomas and he ran from the room to laugh elsewhere. Mr. Klonsume was too taken up with his incoming knighthood to notice.

"Sir Morus," he said reverentially. "I suppose it harms nobody if I take on the title at once. After all, it sounds so natural to my ears, as if I've been Sir Morus all along. I suppose it was always my fate to be a knight; I've somehow felt it inside since I was just a lad. Yes, it could not be a harm to adopt the title at once."

"Certainly not, Sir Morus," Mrs. Right said.

"Should you be curtsying? I hardly know," Mr. Klonsume said, tapping his chin.

"Not in the servants' hall, I believe is the tradition."

"That makes sense. Yes, of course it does. Why would a Sir even be in the servants' hall?"

"Why indeed?"

"And then, I've got the break the news to the duke that I will be off on the morrow. One English maharajah to another, as it were."

Mrs. Right would like to correct that statement to "as it were *not*." Instead, she said, "Leave the duke to me, Sir Morus. He does not like change of any sort, as you probably ascertained when you got here. I know how it will be best handled. In any case, I imagine you might like to spend your time packing your things. When the carriage arrives on the morrow, you will not wish to keep them waiting. It would be bad form."

"Excellent points, Mrs. Right," Mr. Klonsume said with a tone she imagined was meant to signal some sort of newfound gravitas. "Gad, I've got to learn all about good form and bad. Goodbye, Mrs. Right. We will no longer travel in the same circles, I'm afraid. Can't be helped—when one moves up in the world, one leaves people behind. Nature of the thing."

Mrs. Right was itching to inquire what happened to his idea that there was no rank in America. Nobody was above anybody else. Now that Mr. Klonsume imagined he was to have a title, he did not seem so opposed to the idea of rank. She kept her own counsel on it, though.

Head held high, Mr. Klonsume went off to pack his things. There was silence in the servants' hall until he was well out of hearing. Then the hysterics that took over could not be contained for some minutes. Cook came in to join them, as he'd been listening from the kitchens. He said he'd laughed so hard he cried and was planning to blame it on chopping onions if he were caught.

On the morrow, Mr. Klonsume would be taken to The Albany in a carriage that would fly a few ridiculous flags to hammer in the pomp of it all and he'd be given the keys to Lord Charles' set. There, he would find instructions to pray all night to prepare himself for the royal bestowing of a knighthood of the Order of Owen, which she had entirely invented. Saint Nicholas Owen was known as the saint of ingenuity, which was very apt to bestow upon a fellow very impressed with his own ingenuity.

Mr. Klonsume would also be left with preposterous clothing to wear to the nonexistent ceremony, all dug up from the attics. With any luck, Mr. Klonsume would don a frock coat, colorful waistcoat, breeches, silk stockings, shoes sporting a heel and gaudy buckles, and top the whole thing off with a patch and a powdered wig. He would set off to collect Lady Marchfield to be witness to his knighthood.

And that would conclude the satisfying return to Lady Marchfield of yet another butler.

Though Mr. Klonsume was generally oblivious, Lady Marchfield would see Mrs. Right's hand in it at once. She only wished she could be there when the fellow arrived in all his splendor and explained he was to be knighted into the Order of Owen because of his American confidence and ingenuity.

CHAPTER EIGHT

L ILITH HAD EXPERIENCED a very unsatisfactory evening at Lady
Herring's rout. She had been certain that Lord Wembly
would be there. After all, he'd been there last year, as Lady
Pegatha was a longtime friend of Lady Herring.

Neither of them had been there. Of course, there were plenty
of single gentlemen roaming about, but Lilith had begun to
notice that she did not attract *their* notice. She was not so modest
or bashful as to blame it on her looks. Her looks were quite good,
and she knew it.

No, it was the finances. She did not come with a large dowry.
In truth, it was rather a pittance, more for form than for any good
it would do anybody. She understood that many of these eligible
gentlemen had pressing needs in that department, just as her
father's son would have, had there been a son. As it was, the
estate was not entailed. Her cousin would inherit the title, and
she would inherit…a large mortgage.

Nobody would ask for her hand that could not afford to. That
was one of the reasons it was so pressing to find some way to
become alluring to Lord Wembly. He did not need anybody's
money, and she was certain he did not give a second's thought
about it.

She'd encountered Lord Westerby, a rather cranky old bachelor who was forever lecturing people on whatever occurred to
him. What generally occurred to him was some esoteric and

tedious subject. Lilith might have pretended she did not see him and turned in the opposite direction, but Lord Westerby had one thing going for him—he was a member of The Royal Society. He was an associate of Lord Wembly's and might even know why he had not come.

"Lord Westerby," she said, "how do you do these days? I do not believe I have seen you since last season."

Lord Westerby harumphed and said, "Here I am, very predictably a year older. Time will not be slowed or stopped, nature of the thing."

Lilith nodded as if she'd been thinking that very same thought. She hurried on, lest she become caught in a long lecture about time. "I am surprised to note the absence of Lord Wembly this evening. I believe he has the habit of attending every year."

This, for some reason, seemed to strike Lord Westerby harder than it ought. He shook his head and said, "Bad business, that."

Bad business? Had something happened? Had Lord Wembly been injured or taken ill?

"Saw him on the street this morning, could hardly believe my ears," Lord Westerby said, shaking his head in a disapproving fashion.

"What has happened?" she asked.

"Now, do not play these games with me, Lady Lilith!" he said. "I know what I am looking at when I look at it. Not much gets past me, I've seen too much of this world!"

"What were you looking at, though?" Lilith asked, entirely aggravated with the lord's opaque manner of speaking. She hardly cared how much of the world he'd seen if he could not explain a simple fact. What in the world had happened?

"Consider this: a fellow dines at a lady's house and then has the temerity, the *temerity* I say, to claim he must go riding on Monday? Riding? At the very time of Mr. Bell's lecture on his final volume of the principles of surgery? I see what's going on— another man defeated by urges and sentimentality and thereby lost to science."

Lilith was thinking as quick as she could to unravel Lord Westerby's opaque speech. As far as she could gather, Lord Wembly had dined somewhere and then engaged himself for a ride in the park. With who, though?

"I am well aware that the world needs to be populated," Lord Westerby said, "but I also know there are plenty of people to do it! A man of science must not allow his time to be taken up with domestic concerns."

"Might I ask the name of the lady?" Lilith asked, praying he would remember it.

"Another one of those Nicolets," Lord Westerby said. "That really does prove my point too—there are plenty of folks who can populate the world. It is what they should be doing, as they're not good for much else. That duke has never had a rational thought in his life, quite right that he's spent his time populating the world. Though why he went with seven daughters and no sons entirely escapes me."

From that, Lilith gathered he referred to the Duke of Pelham and his endless string of daughters, the latest being Lady Verity. Lord Wembly had gone to dine there? He'd gone to Grosvenor Square to dine?

The idea irked her from head to toe. It must be very nice to have a house on Grosvenor Square, and not even rented as far as she knew it. She would not have thought Lord Wembly would be bowled over by an address, but then apparently he'd arranged to go riding with Lady Verity. Perhaps he was bowled over by Lady Verity herself, which was an even worse thought.

"These women are so crafty!" Lord Westerby went on. "Wembly wished to know from me if I were aware of any research being done into the eyesight of fish, on land no less, because *she* is looking into it. Hah! If she'd done anything more than peering into a goldfish bowl, I would be surprised to know it. Wembly's been taken in by sly feminine wiles. I fear we are to lose another man of science to the pedestrian confines of matrimony. I really do not know how humankind expects to advance with all these distractions on hand."

So that was Lady Verity's gambit. She was posing as if she was as scientific-minded as Lord Wembly. Or maybe she actually was, which would be exceedingly odd. No, she could not be. She invented it to gain his admiration. The eyesight of fish indeed. Why would a fish need eyesight out of the water? Just to see it was on the verge of landing in a frying pan? It was absurd. Certainly, Lord Wembly could not put any stock in the idea.

"Did Lord Wembly say what time he would go riding?" Lilith asked.

"Say what time?" Lord Westerby said, as if it were a deranged sort of question. "He did not need to say what time! It's the same time as Bell's lecture, which is four o'clock!"

Lord Wembly would ride in the park on Monday at four o'clock. She must be there. She would dearly like to ride herself, but she did not have her mare in Town. Even if she had, her riding habit was a bit on the threadbare and faded side. That was perfectly fine in the country, where one could pose as an unfussy country sort of person, but it would never have done in London. She would go in her father's carriage, and she would take Clara as her companion. Somehow, she would find Lord Wembly there and attempt to extricate him from Lady Verity's clutches.

How she would extricate him, she did not yet know.

Of course, maybe there was something to be done with this absurd idea of pretending to study the eyesight of fish on land? There might very well be. One thing she was certain of when it came to the baron—he was a no-nonsense sort of person relying exclusively on facts. Were he to conclude that Lady Verity spouted off nonsense, he could neither like nor approve of it.

Perhaps it would be Lady Verity herself who would extricate Lord Wembly from her clutches.

FOR THE FIRST time in her life, Verity had admitted to someone that she could not read. She'd said it aloud. To Winsome. It had felt very odd to say it aloud, as it had been all her life such a close-held secret.

At first, Winsome had not believed her, or at least thought she exaggerated. Her sister had even grabbed a book from the shelf and opened it to a page and put it under her nose. She'd said, "Surely, you can read a page."

She'd tried. She'd recognized a word here and there. Then she gave up.

She told Winsome the whole of it. How many times she'd tried, books by candlelight, the terrible lessons with Miss Pynchon, and the inventing of facts to cover that she knew so little.

Verity had thought Winsome might feel rather victorious over all the times she'd challenged her sister and accused her of inventing something. After all, it must be gratifying to discover that one had been right all along.

She'd been surprised when Winsome had wept over it. She said she never would have teased if she'd known. Then they'd both wept. Then Mrs. Right came in, wanting to know what they were weeping about.

They did not tell her, though.

After that, they'd had a lengthy conversation about it. Most particularly, Verity wished to know if there was some trick to it. Some strategy she didn't know anything about that might solve the problem.

Winsome did not have any tricks to tell her. Nor did she understand where Verity's problem was. If her sister knew her alphabet and she knew words, why could she not read them all together?

Verity did not know. She'd hoped for some sort of answer, some clue, but it was not to be had. It was a relief to tell some-one, though, even if neither of them could think what to do about it. Or what to do about Lord Wembly. Verity had almost hoped that Winsome would tell her that the lord would not care a jot about it. She had not, though.

Of course she had not. He was an intellectual who said the first thing he'd admired about Lady Verity Nicolet was her mind.

Now it was Sunday. As was their usual habit while they were in Town, they'd all spent an hour in the morning reading their bibles. Verity could see well enough that was another thing that had struck Winsome. They sat in the drawing room with their father and Valor. Verity, as she always did, pretended to read. Now Winsome knew it was all a façade. Now Winsome knew that her sister could not even read the word of God! Even Valor could do it, but she could not.

At least Valor had provided some entertainment to pass the time. She'd searched the passage about Noah for any mention of bringing pugs onto the ark. Then she had to explain to Sir Galahad that while it was not outright said, Noah must have done. Sir Galahad seemed satisfied with the explanation.

Afterward, they'd had a tea tray and the duke's married daughters brought his grandchildren for a visit. Grace's son, Miles, was a chatterer going on five years old who had questions about everything, including inquiring of the duke how his stomach got so round. For good measure, Miles pushed out his own stomach out so they could look alike. Then when the amusement of that faded, he inquired if the duke knew he had hair inside his ears.

Felicity's daughter, Isabelle, was just up on her feet and causing the usual amount of chaos that can be expected from such a development. She also seemed to have inherited Felicity's temper and would get very red in the face if opposed.

Lily was just a few months old and slept like a little angel, though Patience mentioned she was a bit of a night owl and liked to keep everybody awake with her. Stanford had insisted that the nursery be right next to their suite of rooms in case of an emergency. No emergency had arisen, but the earl was going round a bit bleary-eyed these days.

Felicity said, "Verity, I presume you look forward to riding in the park with Lord Wembly on the morrow?"

Verity nodded, as of course she did, though she was a little frightened too. He might ask her questions she had no answer for.

"I am so sorry I missed the dinner," Grace said, "did you put him through Fact or Fib?"

"What else would we do?" the duke said, laughing. "To take a man's measure, it is one of the finest games in the land."

"I left before I had an outburst," Valor said, "because I'm older now and can feel them coming on."

"So she did," the duke said, giving Valor an approving nod.

"Lady Pegatha thinks Sir Galahad is tremendous," Valor said.

"No dog more tremendous. Come now," Grace said, "you will all know what information I am interested in. What was Lord Wembly asked and what did he answer?"

"I asked him what he first noticed about Verity, and he said her mind," Winsome said. She said it rather dejectedly, Verity noticed. Now that Winsome knew her secret, she understood that Verity's mind should be the last thing the baron should admire.

Grace looked surprised to hear it, which did not surprise Verity.

"We told him he was a fibber because it's her eyes," Winsome said.

"At dinner, he almost made Serenity cry," Valor said. "I would have cried too, but I wasn't sure what it was all about."

Grace looked expectantly around, waiting to hear more about it.

"Well, he mentioned a dissection of a monkey," Verity said, glancing at Winsome, "but he was able to assure Serenity it had not actually happened. It was, well, he said it was only predictive research."

"Yes," Winsome said, nodding, "it was only speculation about what would have happened. If there had been a dissection. Which there was not."

"What is a dissection anyway?" Valor asked.

Verity stared at her father. The duke said, "It's when you scold an animal very severely for something."

"Oh, yes, Serenity *would* cry about that," Valor said. "I wouldn't cry if someone scolded Sir Galahad. I'd ask Thomas to wallop them in the face. *Then* who would be crying?"

Of all of them, only young Miles and the duke seemed to see the hilarity of the idea.

There was the clatter of horses' hooves out of doors, coming to a stop. Verity turned on her chair, which was by the window, and shifted the curtains.

"Who is it?" the duke asked. "If it's Lady Misery come to ruin our Sunday, tell the footmen to bar the door!"

"It is not," Verity said. She did not really know who, or what, it could be. It was a fine carriage, but on either side of the coachman it sported odd flags in royal purple with yellow lions, whipping in the breeze. The coachman himself, and the groom too, were dressed rather ludicrously in brocade frockcoats embroidered with gold and silver thread.

The drawing room doors were flung open. Mr. Klonsume strode in carrying his traveling case.

"Your Grace, I know you do not like change, but change it must be."

"Going somewhere, Klondike?" the duke asked.

This seemed to strike Mr. Klonsume as a great joke. "Ah, yes, now that we are to be on more equal footing, we can jest with one another. Good form! Jesting aside, I take this new step up in life very seriously. England shall be proud to name me among their titled society. I will avoid bad form as if my very life depends on it. It is as if the great traditions of our two lands have come together in my person. Adieu, my fellow noble men and women."

With that, Mr. Klonsume bowed deeply, turned, and strode out the door.

Incredibly, the oddly-styled groom opened the carriage door, which seemed to be empty of anyone else, and admitted Mr. Klonsume. The coachman smartly snapped the reins and they were off. Whose carriage it was and why they sent it for Mr. Klonsume was a complete mystery.

The duke snorted. "I expect what we have just witnessed is the conclusion of a cracking good story. Mrs. Right will tell us all about it when she's ready. Goodbye, Mr. Klondike!"

HENRY HAD MADE arrangements with the duke that he would ride his horse to Grosvenor Square since it was so close to the park, and then they would proceed on together. He had not expected to find a line of carriages and horses outside the duke's door.

When he was admitted to the drawing room, he found it rather filled. With both gentlemen and flowers. What were they all doing there?

Of course, as soon as he asked the question, he knew the answer. He'd suspected Lady Verity would be the diamond of the season and here was the proof. The proof made him uncomfortable.

The lady herself was nowhere to be seen. Lady Valor seemed to be holding court with a stout lady beside her. He approached the pair. "Lady Valor, good to see you again."

"*Again*? What ho?" Mr. Rusherton exclaimed, pushing in.

"Lord Wembly came to dinner," Lady Valor said. "I didn't invite him," she added for further clarification.

"Trying to get a leg up, eh, Wembly?" Lord Froggerdon asked.

Lady Valor wrinkled her brow. "Maybe he won't," she said. "Verity doesn't have to get married if she doesn't want to." She leveled her gaze at Henry and said, "These gentlemen have come only because they want to know about Verity's studies. Something about fishes' eyes. That's all. You could keep your attention on things like that."

"Lady Verity and Lady Winsome have gone abovestairs to don their riding habits," the matron beside her said.

Henry did not know what to make of it. How would any of these people know anything about the fish eyesight story?

He paused. He had mentioned the thing to Lord Westerby in passing. But only out of curiosity over whether any research of the sort had been done. Why would he tell anybody?

His Aunt Pegatha was certain Lady Verity had invented the whole thing because she was put on the spot. His aunt rather regretted putting the lady in such a position. She said that if she'd known the girl would come up with such a preposterous story, she would not have urged her to it.

Now, somehow, the word had spread. What were these fellows really doing here? It could be they were interested in becoming more acquainted with the lady, or it could be they wanted to hear about fish eyesight and gather an amusing anecdote for their clubs. It could be both. It was impossible to know.

"I'm to go to the park too," Lady Valor said. "But I don't have to change because I will go in the carriage."

"To the park, eh?" Lord Munson said. "Well, perhaps I would not mind a ride myself—got my horse right outside. Could do with a gallop."

"If you are thinking of tagging along," Henry said, now beyond irritated, "I suggest you get permission from the duke."

That seemed to dampen enthusiasm, as he thought it might. He did not suppose the duke would be interested in having a slew of unseasoned fops and dandies following him round the park.

Lady Verity and Lady Winsome came into the drawing room, followed by the duke himself.

She was looking terrific in a dark blue worsted wool habit and charming hat with a jaunty feather. She really was so very pretty. It should come as no surprise to him to find these young dogs sniffing around her door.

"I think we're ready to go, Wembly," the duke said, coming in behind his daughters. "The rest of you, whoever you are, be off to your clubs or wherever you should be."

Henry was rather gratified at this curt dismissal. He went forward to escort Lady Verity to her horse.

"Come, Val, Mrs. Right," the duke said.

So the matron on the sofa was Mrs. Right. She certainly did not have the look of a mistress. Perhaps she was a female relative and had been engaged elsewhere on the night of the dinner. Certainly that was it. It would make sense that a relative might be intimately involved in the management of the duke's household. It had been mentioned by Lady Winsome that Mrs. Right was to rid the house of the duke's butler.

Though, now that he was looking around, he did not get sight of that interesting fellow. Perhaps he'd been got rid of already?

Henry walked Lady Verity outside, getting ahead of the groom coming her way, and helped her up on the mounting block. He debated whether to cup his hands for her foot or boost her from the waist. He boosted her and hoped he did not offend the duke.

He heard a few grumbles from the departing fops and dandies so presumed he *did* offend them. Lady Verity herself did not look offended, though. She rather prettily blushed, which must be a good sign.

Henry's hands around her waist, even for just a moment, did prompt some ideas. Ideas that were probably best left behind at this particular moment.

His attention had been all on Lady Verity. Now he took in her horse. A Dales pony. The animal really was something to see—it appeared both stout and surefooted, and yet somehow graceful. It had a shiny dark coat and intelligent eyes full of life. Lady Winsome rode a near identical creature, as did the grooms. They were a regular matched cavalry.

Henry mounted his own horse, the duke and his passengers were got in the duke's carriage, including Sir Galahad, and they were off. He rode next to Lady Verity, with Lady Winsome just behind and the grooms following.

They trotted the short way to the entrance of the park and the duke's carriage stopped. He put his head out the window. "We'll take the carriage road; you can have a gallop across the open fields to the Serpentine. Verity knows the way."

With that, the duke's carriage set off.

CHAPTER NINE

A S THE DUKE'S carriage trotted down the road to meet with them again at the Serpentine, Lady Verity said, "Let's be off," and spurred her horse across the green.

Henry did not know what he had been expecting when the duke mentioned a gallop. He'd thought it might be more of a trot, as there were ladies involved. That was not the case.

Lady Verity and Lady Winsome spurred their horses into an ever-faster gallop. Good God, it was like they were at a race at Newmarket. He had a bit of trouble keeping up.

Skirting round trees and bushes, everything went by in a blur. At one moment, Lady Verity galloped underneath some low hanging branches, ducking and just barely clearing them. Mercifully, they began to slow as they approached the Serpentine.

"That was lovely," Lady Winsome said, breathing hard as she reined in her horse.

Lovely? It was downright hair-raising.

"It is not the Dales, of course, we could go so much further if we were there," Lady Verity said, working to catch her breath, "but it is nice to allow our horses to stretch their legs."

Henry could only wonder what their rides looked like in the Dales. His horse was heaving in air after that little adventure. For that matter, he was too. They had stopped by the side of the carriage road waiting for the duke, who was just taking the turn south. It was not too overcrowded, it being just a little of the early side. In an hour, it would be positively mobbed.

Both ladies had jumped off their horses without waiting for a block. He supposed ladies from the Dales were sturdier than he'd been expecting. It was rather attractive. He dismounted too. The duke's carriage rumbled to a stop, and the duke and his passengers clambered out of it.

"I thought we might have a picnic of sorts," the duke said.

One of the grooms was already untying a folding coaching table from the back of the carriage. Another brought out a basket and began to unpack it of jars of lemonade, a ham, a jar of mustard, rolls, and biscuits.

"Nowhere to sit, but that's the park for you," the duke said. The grooms poured lemonade into glasses and handed it round.

"You are quite the horsewoman, Lady Verity," Henry said.

He was pleased to see a faint blush. The second blush of the day. Certainly if a lady blushed over a compliment, it must mean something well.

"We all are," Lady Winsome said.

"I'm not," Lady Valor said. "But that is only because my pony likes to walk. She gets nervous to go fast."

Henry assumed the real case of it was that Lady Valor got nervous to go fast. He could hardly blame her. He'd fox hunted all his life, which was always a rather mad dash, but he'd been on very few rides like the one he'd just been on.

"Lord Wembly?"

A carriage had slowed to a stop and he heard his name called. He turned and found Lady Lilith leaning out her carriage window.

"Lady Lilith," he said with a bow. He did not know what had brought her here but was hoping she would not stop long.

"Goodness, what have we here?" she asked, looking over at the table with the picnic items.

She'd backed him into a corner. There was really nothing else to do but introduce her. "Lady Lilith, the Duke of Pelham, the Ladies Verity, Winsome, and Valor, and Mrs. Right."

He still was not certain how to introduce Mrs. Right, as he did not understand the connection.

"Your Grace, ladies, Mrs. Right," Lady Lilith answered. "You've made yourself very comfortable in the park, what a charming idea."

"You are welcome to stop, if it suits you, Lady Lilith," the duke said.

It seemed it did suit, as Lady Lilith was out of the carriage in a flash. She approached the party and said, "This day is one coincidence after the next. I just encountered Lord Munson on the road and he told me he was coming from the duke's house."

"I do not know where all those young bucks came from," the duke said. "Dashed inconvenient to have my drawing room littered with them."

"Well, they are all very keen to hear from our lady scientist," Lady Lilith said. "It was all Lord Munson could talk about. Lady Verity, you are becoming quite the celebrity."

"I'm sure not," Lady Verity said.

"Goodness, yes. I even heard about it from Lord Westerby last evening. He is a long-standing member of The Royal Society, so I would take that as high praise. I am not scientific-minded myself, so I was a bit lost on the whole thing."

Lord Westerby. He'd been afraid that was where all this talk was coming from. But why did the fellow see the need to talk about it? Henry should not have mentioned it to Westerby. This was all his fault.

Lady Winsome said, "Nobody has any cause to talk about it. It is early days and there is nothing to say."

Lady Verity nodded solemnly.

"I will second that opinion," Henry said. "No good can come of speaking about initial investigations. I am sorry Lord Westerby has put this about."

"Fish eyesight, was it?" Lady Lilith asked.

"I expect it does not matter," the duke said in a decidedly stern tone, "as we have all concluded it would not be wise to talk of it just now."

"I don't even know why anybody would *want* to talk about it," Lady Valor said. "Lady Lilith," she went on, holding up Sir Galahad, "is this the most tremendous dog you've ever seen in your life?"

"Tremendous?" she asked, laughing. "He might be on the small side of things for tremendous."

Clearly, Lady Lilith did not perceive the importance of Sir Galahad. As far as Lady Valor was concerned, her little pug was the most tremendous dog who had ever roamed the earth on four short legs and peril to the person who did not perceive it. Though, Lady Lilith seemed to be finding herself rapidly apprised of it.

Lady Valor glared at her, held Sir Galahad close, and went to stand by Mrs. Right.

Lady Lilith pretended she did not notice the snub. She said, "Mrs. Right, I do not believe we've met anywhere."

Mrs. Right snorted. "No, we would not have," the lady said. "I'm the duke's housekeeper."

Housekeeper? But she was dressed otherwise and had no keys jangling at her waist as his own did. She had been seated in the drawing room and had come in the carriage, which his own definitely did not. She was tasked with getting rid of the butler. How could she possibly be the housekeeper?

"Mrs. Right is the best lady living," Lady Valor said, "and she thinks Sir Galahad is tremendous."

"Of course I do, love," Mrs. Right said.

Then there she was calling one of the duke's daughters "love." She sounded more like their mother. But then, it was Henry's understanding that the duke's duchess had died long ago. Perhaps she had acted as their mother?

Under Lady Valor's stare, Lady Lilith finally decided she ought to depart. Nobody seemed over-sorry to see her go.

VERITY HARDLY KNEW where to look. Lady Lilith had just departed. If she were to be believed, people all over Town were somehow aware of the stupid thing she'd said about inquiring into whether fish could see when they were out of the water.

When all those gentlemen had arrived to the house, they'd brought flowers and compliments, and it had all felt rather odd, but she'd not had any reason to be alarmed. It was her understanding that flitting from house to house was a primary entertainment for young gentlemen. She supposed they would like to come into the duke's house to have a look round it.

Toward the end, just before she went abovestairs to change into her riding habit, some of them had asked about her scientific experiment. But she had really assumed that Valor had said something about it while she was out of hearing. She had answered very briefly that she did not care to discuss it.

But perhaps that was why they had come. Perhaps they had come to confirm the preposterous story of a lady studying whether or not fish could see out of water. How did they know about it? Did Lord Wembly put it about?

"Wembly," the duke said, "Walk Verity down to The Serpentine. She particularly likes the view."

Lord Wembly nodded and held his arm out. Verity laid her hand on it, hoping it was not shaking. What was he to say about all this? Would he ask her more questions about it? She wanted the whole idea to go away—was she to be asked about it everywhere now? Why had she ever invented it in the first place?

They walked under the shade of the plane trees to a bench near the water's edge. The serpentine was quiet and mostly occupied by ducks traveling this way and that. They seemed to have a purpose in their traveling, though Verity did not know what it was. Maybe she should look into it and add it to her stupid list of things she was not actually looking into!

She could barely speak. She was not certain what she waited for, but no words occurred to her.

"Tell me about the Dales," Lord Wembly said.

Verity was entirely startled. She'd been certain he would mention the fact that her ridiculous fish idea was talked of. "The Dales?" she asked.

"Yes, what's it like? I've never been, but for us living south of it, the north carries a certain mystique."

Verity felt herself relax. If there were one thing nobody had to read about in a book, it was the majesty of the Dales. "It is a vast, open place. The first time I came to London, I was struck by how hemmed in I felt, as if I could not see far enough. At home, one can see miles and miles of rolling hills crisscrossed by low stone walls that can be easily jumped on a horse. In spring, you can smell the wild garlic in the air and lambs dot the hillsides. In summer, the hawthorn and wildflowers carpet the meadows. Then the weather begins to turn in autumn and the leaves of the trees turn gold. And then it's winter, all calm and white and austere. It is beautiful, but it can be dangerous too. An inexperienced traveler might lose their way, or slip and break an ankle, or be caught in a deep snowdrift. The winter nights can be colder than one might expect, especially if the wind is blowing."

"It sounds a deal wilder than my little corner of Somerset."

Verity had been on the verge, the very verge, of positing something she'd heard about Somerset, though she'd heard nothing at all. Instead, she said, "What is it like there?"

"I cannot speak for all of the county, as there are differences. My patch is very regulated and civilized, perhaps one might say boring. Grazing land and farmland all very regularly laid out. Though, I should not complain of it being boring—my land has been good to my family and supplies a very good living."

"It has been in your family long, I presume."

Lord Wembly laughed. "All the way back to the Magna Carta—stubborn barons down through the centuries. The house shows it too. I've thought of modernizing from time to time, but

I suppose I am grown too used to its eccentric charms."

"Eccentric? How so?" Verity asked, reining in her instinct to talk of other houses with eccentric charm that she in fact knew nothing about.

"What one might expect when one generation after the next adds their bits and bobs. It began as a very fortified place with the requisite portcullis, ramparts, and murder holes. Then it evolved over time through the Tudors and the Stuarts, and then certain bits added more recently. The end result of it is a mishmash of a house with corridors leading nowhere, secret passages, and closets with bricked up windows. I have a map I regularly hand out to anybody who comes to stay in the house, lest they get completely turned around—when I was a child, Lord Featherby was lost for some hours."

It sounded rather glorious. As well, Verity was glad she had not invented anything, as she could not have conjured such a description.

"Perhaps you might visit sometime," Lord Wembly said. "To see the map."

Verity did not answer that sally, as she hardly knew what to say to it. She wished to say, "Visit? When? Tomorrow?" However-er, she knew she could not be so bold.

They went on to speak of other things, comparing one house to another. Christmas traditions, the inhabitants of the local neighborhood, and the flora of the localities were all discussed. Verity supposed they had the most in common regarding their rather thin neighborhoods. In the Dales, they mostly kept to themselves. Lord Wembly seemed to do the same, as he claimed his only close neighbors were a lady who thought it was still 1750 and a viscount who was forever firing off his gun at nobody knew what.

"Well now," the duke said jovially, approaching from behind, "I suppose you've had enough of a look at the view?"

They both leapt to their feet and Verity was conscious of the idea that they'd been sitting rather close. Perhaps more close than would be expected, at least by her father.

They made their way back and found the grooms had packed up the picnic. Goodness, Verity supposed they'd lost track of time sitting by the Serpentine.

"Wembly, my girls will follow my carriage home," the duke said. "We'll see you at this ridiculous scavenger hunt on Thursday?"

Lord Wembly helped her onto her horse. He helped Lady Winsome on too. Though, he'd hoisted Lady Verity by the waist and only given his locked fingers for Lady Winsome's boot. He supposed that must hint at something and he was happy to hint it.

"Your Grace, I will be there. Lady Verity, Lady Winsome, Lady Valor, Mrs. Right." He bowed, mounted his own horse and set off in the opposite direction.

As she and Winsome trotted behind the carriage with the grooms bringing up the rear, Winsome said, "Well? Did you tell him?"

Of course, she inquired into whether or not Verity had mentioned that she could not read. She had not positively decided to do it. But on the other hand, she could not see keeping it a secret if things were to lead…where she thought they might be leading.

She had to do it, and she could not do it. She was frozen in place.

Verity shook her head and trotted ahead of Winsome. For now, she would put all her thoughts on the lovely conversation that was had at the banks of the Serpentine. She would just enjoy that moment, as she did not know how many future moments there could be. At this particular moment, she was imagining getting lost in Lord Wembly's house and he coming to her rescue using his map.

As they entered the square, an ominous picture came into view. Lady Marchfield's carriage was stopped outside their house.

They entered the house, allowing the duke to lead the way. Verity was not certain why the lady was here, but it could not be ignored that Mr. Klonsume had made an exceedingly odd departure the day before. It was entirely likely her aunt had come to complain about yet another butler exiting the house. Where he'd exited to in such a strange manner, Mrs. Right had not yet said.

If only their aunt would stop sending butlers, she would not find herself half so aggravated.

"This should be interesting," Mrs. Right said as they crossed the threshold.

They entered the drawing room to find Lady Marchfield standing with her arms crossed. Verity glanced behind her and noticed Mrs. Right had disappeared.

"What now, Lady Misery?" the duke asked, throwing himself into his preferred chair. "If you're looking for Klondike, he took himself elsewhere."

"I am perfectly well aware, Roland. What I am not aware of is how you allow that housekeeper to act so outrageously. Criminally, in fact."

"I have no idea what's gone on," the duke said. "Mrs. Right informs me of what happens to all these ridiculous butlers you send at her own convenience."

"At her own *convenience?*" Lady Marchfield asked, as if the idea that a housekeeper was to be afforded any convenience whatsoever was akin to blasphemy.

"That's right, at her convenience," the duke said, "slow to the mark but you're finally catching on."

Verity and Winsome had tiptoed to chairs and sat silently down, not particularly wishing to attract their aunt's notice. Valor had picked up Sir Galahad and very sensibly left.

"If I had not intervened," Lady Marchfield said, "Mr. Klonsume might have caused a difficulty with the queen! He might have turned up to Buckingham House with this ridiculous story! How was he to know any better? Oh, but I unraveled it as soon as I saw that letter. It was on your stationery with your crest. The very idea that your housekeeper would have the temerity to take your stationery and commit a forgery!"

At that moment, Mrs. Right reappeared, carrying a tea tray. She set it down in front of the duke as if she had no notion why Lady Marchfield had arrived or that anything at all was amiss.

"Admit it, you scandalous woman," Lady Marchfield said, pointing at Mrs. Right. "Admit it all. At once."

"Admit what, your ladyship?" Mrs. Right asked.

"Admit how Mr. Klonsume came to receive a letter telling him he was to be knighted. That's what."

The duke snorted. Verity slapped her hand over her mouth to stop from laughing. Mr. Klonsume thought he was to be knighted?

"Oh yes, I did see that letter," Mrs. Right said. "Mr. Klonsume insisted I read it. I was very surprised by its contents, I can tell you. A knighthood, and I had never even heard of the Order of Owen."

"There is no Order of Owen, as you well know," Lady Marchfield said darkly. "You arranged all this. You sent him to The Albany, to Lord Charles' set, I understand. You left the letter directing him to pray all night. You left him those ridiculous clothes from the distant past, replete with stockings and a frock coat. Oh, and a patch and a wig, let us not forget that! And then you sent him to my house in some get-up of a carriage flying flags so that I might escort him to St. James for the ceremony and then on to Buckingham for the reception!"

Verity could see very well that with every word, her father was becoming more and more amused. When the idea of a flag-flying carriage depositing a ridiculously outfitted Mr. Klonsume was relayed, he lost all hope of controlling himself.

The duke heaved with laughter. Mrs. Right said, "Gracious, how is one lowly housekeeper to do all of that?"

Lady Marchfield ignored her brother's hysteria. "One lowly housekeeper can do all that because one lowly housekeeper is employed by the most embarrassing duke that England has ever known," she said.

The duke took a breath from his heaving laughter. "Well,

Klondike's your problem now. Or the Order of Owen's problem—I don't much care. But for entertainment purposes, what do you plan on doing with the fellow?"

Lady Marchfield glared at the duke. "I have had no choice but to buy him passage on the first boat back to America. I've had to pay for a private berth and supply him with funds to resettle himself. He's got it into his head that even though there is to be no ceremony, he has taken on the spirit of a knighted individual and cannot abide steerage. He must be permitted to live as a Sir. I was forced to it, as he cannot stay here. He made threats about approaching the patronesses to be admitted to Almack's! Furthermore, that carriage and his absurd clothes made a positive scene on my square—I still have not come up with a way to explain it and I *will* be asked."

"Klondike returns to New York first class," the duke said, chuckling.

"Perhaps someone should warn New York?" Mrs. Right asked, her tone all full of innocence.

"Mark me, Roland, your disavowment of any sort of regularity will catch up to you and my nieces sooner or later. At the rate you are going, I imagine it will be sooner." With that, Lady Marchfield steamed out of the house.

Verity would never have guessed that Mrs. Right had got Mr. Klonsume out of the house with a ruse about a knighthood. She really was so clever.

CHAPTER TEN

Henry sat in the drawing room with his aunt. He'd kept the conversation going all through dinner by asking her question after question about everything he could think of. How did her steward get on, as he had been poorly last Henry had heard. Had she decided whether or not she would replace her roof on the estate? Or perhaps only repairs would be deemed sufficient? His own steward had suggested he expand his dairy as the cheese they were producing was proving a growing market—what did she think about that?

Now they had fallen to silence as he'd run out of questions.

"Goodness, I really do not understand what could have happened," Lady Pegatha said.

"Happened?" Henry said, sipping his port.

"Certainly there is a reason you have so studiously avoided mentioning anything about your ride in the park with Lady Verity."

Henry sighed. Perhaps he ought to have known that his aunt would not be so easily led. How to explain it all, though?

"Come, now. It is only me. What has that girl done this time? I pray she is not inquiring into whether birds can fly with their eyes closed, but who knows!"

"All right, very amusing. Well, first, I arrived to her house and her drawing room was filled with a collection of fops and dandies. You know the type—too young, too precious, and trying too hard to put on airs and adopt some sort of jocular manner that strikes them as the height of sophistication."

"Ah, yes, London is always littered with overgrown boys at this time of year. They flit, they quip, they ostentatiously peer through their quizzing glasses, and amuse or irritate everybody else, depending on one's mood. But I suppose you cannot be shocked that they have gravitated to Lady Verity—she is strikingly pretty."

"She is," Henry admitted. "But I think those gentlemen were there to collect some amusing gossip. At least, some of them were. Word has got out about Lady Verity's idea of discovering if fish can see out of water."

"Her idea? You mean, her *story*. But heavens, how has it got out? I assure you, I have not breathed a word of it. It seems unlikely that any of her family would have done it. I saw the looks going her way when she posited the idea. Their eyes were almost willing her to stop talking."

"It was me. I mentioned it to Lord Wetherby, just out of curiosity over whether anybody had looked into it in the past. I never dreamed he'd talk about it."

"Oh dear. The *ton* will make hay with it, I am certain."

"Yes, I believe they already are. We had a picnic of sorts in the park and Lady Lilith turned up. She seemed to know all about it."

"Lady Lilith turned up, did she?"

Henry nodded. "She was just passing by and stopped."

"Just passing by and stopped, did she?" Lady Pegatha said, laughing.

"Yes, as I said. What comment do you make on it?"

"Perhaps it was a coincidence, I do not claim to know otherwise. But on the other hand, perhaps it was not a coincidence. Perhaps she continues her pursuit despite lack of encouragement."

Henry hoped not. If the lady were looking to wed, she was looking in the wrong direction. Then a thought occurred to him.

"I do not think, as a general thing, that Lady Lilith has particularly good instincts. That is, I do not think she reads people very well. Lady Valor asked her if her little dog was tremendous. Lady Lilith laughed and said he was a bit small to be tremendous."

"Goodness, that was stupid. One ought not challenge any ideas a young girl has about her dog. I suppose London is filled to the brim with little girls owning the most tremendous dog in England."

"You did not scoff at the idea, though she threw that little pug on your lap several times."

Lady Pegatha laughed. "I certainly did not. There is never a point in challenging a thing that is easy to agree to and no trouble to oneself. Though, my lady's maid might not approve in this case—she was positively shocked over the amount of fur on my dress afterward."

Henry lapsed into silence.

"Come now, the visit with Lady Verity could not have been all bad. Does she comport herself well atop a horse?"

"She is rather expert, actually. I've never seen the like of her and her sister. Not from a lady, in any event. I felt like we were at Newmarket on the final stretch."

"I must commend her for that—there is nary a sight more dashing than an expert horsewoman. And I suppose she was very charming in her riding habit."

"Extremely so. And then the duke suggested I walk her down to The Serpentine. We had a really interesting talk, about everything in the world, it seemed. It felt as if, as if...we had always been talking all our lives. She said my house sounded charming, and I told the truth about it too—I did not attempt to pretty up the facts. She even knows about the map."

"There you have it. Henry, if you are really interested in this lady, and it seems that you are, then close your ears to any gossip that might be going round and proceed." Lady Pegatha paused, examining her sherry in its crystal glass. "Though really, that girl had best stop inventing such preposterous notions."

"You do not suppose that this propensity for invention is some kind of, well, a sort of character flaw? What I mean is, would I always be faced with some new and ghastly idea? Would I be forever wary of what my wife was to say next?"

"One never knows, of course. But my feeling is what you have on your hands is a very pretty and exceedingly awkward sort of girl who will settle into rationality when she feels more secure in things. All of this nonsense is only meant to impress, as harebrained as it has been."

Henry certainly hoped that was the case. Day by day, even hour by hour, his inclinations toward Lady Verity grew. He felt as if he'd passed through some sort of veil and could not be turned back now. He'd actually tried it out. Last night, he'd imagined how it would be if he turned his eyes elsewhere.

His eyes refused to turn. His mind refused to turn. His visions of the future refused to turn.

He was beginning to think that even if he was assured that Lady Verity *would* invent ridiculous stories for all their lives, he'd probably still proceed. After all, inventing ridiculous ideas was not the worst thing in the world. He'd just have to work to tamp down the gossip going round just now. And possibly the gossip that would always be going round. How, he did not know, but surely something would occur to him.

In any case, when she was not inventing scientific research, she was really very charming!

As Sir Jonathan's scavenger hunt had been advertised as an event for families, Verity's father had purchased tickets for Valor and Winsome too. The event was to be held in the North-West Enclosure of the park and it was a fine day for it. There had been a bit of distress over the idea that Sir Galahad must remain at home, as no dogs were allowed in the enclosure. Valor thought that surely Sir Galahad must be exempt from the rule, as he was tremendous and, also, very small. Her arguments were to no avail, though. The duke was happy to flout convention when he saw fit, but he had a healthy respect for rules that made practical sense.

Verity had thought the matter settled, although unhappily, until Valor dragged a picnic basket into the carriage. As the picnic basket, covered on top with a large napkin, had the mysterious quality of being able to move, it was immediately suspect. The duke had opened it, Valor had shrugged, and one of the footmen had taken Sir Galahad back into the house.

There was a crush of carriages stopped by the entrance to the enclosure and they had to leave their own carriage a bit farther than the duke would have liked. Though a duke often got his way and was often given precedence, not so with where one had to leave one's carriage. Coachmen very determinedly turned away upon spotting the duke's crest, preferring to maintain they'd never seen it at all rather than make way.

They walked all together to the entrance and found Lord Wembly milling around nearby it. Verity could only suppose he had been waiting for her, as what else was he doing there?

There was a brief moment when it occurred to her that he might wait for another lady, but that was washed away as soon as he approached.

"Your Grace, Lady Verity, Lady Winsome, Lady Valor. I had hoped to accompany you." He paused, as if he were confused by something. "Lady Valor? I had imagined we might see Sir Galahad this afternoon."

"He's not allowed in, if you can believe it," Valor said.

"Oh, I see," Lord Wembly said. "I did know there was a rule against admitting dogs, though I had not supposed it would apply to such a tremendous specimen as Sir Galahad."

"That's what I said!" Valor cried, looking very triumphant.

The duke winked at the lord, obviously approving of the gambit.

Lord Wembly really was so clever to manage Valor in such a manner. That idea did cause Verity to blanch the slightest bit. He really *was* so clever. And she really was not so clever, though he did not know it. He probably knew everything in the wide world, but for that particular fact.

They went along with the stream of people heading toward a makeshift booth of sorts. "We'll get our clues there," Lord Wembly said. "Then we just wait for the bell to ring and we're off."

On the right side of the booth, there were tables and chairs set up and an old woman was selling mineral water from the spring. "I'll put myself in one of those chairs and hope something better than water comes around," the duke said. "What say you, Wembly? Can you manage keeping track of three of my girls?"

"Certainly, Your Grace," Lord Wembly said.

Verity supposed she should have known her papa would not be inclined to walk all over the enclosure attempting to unravel clues. Still, it was rather thrilling that Lord Wembly was to be their escort.

"Where is Lady Pegatha?" Valor asked Lord Wembly. "I was hoping she would be here because I know she would be outraged that Sir Galahad was not allowed in."

"Ah," Lord Wembly said, "she is not inclined to do much walking."

Valor nodded. "Because she's old. Tell her that I am sorry her old bones could not manage it and tell her Sir Galahad wasn't allowed in. It will make her feel better."

Verity trusted in Lord Wembly's good sense not to send any regards to Lady Pegatha's "old bones." As for Lady Pegatha being gratified to know Sir Galahad was also to sit out the scavenger hunt, she could not guess how she'd view it.

The duke set off to secure a chair. Lord Wembly approached the booth to pick up their clues.

"We'd better win," Winsome said. "I do not like to lose."

"She really does not," Valor said. "Sir Galahad beat Winsome at vingt-et-un yesterday and she was so cross."

"I was not cross about losing, I was cross about the cheating."

"Sir Galahad does not cheat," Valor said, nose up in the air.

"No, but you do," Winsome pointed out.

"Lady Verity!"

Verity turned and found Lady Lilith hurrying toward her with a maid trailing after her.

"How wonderful to encounter you here," Lady Lilith said. "I have been all but abandoned. My father suddenly decided he cannot abide the exercise and stays in our carriage."

"Oh, I see," Verity said.

"You've got your maid," Winsome pointed out.

It was precisely what Verity had been thinking, though she would not have said it aloud.

Lord Wembly returned to them with a paper. He looked questioningly at Lady Lilith.

"Lord Wembly," she said smoothly, "I have been rescued by the Nicolets. My father cannot bear the walking, and they have taken me in."

"Nobody said that!" Valor cried.

Verity laid a hand on Valor's arm, as there really was nothing to be done about Lady Lilith pushing in. Valor was particularly against the lady, as she'd not agreed that Sir Galahad was tremendous.

However, as Verity knew that talk was going round about her alleged scientific research, she'd rather not make an enemy. Especially not because Sir Galahad had been insulted, as the little dog would know nothing about it.

Verity had already noticed a few people whispering while staring in her direction. It was possible they looked behind her or to either side of her, but it felt as if they looked at her. Since she did not know them, and since they were whispering, she was rather afraid of what the conversation was about.

As she knew from her own village, the only thing that got rid of gossip was a new story and a new story often took time to arrive. She must just be everything pleasant right now.

"Of course we are delighted to acquire Lady Lilith's company," Verity said.

"I see, yes, of course," Lord Wembly said. He said it in a pleasant tone, but his expression indicated otherwise.

"You are all very gracious," Lady Lilith said. Despite the fact that neither Lord Wembly, nor Valor, nor Winsome were looking particularly gracious.

Lord Wembly forced a smile. "Now, considering you've not all been to Sir Jonathan's scavenger hunt before, I'll explain how it works. We won't all be going after the same clues, else the whole crowd would be going in the same direction. Some people have other clues, some people have our clues, but set in a different order. There are four clues, each leading to a small colored square of paper—blue, red, yellow, and brown. Once we have collected them all, we race back here. The first to return with all the colors wins."

"What do we win?" Valor asked.

Lord Wembly shrugged. "I am not certain. It is usually something small, as most of the money will go to the charity."

"I don't care what it is," Valor said, "I want it."

Sir Jonathan had climbed atop one of the tables next to the booth. He called, "Get ready, everybody!" Then he rang a large hand bell.

"Lady Verity," Lord Wembly said, holding out the paper, "will you do the honors and read us the first clue?"

Verity felt her cheeks and arms bloom in prickles. Why had she not thought…no, she would not take the paper, she could not.

"Verity's eyes hurt in the sunshine," Winsome said hurriedly. "At least, if she tries to read in the sun. A very usual case."

Verity nodded vigorously to that idea.

Lady Lilith snatched the paper. "Goodness, the sun does not bother my eyes one bit. Let's see, clue number one: Long ago, it was made of bronze, but not in this case. To find it, one must pray and then race."

They stood for a moment, staring at each other. Valor said, "This is too hard. We'll never win."

"Now, wait a moment," Lord Wembly said. "We'll not give up so easily. The clues often hint at more than they might seem to at first. Why must we *pray* and then race? Why not just race? There must be something in that."

A sudden idea came to Verity. She might not know anything from books, but she had paid attention to the vicar's stories from the bible of a Sunday morning. Since praying was mentioned…yes, she thought she might have an idea. She said, "Could it be the bronze snake that Moses made?"

"The Serpent," Lord Wembly said.

"The Serpentine?" Verity said.

"That's got to be it," Lord Wembly said.

They turned and hurried in that direction. Verity was rather stunned. She'd figured out a clue. At least, she thought she had. She'd imagined she'd spend the entire day covering her stupidity but instead, she might have figured out a clue.

HENRY WAS ANNOYED that Lady Lilith had joined their party. Especially since his aunt had put the idea in his head that she might have purposefully turned up at the park. Had she done the same now?

He would not have expected to see her here, as the tickets were expensive and her family were in tight circumstances. But on the other hand, Sir Jonathan never made any particular effort to collect the tickets. He likely assumed everybody would be honorable about it. Perhaps she had not bought a ticket and presumed nothing would be said about it?

If that were the case, then he would really wonder if her father even waited in the carriage. Henry would also be entirely irritated with her pushiness. Where on earth did she think it was going? He had indicated, pretty clearly he thought, that he was not interested. He was not inclined to tolerate this pushing in when he was meant to be spending time with Lady Verity. Having her sisters along was quite enough to juggle.

Though on a more positive note, he thought his alleged shock over not seeing Sir Galahad had gone over pretty well with Lady Valor.

They'd made their way to The Serpentine. It was a brisk and sunny day, and the water rippled with the wind as swans made their majestic way round. He could not help but to notice that the breeze was wrestling with the pins in Lady Verity's hair—a curl had just been delightfully set free.

"I don't see anything," Lady Valor said. "Is it supposed to be in the water? Do we need a boat?"

"Right there," Lady Winsome said, pointing to a tree a few yards ahead. "It's on the water side so you can't see it when you approach."

Henry followed her gaze. There were blue tickets all tacked on the backside trunk of a tree. They hurried to collect one of them. Henry pulled one from its pin and put it in his coat pocket.

"Now let's step away from here so we do not give it away to anybody else," Henry said. "Look dejected, as if we've found nothing."

"Hah!" Lady Valor said. "We're tricking them!"

Henry thought Lady Valor looked a little too triumphant to trick anyone, but there was nothing to be done about it. "Lady Lilith? If you will read the next clue."

"Certainly, Lord Wembly," Lady Lilith said, peering down at the paper in her hand. "It is not changing leaves, nor snowfall, nor hives heavy with honey that grants us the vision of miraculous nature."

"What?" Lady Valor said in a particularly annoyed tone.

Henry did not blame her. This clue did seem a bit more obscure. "What would grant a vision of miraculous nature?"

"Why does the vision have to be granted?" Lady Winsome asked. "Why cannot you just look at it?"

"Oh," Lady Verity said, "but it hints that it is not winter or autumn or summer. It must be spring. And since it mentions vision—"

"The bathing spring," Henry said. "Well done, Lady Verity."

The lady blushed, which complemented her errant curl.

"Are we bathing now?" Valor asked. "I do not think Mrs. Right will like it if we come back wet."

"No, it is the spring people use to bathe their eyes, should they have some sort of malady," Henry said. "Let us be off!"

They hurried toward the bathing spring, dodging various other people going off in other directions. The spring was located under a line of trees with a deal of underbrush. They had to search around before finding the brown tickets laying on a large stone and very much blending in with the surroundings.

The party moved away from the area so as not to give anything away, though other people were beginning to hunt around the spring. Lady Lilith read the third clue.

"For this reason, a Corinthian often picks up the sword."

Henry ran the possibilities through his mind. A Corinthian picks up the sword to do what?

"Is it fencing?" Lady Winsome asked.

"Of course it is!" Henry said. "Now, we'll have to look casual, as if we are not looking along the fence line. We will just be walking along it and looking away from it as if we are interested in something else."

"We'll have everybody bamboozled," Lady Valor said, laughing.

Henry hoped so, assuming nobody was looking at Lady Valor, who had not yet mastered the skill of deception. They meandered along the fence and finally found the smallest bit of yellow peeking from behind a fence post. Henry arranged for everyone to stand in front of him while he retrieved it.

Lady Valor shouted, "Go away!" at somebody while he was

doing it, so he could not say they were particularly successful in the ruse.

"We're on the last clue," Lady Lilith said as they walked away from the fence line.

Before she could read it, there was a loud cheer that went up from the vicinity of the booth and tables and chairs. Then the bell was rung by Sir Jonathan.

"What does it mean?" Lady Verity asked.

"I am afraid we have not won. Somebody has returned to Sir Jonathan with all four colors."

CHAPTER ELEVEN

HENRY NOTICED LADY Verity's younger sisters' expressions upon being apprised that they'd not come out victorious at the scavenger hunt. He could not say they were particularly full of grace.

"What?" Lady Valor asked in an accusatory tone, as if it were he, himself, who had provided this affront.

"That's what I say," Lady Winsome said. "What?"

"I am afraid it is the case," Lord Wembly said.

"Well, it is only a bit of amusement, is it not?" Lady Lilith said. "I suppose it hardly matters who won."

Lady Valor and Lady Winsome glared at her. Henry did not suppose Lady Lilith had quite the same competitive spirit as the Nicolets. She did not seem to understand them at all.

"We must face it with good grace," Lady Verity said, particularly staring at Lady Valor. "No matter how disappointed one might feel. Valor, Sir Galahad would be let down if he were to know you were defeated by it. He will expect more from you, I am sure."

This seemed to give Lady Valor pause. "He does depend on me to be strong. Whenever we hear a noise in the night, he hides his face in my pillow, and I have to pretend I'm not frightened so he won't worry about us getting murdered."

"Quite right," Lady Verity said. "We will make our way back and congratulate the winners for their cleverness."

They did make their way back, despite the various groans from Lady Valor and Lady Winsome. Sir Jonathan stood on a table to address the returning crowds. "Ladies, gentlemen, I am so grateful that you have seen fit to support my little charity by running hither and thither, deciphering my clues. The Sewing Circle will do much good work with your generosity. This will afford the admission of twenty-seven new girls into the program. I am happy for that and I am happy to announce the winners of this little amusement—Lord and Lady Blendwhistle."

Everyone raised an applause for the victorious couple, though Henry could not miss that Lady Valor's clap was exceedingly slow and halfhearted. Even a bit contemptuous, if he was not mistaken.

"May I present Lady Blendwhistle with a looking glass from Rundell & Bridge, which I hope is deemed charming," Sir Jonathan said. He held up a very small looking glass in a round case bejeweled in topaz and small pearls—the sort of thing that might be carried in a lady's reticule.

"Ugh," Lady Winsome said, "it's lovely."

"It really is so beautiful," Lady Valor said. "I'm devastated that we did not win it."

Lady Verity laughed. "It is just as well. You and Winny would have fought over it like cats."

"That's true," Lady Valor admitted. "I would have hidden it and sworn I didn't know where it was and then felt bad for lying."

"Not so bad that you would have admitted to lying about it, though," Lady Winsome said.

Lady Valor snorted over the accusation. "No, not as bad as that."

The duke approached and said jocularly, "Could not get my girls over the finish line, eh, Wembly?"

"We did our best, Your Grace," Lord Wembly said. "We were moments behind the victors."

"But we lost," Valor said, kicking at the grass.

"Yes, yes, it's only a game after all. Lady Lilith, what brings you into our party?"

Lady Lilith appeared flustered to be asked. "Oh, Your Grace, as to that, my father decided to stay in our carriage, declining the exercise."

"Hah! So he sent you out with your maid, eh? A bit of trying work for a maid, running back and forth."

Lady Lilith did not seem to have an answer for that, though her maid curtsied and smiled. She might have even winked, if Henry had not imagined it.

"Well now, I was not particularly expecting to return home victorious," the duke said.

"Papa!" Lady Winsome said. "You expected us to lose?"

"No, I just did not expect you to win, odds of it, you know. Now, as I did not expect a win, I did arrange for a tea with Cook's special apple cakes to soothe your battered pride. Wembly? You'll come along."

"Apple cakes?" Lady Lilith said. "Goodness, that sounds love-ly."

Henry pressed his lips together. If he'd had any doubts about whether Lady Lilith was engineering things, it was gone. There could hardly be a more obvious gambit to be invited along. He really found her boldness unpleasant. There was no point to it!

"And leave your father in the carriage? No, I will not hear of it," the duke said. "I would not like it for myself if my girls left me in the park."

"I will never leave you, Papa," Lady Valor said.

"Yes, so you keep threatening," the duke said drily. "What's say we walk Lady Lilith back to her carriage, say hello to the earl, and then we'll be off."

Lady Lilith looked entirely panicked at this proposal, though her maid looked amused. "Not at all necessary, Your Grace," she sputtered. "Well! I should not like to keep my father waiting. Clara? Let us depart." She curtsied and took her maid by the arm.

Lady Lilith practically ran from the enclosure, dragging her maid along with her.

The duke laughed heartily. "Guess whose earl is *not* in her carriage? Knew it all along."

Now Henry knew it too. Lady Lilith had come with just her maid to escort her, almost certainly had not bought a ticket to support Sir Jonathan's charity, and then pushed into the duke's party. He supposed one might admire her determination, but he did not. It was simply off-putting.

However, Lady Lilith and her machinations were to be put aside. He was invited to the duke's house for apple cake.

LILITH FELT AS if she had escaped certain embarrassment. Not just felt, she knew she had. What if the duke had pressed forward and insisted on walking her to her carriage, only to find it empty of her father? She would be forced to feign surprise and wonder if he'd walked off somewhere while the coachman rolled his eyes. She would never have been believed.

Everyone would know she'd come alone. Lord Wembly would know it, and likely put together that she'd purposely inserted herself into his party. He'd probably guess that she never even had a ticket. He might tell others of his suspicions. Lilith had noted Sir Jonathan looking surprised to see her and hoped he'd forget all about it in the excitement of the day. But if it were mentioned that she'd come alone…She'd be seen as desperate.

She *was* desperate, but she could not bear to be seen so.

Lilith and Clara hurriedly got into the carriage, and she shut the curtains so a nosy duke could not peer inside.

Clara straightened her skirt and said, "Well, that was a pala-ver. So this is what the high and mighty get up to while everybody else is at their work. Hard to believe."

Lilith sighed. Clara was prone to making such statements and hinting that she, herself, was always working. It was not in the least bit true—Clara did a lot of sitting around and ordering her father's maid of all work to bring her things. In any case, what did she expect from Lilith? That she should work as a governess or companion?

She repressed a small gulp, as there was the remotest possibility it would come to that. She had to marry! She thought she might manage it too, if it were not for Lady Verity in the way.

"Clara," she said, "I am an earl's daughter. My only employment can ever be as a wife and the mistress of a large house. It's what I've been brought up for."

"Aye, I can see it from your hands," Clara said, examining her own rather red and chapped hands. "Nice future, if one is lucky. As for the rest of us, well, I only say."

"Your own hands would not look half so bad if you applied Milk of Roses every night," Lilith said. "It is not as if you wash dishes and need to have hands looking like that. You just must care for them."

Clara ignored this tip just as she had a dozen others. "I don't see why you're chasing round that Lord Wembly, though. Not with his eyes turned elsewhere."

"Is it that obvious?" Lilith asked. "That he's turned to Lady Verity?"

"As obvious as the nose on my face," Clara said.

"I don't know what he sees in her," Lilith said.

Clara snorted. "I reckon he sees her face. She's got a pretty one."

This did put Lilith's back up. "She might well be handsome, but I find her coloring rather…well, the point is that she is absurd. And very much a liar. She invents things. He ought to note it and refuse to be connected with her. Looks will fade but truthfulness is forever."

"Is it now?" Clara said, laughing. "Well, you know how men are, bowled over by a pretty face. They think they are so superior in their faculties, but a pretty face will take their brains and send them through a laundry mangle and straight into mush. I know it better than anybody. Mr. Leister, he's training to be a solicitor, looked right by me and made off with Letty Grange. She's a bad-tempered girl, but she's got a good face."

"And you could do nothing about it?" Lilith asked.

"I could have," Clara said. "I just chose not to. After all, if Mr. Leister ain't falling at my feet, I don't want him. Whoever I marry will treat me better than a duchess, he'll be that bowled over by me."

Lilith ignored the idea that Clara was to be treated as a duchess, as she was certain the girl did not have the first idea of what it would entail. "You *could* have done something, though? What could you have done?" Lilith was really grasping at straws now, to solicit Clara's advice. But she had no ideas of her own.

"Well, I did have a bright idea at the time. You know those caricatures you see for sale at print shops and sometimes printed in the newspapers? The ones that poke at the prince and parliament and the like? I know a fella who draws such things and works at a press. I was gonna ask him to sketch Letty Grange as a fishwife shouting at somebody looking very like Mr. Leister and pepper the neighborhood with them. You see, to give a clue to Mr. Leister as to what he was getting himself into. I didn't do it, though."

"The point is, you could have done it. Would it have cost a lot?"

"No, not too much. My friend would've sketched it for free, so then it was just the printing to pay for. I was only to do it on Berwick Street, not paper all of London with it."

Well, that was something to think about, was it not? Lilith very much doubted that Lord Wembly would continue to be interested in a lady if she'd made herself notorious for being a liar. Perhaps Lilith could even assign a nickname. "Lady Fiction" sounded just about right.

"Clara," she said, "might you arrange a meeting with this young man who sketches?"

THOUGH VALOR AND Winsome were beyond put out that they did not win the scavenger hunt and therefore did not win the bejeweled mirror, Verity could not give a toss about it. As far as she was concerned, the thing had come off perfectly. Somehow, she'd solved two clues! She'd been so afraid that she'd be found out as stupid, but she'd solved two clues. It almost felt like a miracle.

It occurred to her that since she was effectively locked out of all the knowledge in books, she'd paid careful attention to any piece of information she'd heard. Winsome might have remembered the vicar's sermon about Moses and the bronze snake, but she hadn't. Her head was too filled up with information she'd read in books to recall a passing word from the vicar. Verity's own head was not so filled up.

Thomas had brought in the tea tray, replete with the miniature apple cakes.

Winsome said, "The apple cakes are special, only our cook makes them exactly like this. But don't try to find out how. Our aunt, Lady Marchfield, tried to get the recipe for her own cook but ours said no."

"Papa calls our aunt Lady Misery," Valor said, laughing, "and she was pretty miserable that day! Also, Papa says she's a polecat sticking her nose into hen houses that are not her own. It's so funny because she gets so mad about it."

Lord Wembly's eyes had gone rather wide at those descriptions. Verity said, "My father and my aunt often…cross swords."

Sir Galahad made his appearance in the drawing room, no doubt having been napping in Valor's room.

"There he is," Lord Wembly said, as Sir Galahad trotted in. "It cannot be denied—he really is tremendous."

"I know," Valor said. "And just think, he could have been drowned in the Thames if I hadn't got my father's gun and put a stop to it. If anybody ever tries to hurt him again, I'll shoot them full of holes. Or I'll have Thomas do it. Then who will be sorry?"

Not surprisingly, Lord Wembly appeared even more startled to hear this information.

"Perhaps no actual guns were involved," Verity said softly.

"They practically were, though," Valor said. "Because I would have got one if I had to. It's the same."

"If not precisely the same," Lord Wembly said, "then at least very like. After all, it is the thought and intent behind the thing that really matters."

"That's what I think," Valor said. "If I *would* have got a gun, then I practically *did* get a gun."

"Quite right," Lord Wembly said.

Valor nodded. Then she paused. "Oh no," she whispered. She pointed at Lord Wembly. "I know what you're doing! You're trying to get me to like you."

Lord Wembly laughed. "Would that be a crime?"

Valor hopped from the sofa and swept Sir Galahad into her arms. "We're going!" she said, marching out of the drawing room.

"Good effort, though," the duke said as his youngest daughter flounced out. The duke had so far been enjoying his second apple cake. He gestured to Winsome. "Why don't you show me that book on the back bookshelf you've been talking about for days. The one with the innocent girl trapped in a damp castle full of ghosts."

Winsome agreed, though Verity knew perfectly well that the last thing her father would be interested in was a book about an innocent girl trapped in a damp castle full of ghosts. She hoped she was not blushing over this obvious gambit to give her a moment alone with Lord Wembly.

Her father and sister went to the back of the drawing room. Verity said, "It was very kind to indulge Valor. And you ought not feel singled out for her disapproval. She's done it to every-body."

"Who is everybody?" Lord Wembly asked, looking amused.

"Oh, well, you know how it is. Any gentleman coming into the house."

"Ah. Suitors, then."

Verity felt very backed into a corner. Yes, of course it was suitors that Valor disapproved of. However, she had not meant to hint that Lord Wembly was a suitor. She thought he was. She hoped he was. But she could not say so!

"All men. All men who come into the house," she said nonsensically.

"I see. As for me, I hope to win Lady Valor over at some point. She now understands my intentions."

"Intentions. Yes," she said. It was a very stupid sort of answer. But what did he mean by it? His intentions to do what?

"I suppose my intentions, in general, would be hard to misunderstand," Lord Wembly said.

Verity smiled dumbly. Was he saying what she thought he said? Or was he saying something she did not comprehend? Was he saying his intentions were toward her? It seemed as if that was what he said. But he did not say that exactly.

She felt she ought to be more sure of what he meant. For all she knew, this type of thing was explained in a book somewhere and everybody knew about it. All she had to go on was her instincts and sometimes her instincts were not very good. She could not make a mistake here.

"I hope I don't flatter myself in imagining our intentions are similar?" Lord Wembly said.

"No, I would not think so," Verity said. If he said what she *thought* he said, then he said that they both had intentions toward each other. Romantic intentions. Which, of course, she could heartily agree with. But why could he not come out and say it? Gracious, this sort of cloudy and roundabout speech would not be put up with in the Dales. There, a person would be directed to say what they meant. Or, as Mr. Wicker was forever shouting, "Say it as it is!" She could not demand it like Mr. Wicker would, though.

They sat in silence for some moments and the awkwardness of it was almost painful. Then, Lord Wembly said, "Have you read any good books lately?"

"Books?" Verity said, her teacup clattering on its saucer. The question had so startled her. It had also brought back around the question of what she was to tell Lord Wembly about her relationship with books, which was no relationship at all. Or when. Or how.

What was she to say? No, Lord Wembly, I've not read any good books lately because I've not read a book in my entire life. I've *pretended* to read them, if that helps.

It was hard to know how to mention it. It was hard to know when to say something. If she were to broach it now, was she presuming an intent on his side that she thought was there, but he'd not come out and said was there? Because, of course, it would be revealing very personal information. But then, if she waited too long…If he proposed and then she told him…He would not be able to back out then.

It would crush her if he turned from her over her inability to read. But then it would crush her more if he were to feel stuck with her. If he were to think he would not have gone forward if he'd known.

But how did one tell somebody that they were stupid? Particularly, how did one tell an intellectual who belonged to The Royal Society that they were stupid?

The duke and Winsome returned to the tea tray, the duke with a book in his hand. "Well," he said, "Winny has finally done it. She's talked me into reading one of these masterpieces of murder and mayhem that she likes so well."

"You'll like it, Papa," Winsome said. "Arabella is such an innocent creature, and she is surrounded by evil forces. I will admit, I was a little bit aggravated with her in the beginning, as who goes to live in a damp and dreary castle with only the old grandmother who never comes out of her rooms, and the baron who looks as if he's thinking evil thoughts all the time, and doors slamming on their own, and a misty lady who keeps disappearing down corridors? I thought, why does she not just leave?"

"Wouldn't be much of a story if she did," the duke said, laughing. "Arabella went to the castle, and it was eerie so she left and went on to live happily. The end."

"That's true," Winsome admitted. "In any case, aside from her lack of judgment about not leaving, it's a cracking good story."

"You hear that, Wembly?" the duke said, laughing. "This is the sort of literature I allow my girls to read. I ought to be more strict about it, I suppose."

The longer the conversation centered on books, the more uncomfortable Verity got. Winsome seemed to sense it and said, "Lord Wembly, my papa and Verity will attend Lady Jellerbey's candlelight picnic on the morrow. I suppose you go too?"

"Oh yes, the candlelight picnic. I've not gone in the past, as I have been too taken up with Royal Society matters. However, my aunt favors it and I will escort her."

"Hah!" the duke said, "not so taken up with that society of yours these days, are you? Well, good thing, is what I say. You're welcome to stay on for dinner today if you like. We eat early. Valor, you know. Gets tired if we run it too late."

Winsome nodded. "Tired Valor is scary Valor," she said with a snort.

"It would be welcome, indeed, Your Grace. But I have promised to take Lady Pegatha to a card party this evening."

"Hard duty, that," the duke said.

Lord Wembly laughed. "I rather think it will be. Things like that never seem too onerous when one agrees to them, but then on the day…"

"Well, nothing for it," the duke said. "Can't let the old girl down."

Lord Wembly rose to take his leave. "I will see you both at Lady Jellerbey's candlelight picnic on the morrow."

"Yes, yes," the duke said. "Dashed strange evening but the

sideboards are good. Find us in the dark!"

Lord Wembly smiled. "I certainly will do." He bowed. "Lady Verity, until tomorrow."

"Yes, Lord Wembly," she said, for utter lack of any other words. What an afternoon! Had he positively said something? Had he not?

Verity had not really understood her older sisters' confusion and bouncing feelings from one thing to the next when it had been their seasons. It had felt as if it were all much ado about nothing. But really, if this is how they'd been talked to, it was not very surprising!

Of course, her sisters did not have the added burden of trying to figure out how and when to acquaint Lord Wembly with her less than impressive intellect.

Verity did not know where she stood. She did not know what to do. She must make a decision, though.

Perhaps if he hinted again about intentions. That must be the right time. Even if she discovered she'd misread the situation.

Of course, she might never know if she'd misread it. He was a gentleman. If he wished to run the other direction upon becoming acquainted with her lack of intellect, he would do so politely.

On the other hand, she could not let it go on too late. She could not trap him into a commitment he'd wish he never made. If the intentions he spoke about were what she thought they were, then he must go into it cleareyed.

Yes, that really was the right choice. The very next time he mentioned intentions or anything at all like it, she would tell him.

The decision filled her with dread. She might lose her chance at real happiness.

Still, it must be done.

CHAPTER TWELVE

HENRY LEFT THE duke's house well satisfied with the day's events. He thought he had hinted at his intentions, and he'd not been rebuffed. As he still had some time before he needed to make his way home, and as he'd had a rather bright idea, he made his way to Rundell & Bridge.

Ludgate Street was its usual throng of people and carriages. Henry looked up and down the busy street to see if there were anybody lurking about who might find themselves nosy as to the reason he went into a jeweler's shop. He did not see anybody he was well-acquainted with or who would be interested in his personal business.

Feeling confident that he was not to create any talk, he went inside. He explained what he was looking for—something similar to the prize Sir Jonathan had given out at his scavenger hunt. He would purchase two and send them to the duke's house for Lady Valor and Lady Winsome, so they might get over their disappointment over not winning.

He suspected, or at least hoped, this would get him further into their good books.

As it turned out, Mr. Rundell was no slouch in the selling department. He'd anticipated that Sir Jonathan's giving away a small looking glass in front of so many people with deep pockets would expand his trade in that item and had well prepared for it.

The clerk brought out a large velvet case with a dozen of

them. Henry chose two he thought would suit. For Lady Winsome, he chose a rose pattern made with small rubies and chip diamonds. For Lady Valor, he chose one that was a bit more gaudy—it was a starburst of citrine and topaz.

And since he was already there, and since he was feeling more and more sure of his intentions, he looked around at some other cases. He looked around for something that would indicate his regard for Lady Verity. When the moment came.

After all, was it not sensible to be prepared?

He ended up selecting a delicate bracelet. It was a brilliant sapphire surrounded by perfectly matched seed pearls, and rows of pearls running all the way to a platinum clasp. It was well proportioned to a lady's wrist, and it was entirely elegant.

He took the bracelet and made arrangements to have the mirrors delivered with a note. Then he made his way back to Berkeley Square.

His aunt was in the drawing room writing letters. "So? How did the scavenger hunt go? Were the Nicolets victorious?" Lady Pegatha asked.

"We were not," Henry said. "However, the disappointment of it seemed to center on failing to win the prize. At least, for Lady Valor and Lady Winsome, it did. The prize was won by the Blendwhistles and it was a small lady's looking glass, decorated with gems. I've been to Rundell & Bridge and purchased two of a similar look and had them sent over with my regards. To Lady Valor and Lady Winsome."

"Ah, clever. You cannot send one directly to Lady Verity before you've declared yourself, but a gift to her sisters will be a heavy hint."

Henry nodded. He took the velvet case from his pocket and showed his aunt the bracelet. "For when things become…more certain."

"It is positively charming. By the by, when will things become more certain?"

Henry shrugged. "Soon, I think."

"Excellent. In the past few years, I had begun to wonder if you would end a life-long bachelor with your head in books. I suppose your doubts about that ridiculous story about the fish looking about themselves when they find themselves on land is gone?"

Henry laughed. "I suppose it must be. In any case, there was not a mention of it today. I expect you were right in your assessment that it was just some odd sort of flirtation."

"Very good," Lady Pegatha said.

"Lady Lilith turned up, and attached herself to our party," Henry said. "Then, she all but invited herself to the duke's house as he'd invited me for apple cakes. They were surprisingly good, by the by. The duke was not having it, though."

Lady Pegatha laughed. "The duke will not be pressured through some idea of courtesy. Apple cakes, you said? I wonder if we might secure the recipe for Cook."

"Not a chance. Apparently, it is a closely guarded secret. Lady Marchfield attempted to get hold of it and was turned away."

"Ah, well," Lady Pegatha said. "In any case, I suppose Lady Lilith will get the hint that you are not interested sooner or later."

"I really hope it is sooner. Today was outrageous, as far as I'm concerned. She claimed her father waited in their carriage, but I do not think he was really there. The duke did not think so either and teased her that we would stop by the earl's carriage to say hello. She practically ran out of the enclosure. Nor do I think she even bought a ticket to the event."

"She stalks you like a hunter after a stag, I'm afraid," Lady Pegatha said.

"I'm afraid so too," Henry said. "I just do not know how to turn her from it. I've hinted enough, she must see I display no particular interest in her. Why does she not turn her view to somebody who might be interested?"

"She is desperate, I imagine," Lady Pegatha said. "I do not suppose young lords with heavy pockets who have no need for a dowry are falling out of the trees at her feet."

Henry supposed that was true. He also supposed he ought to have a bit more sympathy or patience for Lady Lilith's situation. Perhaps she was desperate. He was not certain what desperation would cause a person to do. Perhaps he'd be better served thanking the stars that he'd never been in that situation himself.

Lady Pegatha rose. "Well, this was all very entertaining but now I must go abovestairs and change my dress. We are due to Lady Rareton's card party at seven and her card parties wait for nobody. Perhaps on the morrow, at Lady Jellerbey's candlelight picnic, the time will have come to, as you say, make things more certain."

"Perhaps so," Henry said.

"I only say, the dim lighting of that lady's parties is rather conducive to your aim. I'll leave you with that thought."

Henry nodded. It certainly was a thought.

LILITH HAD NOT realized the thing could be done so quickly and with not too much expense. Clara had finally proved her worth and delivered to her the young man working at a printing press. As it happened, he seemed to admire Clara quite a bit and was eager to impress her. All that Lilith would be charged for was the copper plate for the etching, paper, and ink.

Lilith had described what she wanted, and the young man had quickly sketched some rather glorious interpretations. She'd chosen the one that would irritate Lord Wembly the most, thereby driving him away from any association with Lady Verity.

That had been yesterday. Now, she was in possession of one of the caricatures. The rest were being sent out to likely places to cause talk—gathering places like gentlemen's clubs, and to the talkers of the *ton*. She had even been so daring as to anonymously send a few to some very high-placed ladies. She did not imagine Lady Pembroke and her ilk would be very amused that Lady

Verity had been given a voucher to Almack's after seeing the caricature.

The sketch was positively inspired. It depicted Lady Verity lecturing at a podium labeled Royal Society in front of a sea of gentlemen. The caption read: *After landing several trout on the banks of the River Esk, Lady Fiction concludes that fish cannot see much on land while a certain red-haired gentleman looks on.*

By this evening, there were bound to be several people who'd seen the print and who attended Lady Jellerbey's candlelight picnic. Lilith would be there too. With any luck, Lord Wembly would open his eyes and see that there she was, Lady Lilith Crandall, daughter of the Earl of Berensby, standing there all along. Lady Lilith was not causing embarrassment to him and his family, nor would she ever. By all she knew about him, Lord Wembly was a sensible man. Certainly he would see she was the better choice.

She would wear her best dress to hammer home the idea.

VERITY COULD NOT help but to feel the compliment of it, even if Valor did not quite understand it. Lord Wembly had sent over charming compact looking glasses from Rundell & Bridge for Winsome and Valor. The note had said he hoped these small tokens would ease their disappointment over not coming out victorious at Sir Jonathan's scavenger hunt.

"I'll say it *does* ease my disappointment," Winsome said. "Disappointment is gone!"

"I love mine so much," Valor said. "But, why didn't he send one for Verity?"

"It wouldn't be right," Verity said.

"I see. He doesn't like you as much as I was worried he did. That's all right, Verity. Don't feel bad about it. You can borrow my looking glass sometimes as long as you give it back and don't break it."

"That's not what she means," Winsome said. "He couldn't send her one because it's just not done."

"Why?" Valor asked.

"Nobody knows why," Verity said. "Some things are done and some things are not."

"Who makes up these rules?" Valor said, admiring herself in her glass.

Winsome shrugged. "Felicity asked Papa once and he said they're made up by unhappy people with too much time on their hands. Like our aunt."

"Valor," Verity said, wishing to have a moment alone with Winsome, "I wonder if Sir Galahad has ever seen himself in a glass. After all, he's too short to see into the one on your dressing table."

"That's true," Valor said, considering the idea. She hopped up. "I'll go find out and come back and tell you if he looked surprised. I tell him he's handsome all the time, but he's not really seen it for himself."

Valor left and the drawing room door closed.

"I've decided what to do," Verity said. "The very next time Lord Wembly says anything about intentions, even if it is vague like it was yesterday, I'm going to tell him I can't read."

"What will you say?" Winsome asked.

"I'm not certain," Verity said. "How does one announce that one is stupid?"

"I don't think you're stupid," Winsome said. She paused and then said, "Could you say it was something to do with your eyes?"

"It *is* something to do with my eyes, they make the words all jumbly. But not just my eyes, I do not think. It's my mind too. I just…well, I wonder how an intellectual will view a wife who cannot even read."

"If he loves you, he will not care," Winsome said. "After all, Grace almost killed Lord Dashlend and Felicity almost killed Mr. Stratton, and they didn't care about it. And then Lord Stanford rode through a storm for Patience—he might have been hit by lightning, but he did not care. Also, Lord Thorpe punched his brother in the face to get Nelson back. None of them cared a whit what they had to do for love."

Verity laughed. "I imagine they did care a whit. I just do not know how much more than a whit Lord Wembly will care."

"You have to find out, though. Else, what are you to do? You'd be a positive wreck if you were always trying to hide it and afraid of when he would notice it."

Verity nodded. "I have to tell him. Tonight, if possible. I will see him at Lady Jellerbey's candlelight picnic and try to find a moment for it. I only hope it does not ruin everything."

"Think of this, though," Winsome said. "What trouble to him would it be? He's rich as Croesus, at least that's according to Papa. He could hire a secretary to read to you and do all your writing for you. You'll get lots of letters after you're married— that's what Felicity says, anyway."

Verity nodded. "Well, I've decided. All I can do is go forward and wear my best dress."

HENRY WAS AT once worried and just the smallest bit frustrated. After Lady Rareton's card party, Lady Pegatha had fallen ill. She'd retired early, with the company of her maid to attend her.

He'd thought she'd be right as rain in the morning, but in fact she was a deal worse. Henry had sent for her physician. Doctor Ramsey's conclusion was that she'd eaten something that had been spoiled. Once he'd been apprised of where his patient had been the previous evening, he had no doubt of it. He'd already been on several visits because of it.

Everybody knew that Lady Rareton was inordinately proud of her French chef, and that fellow's signature was his special mayonnaise. The doctor viewed uncooked eggs as the stupidest thing he'd ever heard of and said it was bound to cause illnesses. Or as he termed it: "One might as well roll the dice at Hazard and then be surprised that one's pockets have become lighter."

Lady Pegatha had eaten several small toast points with salmon, dill, and mayonnaise. Henry had avoided them himself as he found mayonnaise revolting. Why anybody would wish to spread it on anything eluded him. Fortunately, his dislike of the stuff had spared him the misery his aunt was currently enduring.

The really worrying part was the doctor had told him privately that a lady of his aunt's age might find the condition much more serious than a younger person would. She would weaken before it was all over and if she could not keep anything down of the fluid variety, it could become very dangerous.

The smallest frustration in all of it was that he would not attend Lady Jellerby's candlelight picnic and would not see Lady Verity. He knew very well that it was low of him to feel it and likely a terrible comment on his character. But then, he supposed he could feel two things at once—worry for his aunt and frustration at missing a chance with Lady Verity. The important thing was what he did about it, and of course Aunt Pegs had need of him, so here would stay.

The doctor had given him a list of symptoms and Lady Pegatha's maid was to alert him immediately if any of them surfaced, especially fever, excessive weakness, or confusion. Doctor Ramsey explained that in the usual case of things he would stay on at the house, but as Lady Rareton had spread her poisonous mayonnaise far and wide, he was certain he would get called out to other houses.

Henry had the stables standing by in case he needed to ride for the doctor. Though what he was supposed to do if the doctor had been called away, he did not know.

Meggy, Lady Pegatha's maid, knocked softly on the drawing room doors and entered. She delivered him a quick curtsy. "I believe I bring good news, Lord Wembly. The dose of laudanum Doctor Ramsey gave to my lady seems to have done some good.

Her stomach does not pain her as much and she was able to take some sips of water. She's resting now, which she did not do at all last night."

That was excellent news. Henry felt himself let out a breath that he supposed he did not know he'd been holding in. "Thank you, Meggy. I've made arrangements with Jane to take over for you at eleven so you can get some sleep."

Not surprisingly, Meggy frowned. Jane was a kitchen maid and the lady's maid would have little faith in her abilities to care for her mistress.

"You will not do Lady Pegatha any good at all if you can barely see straight for lack of sleep," he pointed out. "Jane will wake you if anything changes."

"Yes, my lord," Meggy said begrudgingly. She left and Henry leaned back and sipped his port. It sounded as if Aunt Pegs was coming out of the danger. It was a great relief, and he realized he depended upon her more than he'd ever really examined.

All those months and years with his attention fully focused on his Royal Society inquiries, she'd been his lifeline to the human race. They exchanged letters, she visited him from time to time, and she was always available to lend an ear.

She would be all right, though. He allowed his thoughts to drift elsewhere, and no surprise they drifted in Lady Verity's direction. Certainly, his disappointment at not seeing her this evening was just another indication of his regard.

However, he would look on the bright side of things. Lady Darlington's masque was right around the corner. Lady Pegatha ought to be recovered enough by then that it would be safe to leave her in Meggy's care for an evening.

As they entered Lady Jellerbey's house, the duke said to Verity, "I do not know what's got you so jumpy, but whatever it is, do not fret so much. Girls your age always think the world is ending and it never is."

Verity nodded. Of course, her father was very perceptive and would have noticed her nervousness. He could not know why, though. Perhaps the world was not ending, but it would feel like it if things did not go her way. If Lord Wembly was put off by her mentioning she could not read…she was not sure what she would do. Go home to the Dales, probably, head hung in shame.

Lady Jellerby greeted them at the door. "Your Grace," she said, "have you again come to set my curtains alight while demonstrating how you once set Lady Vanderwake's curtains alight?"

The duke laughed heartily, as he always did when someone mentioned his two encounters with flaming curtains. "I've sworn off it, Lady Jellerbey. One cannot keep doing the same thing over and over—it lacks originality."

"Nobody would ever accuse you of being unoriginal. Now, if I remember rightly, this will be Lady Verity. You look very charming, my dear, and my house is chock full of young gentlemen looking to encounter charming ladies."

As Verity blushed, because it really was embarrassing, the duke said, "I believe we may have reached a point where the attention of one particular gentleman is what's wanted. Is Wembly banging around somewhere?"

"Ah, I see!" Lady Jellerbey said. "I have not seen him yet, but I understand he brings Lady Pegatha."

They moved on to allow the lady to greet more of her guests who were arriving. Verity looked about and noted that Lady Jellerbey's rooms really were as dim as described. The chandeliers were unlit, and candelabras of all sorts were placed on tables and lit up the sideboards. One could see perfectly well up close, but people who stood more distant looked almost ghostly.

It was all very strange. Two gentlemen in the distant gloom seemed to look her way and then put their heads together. Were they talking about her? Were they talking about the strange lady who claimed she was studying if fish could see out of water? It was hard to tell in this lack of light.

"Ah," the duke said, "there's our Grace with Dashlend."

Her father led her over to her sister and brother-in-law. He kissed his daughter on the cheek and said, "What say you, Gracie? You've been chained to this scoundrel for some years now. Any regrets?"

Lord Dashlend laughed, as he was quite used to her father's ways by now. Grace said, "Not one regret for not one minute, Papa."

"And I suppose my grandson gets on well? At least, when he is not commenting on my stomach."

Grace sighed. "Goodness, he gets on well indeed. Though, he has reached an age where we are almost frightened of what he will comment on next. He has recently inquired of his grand-mother why she smells powdery."

"I remember those days very well," the duke said. "Felicity was in the habit of commenting on everything in sight. Old Mrs. Geddy was not very pleased to hear that her nose was the longest Felicity had ever seen in her life."

Lord Dashlend laughed heartily over the picture. "Verity," Grace said, "how do you get on?"

"Oh, very well, I think," Verity said. Which was a little true. Things did get on well, except they might not end well.

"Lady Verity!"

Verity turned and found Lady Lilith approaching. It seemed wherever she went, there was Lady Lilith, ready to join her party. "Lady Lilith," she said. "You already know my father."

"Your Grace," Lady Lilith said with a bob.

"This is my sister and her husband, Lord and Lady Dashlend. Grace, Lord Dashlend, Lady Lilith is the daughter of the Earl of Berensby."

After the introductions, the duke said, "Well now, I suppose I'll take myself to the nearest sideboard, fill up a plate and a glass, and find a quiet corner while you all wait upon Wembly's arrival."

"Lord Wembly?" Lady Lilith asked, looking very surprised.

"Yes, that's the one," the duke said, looking at her quizzically.

Very suddenly, Lady Lilith looked entirely flustered. Why? Why did she look like that at the mention of Lord Wembly? What had happened?

"Gracious," Lady Lilith said. "You have not heard."

CHAPTER THIRTEEN

W HEN LILITH HAD arrived to Lady Jellerbey's house, she'd been fully prepared to gauge the effects of the caricature she'd sent flying around the town. It would take time to really establish a foothold, as she'd only had a small amount of money and so could not purchase as many copies as she would have liked, but surely somebody present would have seen one. That was all that was needed to get the thing going. If there was one thing the *ton* liked to do, it was to relay terrible stories about somebody else.

She'd been waylaid in the great hall by Lady Farthingale and told the tale of Lady Rareton's card party and the poisonous mayonnaise. Apparently, the guests who consumed it were taken ill, including Lady Pegatha, who was said to do very poorly.

That was when she realized the evening would not be quite what she imagined. Lord Wembly would not leave his aunt when she suffered an illness, and therefore, he would not come.

But then she'd had an idea. Might not there be something made of his failing to attend? She'd been all along thinking of driving Lord Wembly away from Lady Verity, but perhaps she could drive Lady Verity away from Lord Wembly as well.

She'd searched the dim rooms and finally found Lady Verity and the duke. They stood with another couple, one of which she believed was Lord Dashlend. That would mean the other was Lady Verity's sister, if she'd got the connections straight.

They all looked exceedingly jolly, which meant they knew nothing of the caricature going round. Certainly it must mean that. Who could be jolly when they were mocked in a print?

Lilith had hurried over and made a great show of things. She thought she'd done a credible job of looking caught out and confused about Lord Wembly's whereabouts, ending with: "You have not heard." Never was there a more ominous statement when it came to London society.

"Heard what?" the duke asked.

"Goodness," Lilith said, maintaining her flustered appearance, "I do not think, rather I am certain, it is not for me to say." She motioned as if she would leave the party, assuming the duke would stop her from doing just that. Which he did.

"Wait a moment," the duke said. "One cannot very well say that we have not heard something and not say what it is we have not heard."

Lilith pretended at being an unwilling deliverer of news. "Well, I suppose, that is, people are saying…he does not come because of the print going round."

"What print?" Lady Verity asked, sounding mortified.

"Oh, as to that, I have not seen it myself. From what has been described to me, it is, oh goodness, I do not like to say."

"You had better say," Lord Dashlend said, looking grim.

Lilith put on a look meant to convey she would not for the world repeat the information, but she was being forced to do it. "As I understand it," she said slowly, "it pictures Lady Verity lecturing at the Royal Society. You know, about the fish seeing out of water, something about the River Esk. And it is noted that a red-haired gentleman looks on. Just a bit of teasing, I'm sure. But then, Lord Wembly is rather prickly about The Royal Society."

The duke, Lady Verity, and Lord and Lady Dashlend all stared at one another.

Lilith curtsied. "I'd really better go." She hurried away, certain she had accomplished something. Lord Wembly did not come because Lady Pegatha was ill, but for all Lady Verity and the duke knew, he did not come because he was offended by the caricature.

Now, all there was to do was drift round the candlelight picnic with her ears open, listening for any news of her prints. She'd done what she could, now she just must wait and see what came of it.

VERITY HAD KNOWN that her ridiculous story of the inquiry into whether a fish could see out of water had been talked about. But an actual print mocking it! That was something else entirely. Lady Lilith had said it mentioned The Royal Society—Lord Wembly's very own society. The society he'd dedicated years to was now mocked and ridiculed. It had pointed to Lord Wembly himself by mentioning a red-haired gentleman.

She'd thought telling Lord Wembly that she could not read would be the real test. But it was not. This was the real test. Could he possibly overlook being personally mocked? Could he overlook his society being mocked? The answer stared her in the face—he had not come.

One minute, he was sending her sisters a thoughtful gift and the next he was avoiding her. That really said it all.

Her whole body felt heavy and there was a very good chance she was going to cry, though she was working hard against it.

"All right," the duke said after Lady Lilith hurried away, "I do not know quite what has gone on, but I think we will not like to stay."

"I will make inquiries into this matter, Your Grace," Lord Dashlend said.

"Papa," Grace said, "go and give our excuses to Lady Jellerbey and call the carriage. I will take Verity to the retiring room until she can leave."

"Right," the duke said. "I'll claim she has a headache."

As all these arrangements were made, Verity only nodded. She would agree to anything, as she did not know what ought to be done. Grace took her by the hand and led her down the corridor. They entered the lady's retiring room, which was a long room of small and private apartments. Grace smiled at the attendant as if there was not a thing wrong, though it must seem odd that they entered the last of the apartments together.

Aside from the chamber pot covered by an ornately decorated wood lid, there was a small sofa and a looking glass. "Now," Grace said, as they sat down, "at times like these, it is very important to think of nothing. Nothing at all. Empty your mind. You'll have time to think when you are in the carriage."

Verity nodded.

"I will tell you about Miles and that will keep your mind elsewhere," Grace said.

Verity's sister went on to tell her stories of her young nephew. On the estate, he'd one day hidden his grandfather's humidor as he did not like the smell of cigars. He'd also brought home a cat who looked very unhappy to be there and had scratched up his arms. It turned out to be a neighbor's barn cat and had to be returned. He'd also been discovered as the culprit of a disappearing tray of marzipan, which was finally located, empty, under his bed.

She listened closely to these stories, following Grace's advice to keep herself from thinking of what had happened.

"I think Papa will have got the carriage round by now, so let us go," Grace said. "Dashlend will get to the bottom of this, and we will come and see you on the morrow."

Grace led her out to the great hall and Verity found herself grateful that the rooms were all so dim. If there were people staring, she could not see it. Soon enough, she would be home. Then the flood would come, but not before she was away from here.

Mrs. Right could only be grateful that Valor had been abed when the duke and Verity arrived home early. As Verity wept and was consoled by Winsome, the duke poured his housekeeper and himself large glasses of brandy and told her what had happened. At least, as much of what happened that they understood at this moment.

It was well that the duke had filled her glass generously with brandy, as her rage over her girl being hurt was near overwhelming. As far as she understood it, somebody in society had made it their business to mock Verity by printing up a caricature and spreading it about. As if that were not bad enough, Lord Wembly had seen fit to avoid her over it.

What sort of man was he? What sort of lord could not stand up to a teasing?

It was true that Verity often invented a fact or two. It was definitely true that she'd invented the idea that she was examining fish eyesight. Mrs. Right had been hoping she'd outgrow the habit. She was not even sure why or how she had acquired the habit. But what a small thing to fall apart over! Lord Wembly was so struck by the print mocking the idea that he could not even meet her? What was he doing? Hiding in his house?

As always seemed to be the case, Mrs. Right's mind began drifting toward how to make Lord Wembly pay for his perfidy.

It was true that she'd made a few slight mistakes in past years with Mr. Stratton, Lord Dashlend, Lord Stanford, and Lord Thorpe. But that was all water under the bridge now. This time, there could be no mistake. Lord Dashlend was out hunting down a copy of that print and there it would be as irrefutable evidence of Lord Wembly's crime.

Mrs. Right tapped her chin. If Lord Wembly was so affected by Verity being teased and mocked, she wondered how he would stand up to being teased himself? She did not know anything about how one went about getting one of these prints done, but she supposed she could find out.

Yes, she very well thought she could work out how to arrange it. Let Lord Wembly feel the sting of it. Let him pay.

In the meantime, she would take Verity above stairs and soothe her to sleep. Her poor girl had been through the wars, and she must be reminded that whatever went on out of the house, she was perfectly safe and protected inside the house. On the morrow, she would set out to have a print made mocking that feckless and fearful Lord Wembly. She would make arrangements to paper the town with them. Then they would all see how he stood up to *that*.

HENRY WAS PLEASED that his aunt had felt well enough to descend to the drawing room. She was still looking piqued, but her spirits seemed well recovered.

"I am sorry you missed Lady Jellerbey's candlelight picnic," she said. "I had hoped it might be the night you went forward and secured Lady Verity."

"It is no matter," Henry said. Though he had not liked to miss it, he would never wish for his aunt to feel as if she'd been any sort of burden. "I believe Lady Verity attends Lady Darlington's masque. That will be time enough. Now, I suppose you are done with Lady Rareton's card parties?"

"Goodness, no," Lady Pegatha said. "I have known Leticia forever. As for that cook of hers, I can comfortably say I am done with *him*. Did I say she sent over a note claiming the mayonnaise had been made correctly but a kitchen maid had taken it from the icehouse too early? As if that would ever induce me to try it again! What does she imagine? That I will keep a close eye on her kitchen maids to determine if they are taking items from the icehouse at the right moments? Leticia is clutching at straws with that idea."

"I suppose her cook keeps his employment then, despite

poisoning a half-dozen of her guests."

"And that kitchen maid too, as far as I can gather. But then, whenever something goes wrong in a kitchen, the fault is always laid at the most junior person in it, as if they are secretly running the place. Almost always nonsense."

Just then, a footman brought a letter in on a salver. Henry picked it up and opened it. What he read next was startling, to say the least.

Lord Wembly—

I would request you visit me at your earliest convenience regarding the caricature involving The Royal Society. Several of our members have already been to see me to voice their complaints. I have not yet decided if we ought to make a public pronouncement about it or ignore it. I would like to hear your opinion before going forward. I currently stay with Lord Kenilworth on Curzon Street.

Sir Joseph Banks

A caricature? What caricature? Was it about Sir Richard's frogs? The only thing Henry could imagine would end up being laughed at by the *ton* was Sir Richard's rather ridiculous observances of frogs in different ponds. Henry could just imagine the mockery if someone outside the society overheard Sir Richard say: "The study of herpetofauna rather depends on our finding it out!" But why should any of that concern Henry? Why was he being called in by Sir Joseph? He was not the one going round spouting off about gazing at frogs all summer.

Lady Pegatha must have noted his confusion, as she was staring at him. "Well?" she said. "What is it?"

"I am not certain what exactly it is, but for being exceedingly odd. Sir Joseph wishes to see me."

"Ah, he is the president of your little club, is he not?"

"The Royal Society is not a little club, though I know you say it to tease. And yes, he is our esteemed president. It seems there is a print going round about the society, and not a favorable one, I will guess. But why should he wish to see me about it?"

Lady Pegatha shrugged. "You will not know until you see him, I presume."

"I will write him back that I am currently unable to leave the house due to an illness in the family."

"Bah, get going and find out what he wants. I am exceedingly unlikely to experience a setback from an assault by mayonnaise."

"If you are certain?" Henry asked. He did not wish to leave his aunt's side until he was sure of her permanent recovery. On the other hand, he was curious to know what this summons was all about.

"As certain as I am that I will dine *before* Lady Rareton's next party and avoid her adventurous cook's creations as if he is Henry the Eighth and I am a lady of his household."

Henry laughed. Lady Pegatha had often wondered why none of the ladies who'd caught the eye of that monarch had not run for the hills. She supposed they had not the means, as why else would a lady wed a king in the habit of killing off his queens? He said, "Sir Joseph is staying just on Curzon Street. I can walk over and be back soon enough."

"Go, take the air. You are a young man; you cannot spend an entire day staring at an old woman who has done battle with a mayonnaise."

Henry stood and kissed the top of his aunt's head. "Do not do anything strenuous while I am gone."

Lady Pegatha laughed. "I do not do anything strenuous when you are here."

"You know what I say."

"Yes, yes, I will try to avoid a mortal injury from my embroidery needle. Go on, I would like to hear news of what's buzzing under Sir Joseph's hat at the moment."

Henry strode out of the room. A footman fetched his coat, and he set off for Curzon Street. It was not ten minutes before he arrived at Lord Kenilworth's door. He was admitted and led to the lord's library, where he found Sir Joseph in his wheeled chair, deep in a book.

Sir Joseph laid the book on his lap. "Ah, Lord Wembly, I desired that you come as quickly as you might, but had not had hope it would be quite this quick."

"Sir Joseph. I stay with my aunt on Berkeley Square."

"Lady Pegatha. Very good. Now, what do you make of this print that's going round? It could be, of course, that there is another red-haired gentleman I ought to think of, but I've been told it is most definitely you."

Red-haired gentleman? There had been nothing in the note about a red-haired gentleman. Was this not about Sir Richard's frogs, then? "I've heard nothing of it until I received your note," Henry said.

"You have not even seen it?"

"No, I have been at home. Lady Pegatha had been struck ill."

"Do not tell me she attended Lady Rareton's card party."

"She did."

Sir Joseph let out a small laugh. "I will not be surprised to see a print about *that*. A dozen matrons of the *ton* struck down singlehandedly by a certain chef and a certain mayonnaise."

"But the print you refer to?"

"Ah, yes, it is on the desk. Lord Westerby claimed it all made sense. Something about the perils of a man of science becoming distracted by a woman and how there were already plenty of gentlemen who could people the world. Really, I can hardly follow half of what that man says."

Henry went to the desk. The print lay on top of a stack of scientific journals. He could hardly believe what he was seeing. A lady stood behind a lectern labeled Royal Society while an audience of gentlemen looked on. He read the caption. *After landing several trout on the banks of the River Esk, Lady Fiction concludes that fish cannot see much on land while a certain red-haired gentleman looks on.*

My God, it was ridiculing Lady Verity and her story of inquiring into fish eyesight. Word must have spread very widely about it. It was his fault; he'd mentioned it to Westerby. As it was looking, Westerby had no sense at all and had gone round repeating it. Then somebody had decided it was too amusing to let pass.

Lady Verity was named Lady Fiction. It was such an insult! It was an insult and a humiliation that he'd brought down upon her head. It was true that she'd invented the preposterous notion that was mocked in the print, but it should never have left her father's house.

Did she know? What must she feel? She was likely to conclude he was the one who had spoken of it after the dinner at the duke's house. She would know that he'd brought this down on her head. After all, who else could it be? Lady Pegatha would hardly have gone round discussing scientific ideas.

"What do you make of it, Lord Wembly?" Sir Joseph said, interrupting his thoughts.

"Yes, what do I make of it. Well, I think this is one of those cases where a very small thing has been blown up to a much bigger thing. Unnecessarily. Lady Verity Nicolet mentioned in passing that she wondered about whether fish might see as well on land as they do in water."

"I see. I've wondered that on occasion myself. Perhaps the various species' different shapes and structures of eyes have to do with typical depth? Meaning how much light is generally in their milieu?"

Henry was rather startled by the comment. He'd not thought anybody wondered about it. But perhaps he had not carefully considered the matter? It seemed Sir Joseph had.

"What should we do?" Sir Joseph asked. "I do not like that The Royal Society has been caught up in this."

The Royal Society. So far, Henry had not given a thought to The Royal Society. The society could weather this storm. Lady Verity perhaps could not.

"I think it would be wise to say nothing," Henry said. "If we make some statement about it, it just puts more fuel on the fire. It is a little bit of teasing and will not take up people's attention for long."

That was partly true, Henry thought. The *ton* would not occupy itself with this print overlong, he did not think. As for Lady Verity herself, that was a much different matter. For a lady to be named Lady Fiction! It was almost as bad as Lady Jersey's nickname—Silence—for her habit of incessant talking. Lady Jersey's nickname had stuck, people delighted in it. Would it be the same for Lady Verity? Would she be known as Lady Fiction forevermore? What was he to do to fix this?

Sir Joseph nodded thoughtfully. "I am of the same mind myself. Starve the thing of air, as it were."

Henry nodded. Really, though, he'd like to choke the thing to death. And possibly choke Westerby too.

"Nicolet, you said?" Sir Joseph said.

Henry nodded. "The Duke of Pelham's daughter. One of his daughters, anyway."

"Let us hope he does not feed the gossip with too much air, then. I understand that gentleman is rather…unpredictable."

The duke. Good God, what would the duke do about this?

IF VERITY COULD have escaped the drawing room before Lady Marchfield got in it, she would have. It occurred to her that drawing rooms should have a secret door at one end where one might make a quick exit.

As it was, she was trapped.

Lady Marchfield waved the print around dramatically. Verity had already seen it in all its horrifying glory. Lord Dashlend had located a copy and sent it over with a note. As far as he could gather, Lord Wembly had inquired of Lord Westerby whether there had been any prior research on the vision of fish because

Verity was looking into the matter. Westerby had repeated it to somebody or other and it had taken off from there. Lord Dashlend did not think Westerby had anything to do with the print, as that gentleman did not get up to such things.

"I've said and I've said and I've said it would come to this," Lady Marchfield cried.

"It's only a joke, Aunt," Winsome said in Verity's defense.

It *was* only a joke. But a cutting joke and a nickname, Lady Fiction, that might stay with her forever. Why had she ever invented such a story? Or any of the stories she'd invented? It would be far better for people to know she was stupid rather than a liar.

"A joke?" Lady Marchfield said, her tone expressing her outrage. "Do you suppose Lord Wembly will be laughing over it?"

Winsome glanced at Verity, as they both knew Lord Wembly had not laughed over it. He'd not come to Lady Jellerbey's candlelight picnic because of it. He'd essentially washed his hands of her, and she was heartbroken over it. She would not allow her aunt to see that, though. The very last thing she needed was her aunt gloating that she'd been right all along. Perhaps she had been right, but Verity did not wish to hear about it.

There was a quick knock on the drawing room doors and Thomas came in, looking almost frightened. Verity had expected a tea tray but what, or rather *who*, he brought in could not have been further from that comforting item.

CHAPTER FOURTEEN

VEN LADY MARCHFIELD was startled. "Lady Pembroke!" she said. Then she looked around the room as if she were a cornered animal.

Verity and Winsome had leapt to their feet and curtsied. Valor, fortunately, had long ago hightailed it out of the room the moment Lady Marchfield had arrived and was hiding abovestairs with Sir Galahad.

"Lady Marchfield, Lady Verity," Lady Pembroke said, eyeing Winsome.

"That is Lady Winsome, Lady Pembroke," Lady Marchfield said. "She is not yet out. We are honored by your visit. Naturally. Might I ring for tea?"

Verity thought it might be the first time she'd ever seen her aunt rather awed by rank. Lady Marchfield seemed perfectly comfortable meeting Lady Pembroke at Almack's, but it was somehow different to find the lady arrived to one's drawing room.

"No," Lady Pembroke said. "I will not stay long."

Lady Marchfield was going very red in the face. "Now if it is about that ridiculous caricature making the rounds, I can assure you..."

Verity's aunt trailed off and she did not have the first idea of what Lady Pembroke could be assured of. The print was terrible and now it seemed to have come to the attention of one of the leading ladies of society. It must have—why else would she be here?

Verity waited to be told her voucher to Almack's was rescinded, or that she ought to leave Town, or she did not know what. Whatever it was, it would be awful. Queen Charlotte's Lady of the Bedchamber had not arrived to congratulate her on her recent accomplishment of being named Lady Fiction.

"The queen requests Lady Verity to attend her. Now, presuming that is convenient."

Verity sank down in her seat, hardly realizing that she'd done so. The queen wished to see her? Why? Could she say it was not convenient? Was that allowed? Why could not her father be here? He would know what to do. He'd left for his club hours ago. Could they send Thomas or Charlie to fetch him?

"Oh dear," Lady Marchfield whispered. "I suppose I'd better escort her."

"No need, Lady Marchfield," Lady Pembroke said, "I am fully capable of that myself."

She would go. She would have to go. She glanced at Winsome with the hopeful idea that perhaps it was not as bad as she felt it must be. Winsome's horrified expression did nothing to reassure her.

Verity felt very much like flying from the room and hiding in a closet. She could not do it, though. "I ought to change my dress," she said shakily. She thought she ought to, but change into what? What did one wear when one was brought to the queen? An angry queen, no less. Certainly, Her Majesty was angry, why else would she send Lady Pembroke for Verity Nicolet?

"That simple muslin will do very well, Lady Verity," Lady Pembroke said. "Let us be off. Lady Marchfield can inform your father that you are safely in my care, and I will personally return you here."

Verity found some comfort in the idea that she would be returned home, because really, she felt herself on the way to a hanging. Winsome had sidled up to her. She squeezed Verity's hand and whispered, "It will be all right."

Just then, the doors burst open, and Valor hurried through them carrying Sir Galahad. She stared at Lady Pembroke and sighed. "I thought it might be Lady Pegatha. She thinks my dog is tremendous."

"Valor!" Aunt Marchfield hissed.

"Indeed, he does look tremendous. Lady Pegatha knows what she's about," Lady Pembroke said. "Lady Verity?"

Verity stood. She had no choice but to go forward and face whatever must be faced. As she proceeded to the great hall to don her pelisse and bonnet, she noted Charlie wide-eyed as Thomas went to fetch those items. She supposed she was rather wide-eyed herself.

Her sisters might have run into difficulties here and there and caused some amount of talk, but none of them had been taken to the queen to answer for themselves. No, that achievement must be Verity's alone.

She remembered what Mrs. Right always said about facing something that needed courage—however frightening it might be, it would not last forever. Time would pass, the moment would pass, and calm would reign once more.

Lady Pembroke said she would bring Verity back home. All she had to do was get through the time until she was safely back through her doors. She could convince her father that they must leave Town and then disappear into the Dales.

She had to force herself to get into the carriage as Winsome weakly waved from the drawing room window. Just then, she wished Buckingham House was as far away as her home in Yorkshire. She wished it would take days and days to get there.

As it was, not a quarter hour passed by before they arrived. During those fifteen minutes, Lady Pembroke was inscrutable. She said nothing and simply looked out the window with a look of complacence, watching the world go by.

The gates were opened, the carriage trotted round the central fountain and came to a stop. They were met by the Earl of

Dartmouth standing on the steps. Why? Why was she so important that the Lord Chamberlain himself met the carriage? She was only a silly young lady making up even sillier stories. Why should he concern himself with it? Why should anybody? Why did he look so grim?

"This way, Lady Verity," he said gravely.

As she followed him down the corridor, she began to wonder if all this was because The Royal Society had been noted on the print. Perhaps it was some sort of crime to embarrass anything that had been given a royal seal? It very well could be. In fact, it was bound to be. To insult something that had been given the royal nod must be an insult to the palace itself.

But she did not create that print! Why did they not drag in whoever had done it?

Perhaps she had not created it, but she had caused it.

Verity felt a terror begin to overtake her. Was she going to prison? Or perhaps she would be banished from London. Just this moment, she would not mind running home to the peace of the Dales.

Two footmen, who appeared far more stern than Thomas and Charlie ever did and were dressed in exquisite royal equipage, threw a pair of massive double doors open.

"I leave you here," the Lord Chamberlain said.

The room was of large dimensions. Everything in it seemed oversized, the chandeliers seemed to stretch five feet across, each of the sofas could accommodate ten people. Largest of all, though, if not in size than in effect, was the queen.

She sat in a gilded chair, cushioned in a lively Indian print. She was, perhaps, not the most handsome woman, and she was past her middle age. However, none of that dampened the effect of her—she was a queen and it seemed to radiate from her very being. Her eyes were a little sharper, her chin a little higher, her expression eminently composed.

Lady Pembroke pushed Verity through the doors, took her by the arm, and marched her in front of Queen Charlotte. Verity curtsied low.

"Lady Verity Nicolet, Your Majesty," Lady Pembroke said, rising from her own curtsy.

"Ah, Lady Pembroke, you always carry out my requests so efficiently. Well, I suppose we had better have tea."

Tea? Verity watched a footman slip out the door to fetch it. It seemed they listened closely to everything the queen uttered and then ran to do her bidding when they heard a comment about what was wanted.

Queen Charlotte had nodded, and Lady Pembroke sat down. Verity remained where she was. What was she supposed to do? Stand or sit?

"Sit down," Lady Pembroke said softly.

Verity curtsied again and hurried to a place on the sofa. To her amazement, a cart wheeled in. Tea. When it had just been asked for not a moment ago. The kitchens must keep water on the boil all day, waiting for a summons.

The accoutrements of the tea tray were rather astonishing. The teapot itself was silver and enormous. It was accompanied by a very large and tiered silver tray, stacked with pastries that appeared flaky and had layers of cream.

"Ah, mille-feuilles," the queen said. "Always a favorite."

So that was what they were. A bit fancier than the apple cakes to be found in her father's house. Verity continued to stare at the pastries, as she did not know where else to look. She had not been addressed, nor told why she was there. She certainly had not been told why she was to have tea. She had grown more and more certain that she'd broken a law about respect for anything given the royal seal. But if that were the case, why should she be given tea?

Perhaps she was not to be given it, though. Perhaps it was only for the queen and Lady Pembroke. Nobody had ever told her what to do in such a situation. Of course, that was probably because nobody else had ever been in such a situation.

Another footman had come behind the one who'd wheeled in

the tea service. He carried a silver tray with three delicate China cups and saucers. So she was to have tea? It was all so confusing and she wished something would be said. Most of all, she wished Mrs. Right was by her side, holding her hand and ready to do battle in her defense against all comers. Even the queen.

The cups had been set down. Rather than the queen pouring, one of the footmen poured. That was probably because of the size and weight of the teapot. Or maybe it was royal protocol. She did not know.

The footman finished his work, the wheeled cart was removed, and the footmen went to stand by the doors once more.

"Well, Lady Verity? What do you have to say for yourself?" Queen Charlotte said.

"Say, Your Majesty?" Verity repeated, playing for time.

Queen Charlotte reached into the myriad folds of her silk robes and pulled out the print. "About this?"

Yes, of course, that. What to say about it, though? As she was certain the real offense was involving The Royal Society in her nonsense, that was what she must apologize for.

"Your Majesty," she said, "I never meant to involve The Royal Society. I cannot even understand how the society became involved. I never claimed to know anything about the society or espoused any views on it. Naturally, as it is The *Royal* Society, with a royal seal, I hold it in the highest regard…Without knowing anything about it. I am entirely sorry to have involved anything royal. I hold all things royal in the highest regard. The very highest. As I've said."

There was a moment of silence.

Verity hurried on. "I understand that Wedgewood is preferred by Your Majesty and called Queen's Ware. Rest assured, whenever my father needs new plates, those will be the plates he purchases. I believe I can confidently speak for him on that front. Because they've been given the royal seal of approval, so what else would we buy?"

Verity was well aware that she was babbling now. It was very hard to stop under the intense gaze of these two formidable ladies. She forced herself too, though, as she could not think of a single other thing the queen might have endorsed. Was she even right about Wedgewood? She was not entirely certain!

The queen and Lady Pembroke roared with laughter. Verity hardly knew what to think. She weakly smiled, as that seemed to be the best approach since they were laughing. But what were they laughing about?

After their laughter settled, the queen said, "I believe what Lady Pembroke and I were more interested to hear about was the quip on the print. What does it mean? Fishing for trout on the River Esk and concluding that fish do not see very well out of water? And who is the red-haired gentleman?"

Verity was taken aback. She had really grown very sure that the offense was to do with The Royal Society. What should she say? What *could* she say?

She realized that the only thing to be said was the truth. The very stupid truth.

The queen selected a mille-feuilles from the tray and sat back, waiting.

"I am afraid, Your Majesty, it is all very stupid. I have been very stupid."

"Excellent, just what I was hoping for," the queen said. "Amuse me."

Verity swallowed. "Yes, well, you see, the red-haired gentleman, that would be Baron Wembly. He is a member of The Royal Society and very scientific-minded. So when I met with him at Almack's, he mentioned looking into the circulatory systems of slow-moving animals and I…well, I said I was too."

Lady Pembroke snorted. Queen Charlotte said, "Did you, indeed?"

Verity nodded. "It was not true, though."

"Not true?" the queen said. "I can hardly believe it."

Verity understood that comment to be the mockery it was meant to be.

"But how did that lead to the print about fish?" Lady Pembroke asked.

"Yes, well, I decided that I ought to find out about these slow-moving animals and their circulatory systems so I could speak on it and then claim I'd lost interest. To never mention it again after that. So I did, when Lord Wembly and Lady Pegatha came to dine. But then somehow it led to claiming I had developed another interest—"

"Another one," the queen said to Lady Pembroke, her shoulders shaking with laughter.

"You see, Lady Pegatha did really press me to know what it was, and just then one of our footmen had come round with broiled cod…"

"No," the queen said, clearly enjoying the recounting of Verity's idiocy.

"And that's when I said I was looking into whether fish could see out of water."

"A calamitous series of events," the queen said, dabbing her lips with a napkin. "Gracious, why did you begin with it?"

Verity shifted in her seat. "I suppose I wished to seem intelligent to Lord Wembly."

"You could have just read a book and reported on it," Lady Pembroke pointed out.

Of course, the lady could not know that was precisely what Verity could not do.

"Might I venture to guess that there was interest between you and Lord Wembly and that caused you to claim these absurdities," Queen Charlotte said.

"Yes, I believe so, I am afraid I was trying to impress him."

"I have been most amused," the queen said. "I suppose Lord Wembly takes the whole palaver in stride?"

Verity looked down at her hands, certain she turned twenty shades of red. "It seems he has taken great offense to it. Which, of course, I understand. He is very dedicated to The Royal Society. He was meant to meet me at Lady Jellerbey's candlelight picnic, we had made arrangements. But he did not come. Understandably.”

“You understand it?” Lady Pembroke asked.

“I do not understand it,” the queen said. “What lord cannot stand up to a bit of teasing?”

Of course, Verity had no answer to that.

“Quite a few, I believe, Your Majesty,” Lady Pembroke said. “Taking oneself seriously has become a sport for a certain type of gentleman these days.”

“I do not like it,” the queen said. She tapped her chin. “Perhaps Lord Wembly ought to be taught to laugh at himself. Yes, leave it to me.”

Verity was certain she’d gone wide-eyed. What did the queen mean by it? She could not guess, though Lady Pembroke had nodded approvingly.

“What is the next society gathering you attend?”

“Oh, that would be Lady Darlington’s masque, Your Majesty. If I am in spirits to attend.”

“Chin up, Lady Verity. It does nobody any good to weep in a corner, you may take my word for it. Lady Darlington’s masque is in two days from now, if I am not mistaken. Until then, you are to sequester yourself at home. Go nowhere, admit nobody, see nobody. Tell your father I will take you both to the masque. Now be off, you ridiculous girl. On no account invent one more story about what you are studying. No slow-moving animals, no fish, nor any other living creature. Do you understand?”

“Yes, Your Majesty,” Verity said, her thoughts racing ahead. Why was she to hide away? Why would the queen escort her to the masque? What in the world did the queen have in store for Lord Wembly? She burned to know all of it and could ask none of it.

“What costume do you intend on wearing?”

“Oh, as to that, I was only to wear a simple domino,” Verity said. Her older sisters had given much thought to their costumes, but there was something that had put her off it. Wearing a costume felt akin to being a fraud and she was already a fraud with a terrible secret. It seemed somehow wrong to don a costume—a fraud acting as a further fraud, she supposed.

Madame LaFray had been very put out over Verity not wishing for an elaborate costume made, but she felt almost repelled by the idea. It would have felt as if she were strutting around with her head held high when she had no right to do it.

"No, a domino will be entirely unacceptable," the queen said. "I will send something to the duke's house. Lady Pembroke will assist me in the effort."

"Ah, we do like a project," Lady Pembroke said.

She was to wear a costume from the queen. Should she say she was a fraud? Should she say she could not even read and had hidden it, lied about it really, all her life?

"Off with you," the queen said. "Return to your father and follow my instructions."

Lady Pembroke rose, and Verity hurriedly did too. They curtsied and were dismissed from the queen's presence. She was on her way home. Verity supposed she should look toward the positive aspects of it. She was not being sent to prison, she was not banished from Town. What was to come next, she could not know.

However, she had come out of Buckingham House for the most part unscathed. It was a far better outcome than she'd imagined when she went into it.

CHAPTER FIFTEEN

Lilith was not entirely sure what she had unleashed. She had simply meant to turn Lord Wembly from Lady Verity. She supposed she had, though it seemed to be accompanied by some unintended consequences.

It seemed there was a new print going round that she'd had nothing to do with and it was very unfavorable to Lord Wembly. Certainly it must be aimed at him. It was a red-haired gentleman with his posterior in flames who appeared to be running from the doors of The Royal Society. It said: "Not very stoic."

Was it a comment on Lord Wembly's courage? Was he to be expected to carry on his courting of Lady Verity despite her being named Lady Fiction? She had really not predicted that as a consequence.

What if he discovered she had been the author of the original print naming Lady Verity as Lady Fiction? It would ruin everything.

She must not allow that to happen. The only other gentleman who had taken an interest in her was Mr. Grantley. He was rich, very rich, but he was ten years too old. And, worst of all, his money came from trade. He had some sort of factory near Bristol that made yarn and thread.

Lilith knew very well why she was of interest to that gentleman. She was an earl's daughter and Mr. Grantley had aspirations. He was well read and well mannered and was invited to certain things, but there would be places where the doors would always be shut against him. He imagined that an earl's daughter would polish him up in the eyes of the *ton*. Or perhaps his children would benefit.

It was not what she wished for, though. It would be a step down when she was determined on a step up.

Her temporary maid, Clara, was snorting over the print. "I guess a person never knows how a thing will take effect," she said. "According to this, Lord Wembly ran the other direction from Lady Verity, but then he's also revealed himself to be a feckless lothario."

"Lord Wembly is not feckless and certainly not a lothario. He is sensible," Lilith said. "Whoever sent this print around is an idiot."

"It's still funny, though," Clara said. "His posterior in flames is funny."

Lilith did not answer, as she did not think Clara had the least understanding of the situation.

HENRY COULD NOT work out what was happening. Was he shunned? Was Lady Verity ill? He did not know.

He had called on the duke's household twice and not been admitted. He wished to apologize and take full responsibility for the damnable print that had gone round naming her Lady Fiction. If he'd not said anything of the matter, the print would not exist.

Certainly she must have concluded the fault was his, but he must be allowed to state it aloud and take responsibility for it.

And yet, both times he'd gone to the house, the housekeeper, Mrs. Right, had met him at the door. That was odd enough in itself. That lady had positively glared at him and told him Lady Verity was not at home to visitors. He supposed that meant she was at home, but he was not to be let in.

If he would only have an opportunity to apologize.

Would she come to Lady Darlington's masque? If she did not, that would indicate a retreat from society. The duke might well pack up his family and return home for the year.

Perhaps he should send flowers? What could he send to indicate regret? Marigolds? Or send a note and hope it got past the duke?

As for the duke himself, how did he view his daughter's current circumstances?

He would ask Lady Pegatha her opinion of it all.

Just now, he was milling round Lord Ledwell's rout. He had no prior indication that Lady Verity would attend, as he did not have access to her full calendar. However, it was one of those parties people liked to call 'the event of the season.' Henry was not certain why. The only thing this crush of an event had to offer was a punch Ledwell served each year of rum, sugar, lime, and nutmeg. However, he could be reasonably assured that the duke and his family had received an invitation. If there was the smallest chance she would turn up, he would not miss it.

Sir Reginald, a loud and voluble member of his club, suddenly slapped him on the back. "What's it all about, Wembly?" he asked.

Henry presumed he inquired into the Lady Fiction print. It seemed there were so few lords in Town with any shade of red hair that he'd been easily identified.

Before he could compose an answer, Sir Reginald said, "Pants on fire, eh?"

What on earth did he say? What pants on fire?

"Mind you, nobody can blame you for running from a lady inventing strange stories about fish. I understand the duke has raised them all in the wilds, somewhere up north—no surprise they come out of it with strange habits.

Lord Frederickson pushed his way into their conversation, though Henry had not much of an idea of what they were talking about to begin with. "Wembly, brave lad," he said.

"Brave? Why?"

"Somebody's got it out for you, eh?"

What was going on? Was he talking about this pants on fire idea too?

Just then, Lady Caroline tapped his shoulder with her fan. "Gracious, Wembly," she said. "Whatever it is you've done, do fix it. I do not care for a gentleman of my acquaintance to be named spineless. You have not refused a duel, I hope?"

Spineless? "Lady Caroline, I have not the first idea of what you are referring to. For that matter," Henry said, turning to Sir Reginald and Lord Fredrickson, "I do not know what either of you are referring to either."

Those three people looked at one another. Lord Frederickson said, "I was talking about that print going round where you are lying on a fainting couch, waving a vinaigrette under your nose. I mean, I assumed it was you, what with the red hair."

"His hair is an auburn shade, really. However, a print of a fainting couch is not at all what *I* referred to," Lady Caroline said. "I spoke of the print where Lord Wembly is slumped in a chair as if he cannot sit up straight and it simply says: Spineless."

Sir Reginald laughed heartily. "Now this is amusing! *I* was talking of neither of those. I meant the print where Wembly is running out of The Royal Society with his posterior in flames. It says: Not very Stoic."

"Good God, Wembly," Lord Frederickson said. "How many prints are going round about you?"

"I've no idea," Henry said softly. "Gentlemen, Lady Caroline," he said hurriedly. He excused himself and made his way out of the house, lest somebody mention another print meant to mock him. How many were there?

Why was he being mocked in the first place? He hadn't done anything.

Perhaps it was because he'd caused Lady Verity so much trouble by mentioning her research into fish? But he was not running away with his backside on fire and he was not spineless and he certainly had not fainted over it.

Had he failed to do something he ought to have done? Was that the problem? Was he being mocked because he'd not yet done anything? He'd tried to apologize but had not been let through the door.

He'd better find a way to get hold of these prints and see exactly what he was up against. With any luck, Lady Verity would attend Lady Darlington's masque, and he could apologize there. He would also make a show of seeking out Lady Verity to prove he was not running away or slumping in a chair or fainting on a couch.

Really, when his thoughts had turned to finding a wife, he'd thought it would be a deal more straightforward!

NOBODY BELONGING TO the Nicolet household had ever been called to Buckingham House to answer to the queen. Of all of them, only the duke was really acquainted with her. Some of her sisters had met her at various events, but she was not nearly as out and about as she had once been, due to the king's illness, which seemed to come and go. Though it seemed these days it mostly came and rarely went.

The duke had been in the habit of writing a letter to the palace, excusing his girls from arriving for the formal curtsy. Because of the king's illness, some years it was held and others it was not, and it was the duke's opinion that Queen Charlotte did not give a toss about it anyway. Verity's father thought there could be nothing sillier than to have a monstrosity of a gown built and secure wildly large ostrich feathers for a lady's hair, all to go and curtsy to a lady who would rather be elsewhere with a tea tray.

As the queen had not brought up the Nicolets' absence over the years, Verity presumed he'd been right in his judgments. Or at least not condemned for them.

All that did not wash away the idea that Verity Nicolet, of all of them, had been called on the carpet to answer for herself. It prompted an immediate family dinner so they might discuss what had happened, what might happen, and how to go forward.

Just now, they were seated round the duke's dining table, with Thomas and Charlie expertly managing the sideboard.

As the two footmen brought round the wine, Lord Thorpe said, "The American butler is gone, is he?"

This caused snorts from Thomas and Charlie. The duke said, "Gone back to America where he belongs. I'll tell you the story one of these days, but suffice to say that Mr. Klonsume left here in high style and Lady Misery was off her head over it. Very amusing."

"Sir Morus," Thomas whispered, his shoulders shaking.

"Now, why do not we start off with Verity relating what occurred," the duke said. "That will give us a direction, I think."

All eyes turned to her. Verity took a sip of wine to fortify herself. "Well, it seems there is a print going round. Lord Stanford's seen it."

Lord Stanford nodded. "It names Lady Verity as 'Lady Fiction.'"

"Because of when she accidentally said she was studying whether or not fish could see out of water," Winsome explained.

As most of her sisters and their husbands, but for Grace and Lord Dashlend, had been on the scene when she'd blurted out that ridiculous idea, they all nodded sadly.

"It's our understanding," Valor said, "that Lord Wembly got mad about it. But I really think, Verity, that if he wants to be mad and go away, you should let him."

Verity ignored that bit of sage advice. Of course Valor would wish him away.

"I'd like to know why he repeated it, though," Mr. Stratton said. "He must have done, as I do not think Lady Pegatha would have had cause to."

"I'd like to know why too," Verity said. "He's come to the

house twice and maybe he came to say why, but I could not see him."

"The queen's told her to stay indoors and see nobody," Serenity said.

"I like the queen," Valor said. "You should stay inside forever, Verity."

"It's only for a few days, Val," Grace said.

"It could be longer!" Valor said. "The queen might mean longer."

"I'm sorry," Lord Dashlend said, "are we not to mention the other three prints going round?"

Other three prints? Why would there be others? Was she to be mocked incessantly? Was not one caricature enough? Who were these spiteful people making up these prints to ridicule her just because she'd said one stupid thing?

"What other three prints?" Mr. Stratton asked.

"The ones depicting Lord Wembly," Lord Dashlend said. "One has got his posterior on fire and names him not very stoic, another has him slumped in a chair and named spineless, and the other has him on a fainting couch with a vinaigrette."

Verity felt her insides go cold. It was bad enough that she was mocked, but now there were direct salvos at Lord Wembly? Three of them? Why?

"Well now, the spineless one was from me," the duke said. "I felt compelled to answer his failing to appear at Lady Jellerbey's dim indoor picnic on account of a teasing. Thought I'd put some starch in him. Of course, if he's come to the house to apologize, that might have been a mistake."

"But Papa," Verity said, "what if he did not come to apologize? What if he is infuriated to be mocked in three different prints? And who made the other two?"

"Calm yourself, Verity," Felicity said. "A gentleman would never come to express his indignation directly to a lady of his acquaintance."

"Quite right," Mr. Stratton said. "If a gentleman wished to

yell about it, he'd yell to his friends, not to the lady in question. It would be very bad form."

"He might see the duke about it," Lord Thorpe pointed out. "If he really wished to take things far."

"Yes," Mr. Stratton said. "He might see the duke about it."

All four gentlemen laughed heartily at the notion that anybody would have the temerity and lack of sense to come to the duke to complain about one of his daughters.

"Then he really would have his posterior on fire, eh?" the duke said, joining in on the laughter.

"Who did make the other two, though?" Serenity asked.

"I can make some guesses," the duke said. "That not very stoic comment smacks of Mrs. Right—we all know how ready to come to the defense of my girls she is. And then the vinaigrette is certainly Queen Charlotte. It is one of her preferred insults. Everybody remembers when Lord Destin was forever complaining about the waltz being allowed into England. She famously asked him if he needed to borrow her vinaigrette and not a word was heard from him after that."

Verity took up her wine. It had been bad enough to wonder if Lord Wembly would be able to see past the print going round about her. Now there were three going round about *him*! She well knew her papa and Mrs. Right, and even the queen, she supposed, had meant to be helpful. But how was a gentleman to see past all of that? And that was before she'd even mentioned the idea that she could not read. There did not seem to be any way he could look past all of it. It would be too much for any gentleman.

"It's hopeless," she said. "I just wish to go home."

"Let's go," Valor said, championing the idea.

"Why do you say so, Verity?" Grace asked. "The rest of us have faced some…circumstances. We've come out all right."

"*I'll* say there were circumstances," Lord Dashlend said with a laugh. Mr. Stratton, Lord Stanford, and Lord Thorpe all nodded in his direction to acknowledge the truth of it.

"I just know that this particular case is hopeless," Verity said.

"There it is. Totally hopeless," Valor said, seeming delighted over the hopelessness of her sister's fortunes.

"It cannot be hopeless," Patience said. "It only feels hopeless. We've all felt it at one time or another, but then it turns out not to be true."

"It is true this time," Verity said. "Winsome knows why."

All eyes turned to Winsome, who in turn peered at Verity. "Should I say? Really?" she asked.

Verity took a rather large swig of wine and said, "Why not? I cannot hide it forever, can I? I do not even care anymore."

That was coming very close to the truth. Her mind was drained of strength. It was tiring to always be on guard, as any moment somebody might thrust a paper into her hands and ask that she read it. It was wearying to sit with her bible every Sunday and pretend to read. Most of all, it was exhausting to always have a secret that somebody might find out. It was akin to acting as a spy in a foreign land, always looking over one's shoulder and waiting to be caught out. She was just so tired from all of it.

"Gracious, what is it we do not already know?" Patience asked.

Winsome looked at Verity once more. She nodded to her sister. She would like to get it over with and stop hiding who she really was. She could not go on with the pretense that she was just like everybody else. She was not. Everybody could know it, and see it, and do what they liked with it.

"Well," Winsome said, "you see, Verity cannot read. Her eyes make the words all jumbled."

"And my mind jumbles it too," Verity said. "I cannot read and Lord Wembly is an intellectual. You see the problem. There. Now everybody knows that Verity Nicolet is the stupid sister."

"I do not think you are stupid," Felicity said. "It is just what you have, and we all have something. Poor Stratton here has been introduced to my temper once or twice."

Mr. Stratton laughed. "I show her my scars and then she remembers I saved her from being eaten by a tiger and she cheers up."

Felicity nodded. "And then Grace has flung herself on the floor more than anybody in England, and Serenity collects dead bees, and Patience is forever toe-tapping, and Winsome is suspicious of everybody. You see? We all have our crosses to bear."

Verity gave Felicity a weak smile, but really, she did not think her sisters' minor peccadilloes rose to the level of her own faults.

"Papa," Valor said, "I am the only one who is perfect, it seems."

"Is that right?" the duke said with a snort.

"Valor," Felicity said, "you have not even managed to get your pony up to a trot and do not tell me it is because she likes going slow."

Valor shrugged to have her fearfulness pointed out.

"Now, Verity, I am not entirely sure why you never mentioned that you have word swimming?" the duke asked.

"Word swimming?" There was a name for it? "I did not want to disappoint anybody, I suppose. But Papa, do you mean to say that other people have it? There are other people who cannot read, even when they've tried very hard to do it?"

"Your mother had it," the duke said. He laughed. "She always said the words got up and went swimming on her so that's what we called it—word swimming. For all I know, there is some other term for it I've not heard."

"That is exactly what happens," Verity said. "The words swim around and then they don't make sense."

"You would have been too young to remember, but Felicity and Grace might," the duke said. "Girls, do you not recall that Mrs. Right used to read everything to the duchess?"

Felicity laid down her fork. "Yes, I do remember. She would read all of Mama's letters aloud and then she would write out the responses. Goodness, I suppose I just thought it was part of Mrs. Right's duties."

"It was," the duke said. "See that, Verity, the whole thing is easily managed. We might have been managing it all along if you'd mentioned it. What a thing to keep to yourself."

Verity drained her wine glass and Thomas hurried over to refill it. It felt a great relief to have everything in the open. Though, she also felt a bit stupid to not have mentioned it before now, as it seemed it was not so unusual, and it might have been managed. She looked like her mother, and it turned out she was more like her than she'd known.

"Well, look at that," Serenity said, "things are coming right already."

Verity stared at her sister. "Serenity, there are four prints going round, entertaining all of society. One of me and three of Lord Wembly. Also, I have not mentioned to him, an intellectual and member of The Royal Society, that I cannot read. That I have word swimming."

"Oh yes, all that," Serenity said. "That is quite a lot."

"Not insurmountable, though," Lord Thorpe said. "What I would like to know is why is the queen escorting you to the masque?"

Nobody had an answer to that. It had been a very informative evening. But nobody had an answer to that.

"What do you wear to the masque, Verity?" Patience asked.

As the queen was sending over a costume, nobody had an answer to that either.

CHAPTER SIXTEEN

"WELL," LADY PEGATHA said, "this is a fine mess."

Henry and his aunt were poring over the three prints that had gone round about him. It was a fine mess indeed. It seemed wherever he went, somebody had seen at least one of them. Had he not sported red hair, there might have been some confusion as to who the gentleman in the prints were, or even if they were the same gentleman.

That was not the case, and everybody had speedily leapt to the conclusion that it was him, in all three prints. But who was behind them? And why?

"I would not put it past the duke to have been the author of one of them," Lady Pegatha said. "Or perhaps all three of them."

"Why, though?" Henry asked. "I have not actually done anything. Why am I accused of...I am not even certain what I am accused of."

Lady Pegatha shrugged. "The duke is a funny creature. Perhaps he thinks you have paid Lady Verity certain attentions and yet nothing firm has come of it."

"How could anything firm come of it when I am barred from his house?"

"I did not say he was a *sensible* man," Lady Pegatha said. "In any case, you are not barred from Lady Darlington's masque. I am certain Lady Verity will attend—a lady does not compose a costume well in advance and then fail to wear it."

"I see. Is that what you have done? Composed an elaborate costume?"

"I have not, I've grown too old for such things. I will wear one of my old standbys. I will go in a simple tunic in the Grecian style. You will wear a domino, I presume?"

Henry nodded. "Yes, of course I will. I do not understand these gentlemen getting themselves up as jesters and sultans and who knows what else. It is all well and good for the ladies, it is their opportunity to create something of beauty—"

"Not always," Lady Pegatha said, with a snort. "Last year, one of Lady Verity's sisters came as a bee. It was exceedingly odd and not at all attractive."

Henry had heard of that, of course. Lady Serenity apparently had an overfondness for bees. It was even said that Lord Thorpe had built a crypt to house any dead bees that the lady came across.

Perhaps that was a clue to the Nicolets, and to Lady Verity herself. It was not just the duke who was eccentric. It was all of them. Perhaps it had been simply eccentricity that had caused Lady Verity to claim she was making scientific inquiries. For all he knew, the whole family had laughed over it afterward.

Perhaps he'd better become more accustomed to taking in a jest? That might just be it.

In any case, he was growing tired of all this nonsense. He'd decided to wed, he'd found the lady he wished to wed, and he thought she was agreeable. Or at least, she *had* been agreeable. That should have been the end of it. There was no reason for these endless complications. He was fed up with it.

On the chance that she was no longer agreeable, or not at this moment agreeable, surely he could change her mind. Surely. There is, or at least was, something between them. He knew it. He was all but certain she knew it. Why were a pile of ridiculous prints circulating to get in the way of it?

"There is no dancing at Lady Darlington's masque, none organized in any case," Lady Pegatha said. "It will just be people milling round in costumes until the hostess names her winners and gives out her prizes. Do you have a particular strategy for the evening?"

"I do, now that I think of it. I plan to be rudely ignoring of every lady but for Lady Verity. If the duke attempts to send me away, I will only move off a few feet. He cannot make me leave the masque, after all. Then everybody will be clear that I am not on fire or fainting or spineless. I will make my apology and state my case. We will see what she says to it."

Lady Pegatha smiled. "I like it," she said. "Just one little note, though. Perhaps you might want to say something more romantic than stating your case, as you term it. Just keep in mind that you will not be speaking to The Royal Society, but a lady deciding if she will wish to hook her carriage to your horses until the end of time."

Romantic, yes, he'd better give that some thought. He'd allowed his mind to be so focused on the scientific and facts that he had no notion of what might be pleasing to a lady to hear at such a moment. "What did Lord Bessworth say to you when he proposed marriage?"

This sent his aunt into peals of laughter. "Gracious, I have not thought of that proposal in years. He told me my eyes were stars and my skin a fine China. It was all going exceedingly well until he told me my lips were tulips. You see how funny that was—my lips were two lips? I quite adored him for it. Why not? I was mad about him, and he could have said my lips were nettles and I would have accepted him."

Henry nodded. He would avoid any mention of tulips. What he *would* mention, he did not have the faintest idea.

"The important thing was, he gave it his best try," Lady Pegatha said. "Really, a lady in love is only looking for effort, not Shakespeare."

Henry supposed that was the real question. Was Lady Verity in love? She might have been, but he really did not know where her mind had gone since he'd last seen her.

He was determined to find out, though.

"It's magnificent, Verity," Winsome said, once more examining the costume the queen had sent to the house.

It had come earlier in the day and even Valor had been bowled over by it, despite holding the opinion that Verity should not go to the masque and they should all go home and live happily together in the Dales forever.

Verity was to go as a swan. The dress was white satin with an overlay of white feathers all positioned to mimic a swan's wings folded. The mask itself was white sequin with a rim of black sequins around the eyes and a dab of orange silk on the nose. It came with white satin slippers and long white kid gloves. The slippers were just the tiniest bit too big, but Mrs. Right had balled up small bits of paper and stuffed them into the toes to solve the problem.

It was not a dress she would have ever dreamed of wearing. Not when she'd considered herself a fraud. Not when she'd harbored a secret.

She felt a little differently now. She was not stupid; she simply had a case of word swimming. It was a condition, not a comment on her intelligence. An odd condition, to be sure, but a condition all the same.

The duke had a long talk with Verity in his library, explaining how her mother was one of the most intelligent people he'd known in his lifetime. Who really cared that words swam in front of her eyes? He had not.

Verity had asked him how and when he'd found it out. It had been early on, during their wedding trip. He'd asked her to read something or other and she'd said, "By the by, I cannot read. The words swim." Then he'd said, "We'd best hire somebody for that then." She'd said, "I suppose that's right."

That had been the entire thing! There had been no grand reveal of a terrible secret. There had been no recriminations or regrets. It had just been an offhand, 'by the by, did I mention?'

Naturally, she did not know if Lord Wembly would be so casual about it, nor how the prints going round would have affected him. She supposed she would get a further hint tonight. Would he be there? Would he approach her? If he did, what in the world would he say?

And then, of course, what would the queen say about it all? Verity had almost expected some sort of note to come from the palace, alerting them that the queen would not attend them after all.

No note had come, though.

"Winsome, Valor?" Mrs. Right said. "Be off with you now. I want a few words with Verity before she goes downstairs."

Winsome laid down the remarkable swan dress. "Come on, Val. We'll take Sir Galahad downstairs so he can see Papa's domino."

Valor giggled. "The one with the red flames at the bottom because he's set curtains on fire two times." She scrambled off the bed and swept up Sir Galahad, that dog perfectly satisfied to be carried everywhere. They left and closed the door behind them.

"Now, my love," Mrs. Right said, "I just wanted to say one little thing about the word swimming. I should have noted it. I read everything to your mother and I should have had a sharper eye out for it. I didn't realize it could be passed down as it has been. If I'd known it could be, I would have had a sharp eye out for it, as you are the picture of her."

"How could anybody know it?" Verity asked. "In any case, I did work very hard to hide it from everybody."

"That you did. Still, when Miss Pynchon complained to me that you were not working at your studies, I should have seen it then."

"I'm glad everybody knows now," Verity said. "Except for Lord Wembly, he does not know."

"If he's got feelings for you, he won't give a toss about it. When the duke came home with your mother, he just said I'd have to read her all her letters as she'd got some sort of eye problem. After that, I do not believe he ever gave it another thought."

"And so you did?"

"Aye, every letter she received, and I wrote the letters going out too. Sometimes she had me read her a novel. I came to know her very well through those exercises. Now, when you go forward to your own household, hire a woman you can trust to do just the same and you should get on very well."

Verity was cheered by the idea, but then she also knew her father to be a particularly superior sort of person and his loyalty to his own could not be questioned. She did not know Lord Wembly so well. Was he as superior a person? What would he think? What would he think about any of it?

"Come now, let's get you into this dress. Your father says you both must be downstairs and ready well ahead of time. Nobody can expect the queen to wait on a latecomer."

LILITH HAD SCRAPED together enough funds to compose some sort of costume for Lady Darlington's masque. She would present herself as an innocent milkmaid and hope that perceptions of her stayed innocent. She had begun with a caricature to drive Lord Wembly away from Lady Verity, but the entire thing had got completely out of hand.

The Town seemed to be papered with prints mocking Lord Wembly. At a card party last evening, it was all anybody talked about.

There were two problems with that. One, Lord Wembly was likely outraged. And two, the talking had made it far more important than it was ever meant to be. When something became important, more and more people started looking into it, inquiring about it, wanting to know who was at the bottom of it. They could not discover that she'd started it all.

She'd never had the wish to do something underhanded, it was not particularly in her nature, but she was desperate. Lady Verity could have anybody. She was undeniably pretty, despite Lilith's claim to her maid that she did not care for the lady's coloring. Lilith did not know the precise details of Lady Verity's dowry, but it was said she was well-funded. She was a duke's daughter. What didn't she have?

Lady Verity might be in the habit of making ridiculous claims, but a well-funded and pretty duke's daughter had that sort of latitude.

Why must she set her cap on Lord Wembly? He was the one person who might give Lilith what she wanted. What she needed, really.

As the carriage rumbled along, on the way to Lady Darlington's masque, her father said, "You'll need to settle on someone soon. We cannot afford to forever come to Town husband hunting. If necessary, you'll have to consider Mr. Grantley after all."

Lilith did not answer. She could not bear to answer.

She would go into the masque head held high and she would do what she'd always done as a child when she'd broken something and was loath to admit it. In those days, she'd run to her governess and pretend to just have discovered the broken item and lamented over who could have been so careless. It had usually worked.

Tonight, she would make a point to sympathize with Lord Wembly over those dastardly prints and denounce whoever these people were who occupied their time in such a ridiculous manner.

With any luck, the very last person anybody would suspect of being involved was herself.

As the queen was going to arrive to the house, the preparations by the duke's household staff had been extensive. Never had baseboards and corners and windowsills been scrubbed so thoroughly. The chandeliers had been lowered for a polish. If a speck of dust drifted into the house looking for one of its own kind, it would find none.

All of that, as it happened, was for naught. The queen did not even descend from her carriage, much less come into the house. Of course, that did not stop Thomas and Charlie and Cook and all the housemaids peering out of windows and trying to get a glance of Her Majesty. Winsome, Valor, and Mrs. Right could be seen lurking at the drawing room windows.

Once they were apprised that the queen would not come inside, the duke and Verity had hurried outside. Verity had thought the lady might ride in some sort of elaborate and gold-plated coach. However, while the carriage was large, it was very usual and did not even display the royal arms.

As they performed the exceedingly awkward exercise of attempting a bow and curtsy while inside a carriage, Queen Charlotte said, "Duke, I've not seen you in quite a few years, though I do recall receiving your letters each year, explaining why your daughters cannot come to make their curtsy."

"Your Majesty, I've made a guess that shortening up the whole procedure by one girl must be pleasing, as I imagine the whole palaver is tiring and tedious."

Queen Charlotte tapped her fan on his knee. "Even if it is, and I will not admit to it, it is not seemly that a duke does not send his daughters. Save your eccentricity for everybody else, if you please."

The duke suppressed a laugh. "I understand, Your Majesty."

Verity supposed that meant that Winsome would make her curtsy next year. She could not imagine the result when Winsome found out she was to wear that preposterous gown while the rest of them had avoided it—she'd be positively livid.

"Lady Verity, you look exceedingly charming."

"Thank you, Your Majesty, for sending such a lovely dress."

"I have decided to come as the Goddess Nemesis. She is known for many things, but restoring balance is what I think of."

The queen was dressed in a gold satin gown with folds hinting at the Greek with a gold holster and dagger round her waist. Her tiara was a glorious platinum and diamonds studded with evenly matched pearls. The dagger's hilt glittered in the passing light coming through the carriage windows.

"You, Lady Verity, go as a swan, and you might recall that the Goddess Nemesis was very kind to a swan."

Of course, Verity did not recall. It was precisely the sort of thing that was buried in a book somewhere. But then, perhaps it was not necessary to recall, but simply agree. "I cannot begin to express my gratitude for your kindness, Your Majesty."

"It is likely well that you cannot begin," the queen said. "One does tire of people expressing gratitude every time one turns round."

The duke snorted.

"We are looking quite well," Queen Charlotte said, fussing with the folds of her gown. "I wish I could say the same for this rather pedestrian box on four wheels. Not even my coat of arms on the door." The queen sighed. "My advisors tell me it would be dangerous to announce my presence while I travel, but really, am I to creep around Town like a criminal?"

Neither she nor her father answered that, as neither of them could hardly know what factors the queen's advisors had taken into account.

"I suppose you might have encountered a certain print of a certain red-haired gentleman on a fainting couch?"

The duke smiled. "Among my many presumptions, Your Majesty, I did imagine your hand in that?"

"Ah, I gave myself away, did I not? Everybody knows I like to offer my vinaigrette when one of my subjects is becoming hysterical over nothing. Now, *is* Lord Wembly still hysterical over what has occurred? Lady Verity?"

"We are not certain, Your Majesty," Verity said. "He did come to the house twice, but as I was to sequester myself and see nobody, he was not admitted."

"Well, we will see what he does tonight. My presence will serve the purpose of throwing my considerable influence on the side of Lady Verity Nicolet. That will close the talkers' mouths, if I am not mistaken. I have found a pall falls over drawing room gossip when I make clear I do not like it. Lady Pembroke is already primed to circulate the room, mentioning that I quite depend upon hearing Lady Verity's views on a whole host of topics."

Verity was not very successful in suppressing a small gasp over that idea.

The queen laughed over it. "Never fear, Lady Verity. If you are asked anything about precisely what I consult you on, you are to say that your conversations with the queen are of a private nature."

The carriage slowed to a stop in the line of carriages in front of Lady Darlington's house.

"Your Majesty," the duke said, "they do not make way because they do not recognize the carriage. Allow me to descend and alert them."

"Not on your life, Duke," the queen said. "I did not tell Lady Darlington I would attend. Would you really deprive me of the amusement of the surprise? They will scramble like mice at sunrise and then attempt to compose some sort of throne or place of honor where I may view the proceedings. It will all be badly done but I will nod in approval so Lady Darlington might sleep tonight."

The carriage did eventually make its way forward and then waited an age while Lady Catherine and her lord came out of their carriage, then the lord went back in to fetch his lady's reticule, and then there was some further delay for nobody knew what reason. Verity presumed they'd be mortified when they realized that the queen's carriage had been behind them, all the while waiting through their disorganized disembarkation.

Finally, at the queen's direction, Verity and the duke descended and then her father helped Queen Charlotte to the pavement. The look on the waiting grooms and footmen when they realized the queen had arrived was amusing. When one of them made to dash inside to alert Lady Darlington, the queen stopped him in his tracks.

She sailed in with Verity and the duke behind her.

Verity, of course, understood that the queen making an unexpected entrance would put people on the back foot, and so it did. Lady Darlington had been almost speechless. After they moved on from the receiving line, Verity could hear the surprised hostess issuing orders for a particular chair to be brought into the ballroom and placed at the top.

They entered the room and the hush rolled across it in waves, one party seeming to notice that the party next to them had stopped talking. Men bowed, ladies made a low curtsy.

Queen Charlotte said, loudly, "I have not been in the habit of attending Lady Darlington's soiree, however, Lady Verity mentioned that it was amusing."

Her father winked at Verity over that particular pronouncement. She supposed the queen, of anybody in England, knew just what to say to manage the *ton*.

Verity scanned the crowd looking for Lord Wembly. It was very hard—what was he wearing? Everybody was in at least a half mask.

Lady Darlington's footmen had run in at the top of the ballroom carrying an oversized chair with gilt arms, racing to get it in place before the queen reached them. The three violinists who'd been there to provide soft music for the party were moved to the other end of the room. Several other footmen brought smaller chairs and placed them on either side of the makeshift throne.

"Come, Lady Verity, we will view the proceedings from the comfort of a chair. You too, Duke," the queen said. As they made their way there, the queen leaned toward her and said quietly, "Let us see if Lord Wembly has a stiff enough spine to approach his queen and request an audience with Lady Verity Nicolet."

Chapter Seventeen

Henry had escorted Lady Pegatha to Lady Darlington's masque. They arrived in good time, very much on the early side of things, actually. He ignored the frowns from the footmen who had to bring them glasses of wine before they felt ready to do so. It was, after all, the time-honored tradition of footmen to advertise any sort of opinion that ought not be said aloud with a deep frown.

He really did not care how much they wished to frown. Henry would be on the scene when Lady Verity arrived, approach her at once, and hopefully secure his aim.

The room had begun to fill but there was still no sign of her. At least, he did not think she had arrived. Some of the ladies were costumed so completely that it was difficult to know who they were.

"My advice," Lady Pegatha said, "keep your eyes open for the duke. He is in the habit of wearing a domino that is decorated with flames at the hem. Does he reference his prior activities in setting curtains afire? Or perhaps he jokes that his vicar goes to the devil? Who knows."

"Lady Pegatha, Lord Wembly."

Henry turned to find Lady Lilith, or a dairy maid, as she was dressed at the moment. "Lady Lilith."

"Charming costume," Lady Pegatha said.

"Lord Wembly," Lady Lilith said, all but ignoring his aunt's compliment, "I must say that I am appalled at these ridiculous prints that are going round. What sort of person spends their days getting up to such tomfoolery?"

"I've no idea," Henry said.

"I only wondered…" Lady Lilith said, trailing off.

Of course, Henry well knew that he was given a moment to press her on what she had wondered. He was not inclined to it, though.

"Wondered what, Lady Lilith?" Lady Pegatha said. "We do not prefer guessing games."

Lady Lilith appeared flustered. "Well, it is just that I think, who would have the daring to do such a thing? Who would not fear any sort of recrimination? Who has made a habit of flouting society's rules and opinions?"

"Who?" Lady Pegatha asked, beginning to look annoyed.

"The Duke of Pelham?" Lady Lilith said. "It just occurred to me that he might be put out about seeing his daughter mocked in a print and decided to…answer it."

Henry did not know if the duke was at the bottom of all these prints. He certainly might be, which added a complication. He'd put all his thoughts toward Lady Verity. But what if the duke would never sanction the match? After all, he was only a baron, and an irritated duke might not deign to overlook it.

The duke was an interesting personality. Henry got the idea that he really was not at all concerned with society's approval or disapproval. He would not have given a thought to the right or wrong of it if he'd decided to revenge himself upon Henry through a series of prints.

Now that he thought of it, he'd heard some stories of the older sisters' suitors running afoul of the duke. Stratton had a pile of chains dropped at his door. And then there was something about Stanford's house being infested with case moths, though Henry could not imagine how the duke could have been involved in it. The joke at the time that went round The Royal Society was court a Nicolet at your peril. He'd not thought much of it.

Perhaps he should have?

The hum of a room filling up with people talking suddenly faded to silence. Henry turned to discover what had caused it.

Then he saw what had caused it. Queen Charlotte had arrived…with the duke and Lady Verity.

The queen was dressed in a very regal gold gown draped in the ancient Greek style, the duke in his domino with flames round the hem. Lady Verity was magnificent. A gown of white feathers, a swan, it could not have suited any lady better.

Why did she come with the queen, though?

"Oh dear," Lady Pegatha said quietly.

He turned to her. "What do you mean? What is oh dear?"

"I have not before heard that the queen and Lady Verity are fast friends. Therefore, a point of some sort is being made. I will imagine the point is the queen throws her considerable favor on the side of Lady Verity and against whoever made that print of her."

Lady Lilith gasped. Henry was not sure why. If the queen had decided to back Lady Verity, certainly that must be a very good development.

"What's thrown you off, Lady Lilith?" Lady Pegatha said.

"Oh! It is just, well, one would hope…" Lady Lilith trailed off.

"Hope what?"

"Um, I suppose one would hope the queen did not assume that Lord Wembly was the author of the print against Lady Verity?" Lady Lilith said.

"Why would she assume that?" Henry asked.

"As to that," Lady Lilith said, "I did hear that the whole idea of fish eyesight was mentioned at a small dinner at the duke's house?"

Of course it had been mentioned at a small dinner. All family attending, but for he and his aunt. Henry did not suppose anybody in their right mind would accuse Lady Pegatha of being the author of it.

But he was not either! At least, not entirely. He'd mentioned it in passing and then the idea had spread, and somebody had the notion it would be amusing to do a print.

If Lady Pegatha was right, if the queen had come to back Lady Verity and denounce the author of the prints, and it was assumed to be him…Well, it was a fine situation.

The queen, the duke, and Lady Verity had proceeded to the top of the ballroom. A throne of sorts, meaning the largest chair in Lady Darlington's house, had been set up, with smaller chairs on either side. The duke took one side and Lady Verity the other. Was she to be trapped there all night?

Lady Pembroke entered on the arm of the Earl of Dartmouth—both part of the queen's retinue. The Lord Chamberlain stood to the side of the makeshift throne. Clearly, he would act the gatekeeper regarding who was to come into the queen's presence, and who was not.

Lady Pegatha snorted. "It seems your damsel is just now locked behind the castle walls. Will you make any attempts to rescue her?"

"I believe I will," Henry said.

"Oh, I am not sure that would be wise, Lord Wembly!" Lady Lilith said, the note of alarm in her voice all too clear. "After all, the queen might be affronted by it."

"I am not certain I care, Lady Lilith," Henry said resolutely. Of course, he did care, but this situation could not be allowed to stand.

Queen or no queen, he must speak to Lady Verity.

VERITY HAD FOLLOWED the queen to the makeshift throne Lady Darlington's footmen had arranged. Queen Charlotte ordered the duke to her right and Verity to her left. Footmen arrived with trays of wine and champagne, as well as the bits of food Lady Darlington was in the habit of sending round.

The queen stared at small rolls of thin ham stuffed with creamed cheese, tiny cheese tarts, and squares of pineapple skewered on thin sticks. She waved them on and satisfied herself with a glass of wine. Verity did the same. She was not at all clear if there was some etiquette involved—could one eat if the queen had declined? Though, she really would not have minded trying out the pineapple.

Whatever the rules might be, the duke did not seem to see the need to follow the queen's lead and filled up a small plate. He took so many, and such was the look of consternation on the footman's face, that if Verity had to guess what the young man was thinking, it would probably be along the lines of: "Why not just take the plate in my hand, as you've nearly emptied it into your own."

The ballroom had gone very quiet, and the crowd stared at the queen as if nobody understood what they were to do next. Queen Charlotte signaled the three violinists to take up their playing again. They did so, and it seemed to break the pall that had fallen over the room.

"Hah!" the duke said, "there's my sister, Lady Misery. Dressed in another high-flown get up—she attempts to look regal but can never quite hit the mark."

"You are exceedingly naughty, Duke," the queen said. "Lady Marchfield is a respected matron."

"Yes, but not a very amusing one," the duke said.

"Well," Queen Charlotte said with a laugh.

The queen leaned in Verity's direction and said, "Here comes Lady Pembroke and my lord chamberlain. Lady Pembroke will circulate the crowd, as I mentioned. Lord Dartmouth will stand by us and make introductions he thinks fit upon being ap-proached. I am hopeful Baron Wembly will take his chance, as he will know Lord Dartmouth from The Royal Society."

Goodness. It was all so formally done. Where was Lord Wembly? Was he here? Did he wish to see her? If he did, why? Was it to scold her for all those prints that had gone round? If she'd never said that stupid thing about fish, there would be no prints.

But perhaps not. He had come to the house twice, which seemed to be a lot of trouble just to complain. She very much wished she could see into his thoughts, but gentlemen were so inscrutable.

"I do not know why you suddenly look like a hare in a hunter's sights," the queen said. "You are a duke's daughter—chin up!"

Of course, the queen was right. Verity lifted her chin and did her best not to appear as a ridiculous person who talked about examining fish eyesight.

As she did so, she saw Lord Wembly. He wore a simple domino and half mask. Now that she'd spotted him, she wondered how she'd not seen him before. That lovely, lovely auburn hair. It really was so superior to every other gentleman's hair. He was walking over, with Lady Pegatha and Lady Lilith trailing him.

"Now we will see what the lay of the land is," the queen said, sounding very jolly about it.

Lord Wembly had a word with the Lord Chamberlain, that gentleman looking very stern and seeming to consider what was said to him.

"Your Majesty," Verity daringly whispered, "he will not be turned away?"

"Certainly not," the queen said, "where would be the fun in that? Though, Dartmouth does terrifically at pretending he is weighing the matter."

The earl really did do terrifically. Verity was entirely convinced that Lord Dartmouth had not positively decided to allow Lord Wembly to approach.

Finally, the Lord Chamberlain gave a grave nod, and Lord Wembly was allowed to proceed, while Lady Pegatha and Lady Lilith remained by Lord Dartmouth's side.

Why was Lady Lilith there anyway? She was dressed as a charming milkmaid. Why should she be one of Lord Wembly's party? Why was she staring at Lord Wembly so intently?

"Your Majesty," Lord Wembly said with a deep bow. "Your Grace, Lady Verity."

"Wembly," the queen said. "I understand you have created quite a lot of talk these days?"

"None that I have meant to, Your Majesty."

"I suppose you've seen the print where you are in repose on a fainting couch?" the queen said with a smile.

"I have, Your Majesty. Though I hope I may be so bold as to point out that I am not in a faint, nor have I ever been. I do not believe the author of that drivel knows my character very well."

Verity felt the blood drain from her face. Perhaps it had drained from her entire. body and was now in a pool under her chair. That *drivel*? The queen herself had composed that print.

Silence had descended on the party.

The duke said, "That's what I like about you, Wembly. If there is a pile of manure within a mile, you'll find it and step in it."

Very naturally, Lord Wembly seemed put on the back foot over that comment.

"I, your queen, composed that print," the queen said, sounding in high dudgeon.

Now Lord Wembly was so far on the back foot that Verity wondered if he would fall over.

"I deeply apologize, Your Majesty," Lord Wembly said. "It was humorously done, of course. But I must insist, I was never in a faint or anything like what those other prints portrayed."

"Other prints?" the queen asked.

"Yes, Your Majesty," the duke said, "there was one with his posterior afire, and another with him slumped in a chair and named spineless."

The queen seemed to lose her irritation over the amusement of it. "Wembly, do you make it a habit of causing so many prints to be made about you?"

"I have not in the past, Your Majesty, and hope never to do so again."

"I see," the queen said. "Well? Beyond insulting my print and making a general spectacle of yourself, was there anything else you wished to accomplish?"

"If I might request to take Lady Verity on a turn about the room?"

The queen looked to Verity's father. "What say you, Duke?"

Verity leaned forward to catch a glimpse of her father and encourage him to acquiesce.

"I'll leave it to Verity, Your Majesty. All my girls have sense enough to decide for themselves."

Verity sprang from her chair. "I'll go…That is, I am agreeable to a turn around the room. Your Majesty." She curtsied. Lord Wembly held his arm out and they set off.

Not a moment later, Verity noticed they were being trailed by Lady Pegatha and Lady Lilith. Lord Wembly seemed to notice too.

He turned and said, "Aunt Pegatha, perhaps you might escort Lady Lilith…somewhere. Perhaps to the tables where Lady Darlington has set out her voting tickets for the costumes."

Lady Pegatha nodded, though Lady Lilith was looking irate about it. Verity was glad, though. She would not be able to discover what was in Lord Wembly's mind if there were other people in the conversation.

His aunt had nodded at Lord Wembly. Rather knowingly, Verity thought—as if they had a secret between them. Lady Pegatha had taken Lady Lilith's arm and steered her in the opposite direction.

"Lady Verity—"

Before Lord Wembly could get further than saying her name, Lord Westerby had him by the arm. Verity did not know him, but she knew *of* him. Her father claimed the elderly gentleman would corner a person and lecture them about some arcane subject for hours at a time.

"Wembly, do not tell me you plan on missing Brande's lecture on the morrow regarding his observations on the effects of magnesia in preventing an increased formation of uric acid?"

"Why should I?" Lord Wembly asked.

Lord Westerby looked pointedly at Verity. "I only say, the world can be peopled by those who do not take an interest in advancing science."

Verity stared at the gentleman. What a thing to say.

"Thank you, Lord Westerby," Lord Wembly said, "but I believe you have been enough help to me over the past weeks to last me a lifetime."

They moved on, though Verity heard Lord Westerby call behind them: "Does that mean you'll come, then?"

"Now, Lady Verity—"

They were again interrupted. This time by Lord Froggerton, one of the gentlemen who had come in droves the day Verity was to ride in the park with Lord Wembly.

"Eh, Wembly?" he said in a jocular tone. "Had to face the queen, eh? All those prints—she don't like that sort of thing."

"Are you an intimate of Queen Charlotte's, then? Are you privy to her private thoughts on a wide variety of subjects?" Lord Wembly said, his tone all irritation.

"Well, no, but I've heard…"

Lord Wembly gave Lord Froggerton a withering stare and that gentleman turned and walked away.

"As I was saying, Lady Verity—"

"Pants on fire!" a gentleman said, stopping them in their tracks.

"Thornton," Lord Wembly said with a heavy sigh, "did you need something?"

"Need? Who needs a laugh after all those prints going round—I've got a whole collection of them."

Lord Wembly turned to Verity and said, "The doors to the balcony are right there—will you consent to step out?"

She nodded. Lord Thornton said, "A bit of fresh air? I do not suppose it would do me any harm."

"Not *you*," Lord Wembly said. He was really looking out of

patience and Verity could not tell if he were in a hurry to scold her and denounce her for bringing him so much trouble…or something else.

He pulled Verity through the doors and shut them in Lord Thornton's face. The balcony was quiet, the doors closing on the babble of guests in the ballroom. The cool air fanned her cheeks and smelled fresh in comparison to the heat and perfume of the indoors.

"Lady Verity, first, I would reiterate that I have not been on fire or slumping or prone on a fainting couch. Though, I do wish I'd known the queen was the author of that last one. Nevertheless, if I have been anything at all, I have been aggravated by all this unnecessary nonsense."

Verity felt her heart slowly squeezing inside her chest. He had got her alone to communicate his ire, and she'd been so hopeful it was something else.

"I should never have said that ridiculous thing about the fish eyes," she mumbled.

"It was not true, was it? You were not really looking into it?"

"No."

"Why did you say it, then?"

"Well, the footman came round with the broiled cod, and I was looking at it…so that's what I said."

It was not really an answer. Lord Wembly wished to know why she would invent such a story. She had not told him she could not read, that she had word swimming. Now she certainly could never reveal it. He'd brought her out of doors to express his irritation, not his admiration.

"In cases such as these, I presume it is the usual…" Lord Wembly paused. "Wait. Lady Pegatha did warn me not to sound as if I were giving a lecture at the Royal Society."

Verity swallowed. He'd told Lady Pegatha he was to give her the what-for and she'd advised him on how to do it? Is that why they'd seemed like they had a secret between them?

"I am not so skilled at finding the right words, it seems. This might do better." Lord Wembly reached into his coat and brought out a velvet box. He opened it to reveal the most charming bracelet Verity had ever seen.

It was a superbly cut sapphire surrounded by seed pearls that went on in rows to form the band of the bracelet. He was giving her a bracelet? She was wrong, then? He might be a little scoldy over…recent events. But he also gave her a bracelet, which was practically a declaration. Or was it definitely a declaration?

He removed it from its case and made to put it round her wrist.

"Wait!" she cried. Now was the time, now she would have to tell him that she could not read. She should have told him earlier. She would have, if he'd been more clear about his intentions. She really would not have waited until this moment.

But now was the time.

The bracelet hung in Lord Wembly's fingers. "There is something I have to say…or rather, inform you of," Verity said. "After you have heard it, you might wish to slip that bracelet back into your coat pocket. You would have every right to do it, too. It is very grave news. Very grave, indeed."

"Good God," Lord Wembly whispered, "are you already married?"

"No!"

"It's not, well, it's not a baby?"

"Whose baby?"

"No, of course not," Lord Wembly said. "What? What is it?"

"Well, what it is, you see, it is a condition with my eyes."

"You're going blind?" Lord Wembly asked. "Well that is nothing. Nothing at all."

"No! At least, I had not considered that a possibility. It's called word swimming. When I look at a book, the words swim on the page. You see, I cannot read because of it."

Ugh, she'd said it. She'd never wanted to say it, but now Lord Wembly knew it.

CHAPTER EIGHTEEN

VERITY HAD FINALLY admitted it. She could not read. She had word swimming.

Lord Wembly wrinkled his forehead. "Is that similar to word spinning?"

"Possibly?" Verity had never heard the term, but then she'd never heard of word swimming before her father had mentioned it.

"The words mix themselves up so it's all a jumble?" Lord Wembly asked.

"Yes, that is exactly what happens. So you see, another gentleman, a more sportsmanlike gentleman, might not mind—"

"I'm sportsmanlike!"

"What I mean is, a gentleman who might always be off fencing or boxing—"

"I fence and I box. Very well, actually."

"You see what I say, though. You are an intellectual. You are a member of The Royal Society. You read and think and conjecture. How could you consider…what I mean is books and the knowledge in them mean everything to you."

"*You* mean everything to me. Why should I care that you have a case of the word spins? For all I know, I might go gouty in my middle age. Would you mind it?"

"Of course not," Verity said. "If you were gouty, I would just put your foot up on a padded stool and give you willow bark tea and make you give up your port." She was babbling now, she knew it. He'd said: "You mean everything to me." And here she was, babbling about the gouty foot he might or might not someday be afflicted with.

The balcony doors swung open, and Lord Kendrickson poked his head out.

"Get out!" Lord Wembly shouted at him. Lord Kendrickson took on a look of alarm and disappeared, the doors closing behind him. "Lady Verity Nicolet, before anything or anybody else tries to stop me, I adore you and could not care less that you get the word spins. Will you consent to wed me and live in my ridiculously complicated house in Somerset forevermore?"

"Yes! Yes, I do," Verity said. "That is, if you are certain—"

"Of course I am certain, you ridiculous girl. I'm an intellectual, at least give me credit for knowing my own mind."

He was sure. It had happened. He'd said it. He'd said it even though he knew she could not read. It was a miracle. What next? What would he do next?

Lord Wembly reached for her and pulled her into his arms. That was next. He pulled her into his very strong arms. He was such a man!

He kissed her gently and whispered, "You will put up with my red hair, then? Realistically, we might even have red-haired children."

"I adore your hair."

He put the bracelet on her wrist, fiddling with the delicate clasp until he'd got it closed. Then he kissed her again, and then again. The cold air did not seem so cold now. The world did not seem so dangerous now. As he kissed her neck and played with the curls in her hair, it really did seem a miracle. She was to marry. Most importantly, she was to marry as she was, not as some invented version she'd pretended to be.

Or even more importantly than that, she was to marry *this* man.

The balcony doors opened once more. Wembly growled, but

then suddenly took a step back.

"That's probably enough now, Wembly," Verity's father said.

"Yes, of course, Your Grace, it's just that things…"

"Got a little out of hand?" the duke asked.

"Papa, Lord Wembly has asked me to wed, and I know you will approve as you are the most darling father that ever lived, and I could not admire you or dote on you more."

The duke laughed. "I suppose I must agree then, given that flowery bit of inducement. Though, I certainly will not approve of any further mauling of my daughter at a ball. Fix her hair, Wembly, and then come back inside."

The duke left them out there to undo any damage that had been done. Lord Wembly did fix her hair, though it took some time to do so as there were considerable interruptions of the kissing variety. He did finally put her into some sort of order, and they reentered the ballroom.

The queen was looking very approving of them, and she gave Verity a little hand wave to signal she need not return to Her Majesty's side.

Wembly led her to one of only three card tables set up at the other end of the ballroom. "Let us pretend at piquet so nobody bothers us," he said.

Verity was exceedingly agreeable to it. Lord Wembly allowed various footmen to approach with wine and bits of the delicacies that Lady Darlington sent round, but otherwise just held his hand up when anybody else thought to approach their table. He was delightfully rude about it. Eventually, all the young gentlemen who no doubt wished to mention the prints and snicker over it got the message.

"What shall I call you?" Verity asked.

He looked as if he'd not considered the matter. "I suppose whatever you like. Wembly, or my given name is Henry."

"All my sisters call their husbands by their title names, but I do like Henry. Perhaps I will use both, Henry for in private."

"I will answer to both then. Now, considering what a palaver this courtship has been, I hope you were not thinking of a long engagement?"

"Goodness, no," Verity said. "Let us wed before anything else happens."

Henry nodded. "Agreed. I shudder to think what could be next if we dare to delay."

Verity giggled. He really did have the most delightful dry wit.

"And the wedding trip—I suppose you have ideas? At least, Lady Pegatha assures me it is a subject a lady will have given a great amount of thought to."

In fact, Verity had no ideas at all. She'd been so wrapped up in her word swimming, and the preposterous story about fish eyesight, and the ensuing prints, that there'd been no room for such considerations. It had seemed impossible that she'd ever get as far as going on a wedding trip. "I've not given it any thought at all," Verity said.

"I am certain there is something extravagant we could arrange—perhaps I might rent a fine house in Brighton?"

"To be truthful, I do not much care. Let us just go somewhere we can be alone." Verity supposed it was a rather shocking thing to say, as ladies were not meant to think of, or wish for, such things. But she was thinking it and she was wishing it.

Lord Wembly's brows raised just a little bit. "That is certainly not Brighton, then. Do you suppose you would not mind if it were a very simple sort of place?"

"I would not mind at all." What did she care where they went? They might hole up in a cave somewhere if he liked it.

"I do have a house on the Isle of Wight; it is old inherited land. The view is terrific, it overlooks the sea from a high cliff, but the house is nothing much. Just a small cottage. I go there sometimes if I look for peace and quiet to conduct my research." Lord Wembly paused. "Which is the other thing you might not like aside from the simplicity of it—it is full of books. Walls and walls of books. I would not like you to feel uncomfortable by being surrounded by them."

"But that is just it—I would like to know everything in books," Verity admitted. "If I could read them. I suppose you realize we will have to hire a lady to do it for me, which I know is an added expense you would not have accounted for."

"Fortunately, I am very rich," Lord Wembly said.

"Yes, you are, I had forgotten."

"We will go to the Isle of Wight, to my little cottage there, and I will read to you whatever you like. We can walk along the cliffs and there is a woman there who arranges for my meals. Our meals."

And so it was settled. They would wed as quickly as humanly possible and then they would travel to the Isle of Wight, and Lord Wembly would begin to reveal what had been hidden away from her all her life by reading to her. She had been wholly dependent on Winsome reading to her and Winsome always gravitated to terrible novels. There was so much to find out!

"Verity?"

It was her aunt, Lady Marchfield. At her approach, Lord Wembly had almost raised his hand to drive her away as he'd done with some others, but then he seemed to think better of it.

"Aunt," she said.

"I would caution you that you have been at this table, alone with a gentleman, for an excessive amount of time. In full view of the queen, no less. I understand she was so kind as to transport you here. I do not think you repay her courtesy with this behavior. It is not seemly. Lord Wembly? I would have counted on you to know better."

"We are engaged, Aunt," Verity said, laughing. "Look." She held up her bracelet for Lady Marchfield to see.

"We are planning our wedding trip," Lord Wembly said.

"Nevertheless..." Lady Marchfield said to no point. Verity thought she looked a little put out over hearing of the engagement. Certainly, her aunt wished for her to be well-settled. But then, perhaps it irked her to be so often proved wrong, especially after her experience with Mr. Klonsume. And then Verity was supposed to have ruined her chances by spouting off about fish eyesight, but somehow, she had not.

"The queen is all for it," Verity said. If there was anything that would affect Lady Marchfield, it was hearing of the approval of a lady more powerful than herself. Nobody had more power than the Queen of England. Not even the king these days.

"The queen approves? I see," Lady Marchfield said. "Well then, congratulations on this…miracle."

Verity nodded at her aunt, and for once the lady was not far wrong. It really did seem miraculous, though perhaps not for the reasons Lady Marchfield thought. Her aunt drifted off, no doubt deciding to save her strength and live to fight another day.

Now that Verity was looking around the ballroom, she could not miss that Lady Lilith was glaring at her. Lord Wembly's eyes drifted in that direction too and he suppressed a sigh.

"Is there a reason she looks so put out?" Verity asked. "Have I done something to offend the lady?"

"I believe she might have had some…hopes…let's call it. In my direction."

"Oh, I see, goodness, that is terrible. She must be heartbroken."

"I really do not think—"

"Never mind it," Verity said.

"Yes, that is exactly what I would wish."

Verity supposed he thought the matter was to be forgotten, though that was not precisely what she'd meant. She would call on Lady Lilith and smooth things before the wedding. After all, she knew what it felt like to be heartbroken, and she did not think Lady Lilith even had any sisters to console her.

And now that she thought about sisters, she would have one to console herself. Valor would not be enthusiastic to discover another sister would leave the house. "Valor," she said softly.

"She will not be pleased, I imagine?"

Verity shook her head. "Lord Thorpe got her a puppy, Sir Galahad. Though, never mention that to her—she does think she rescued the dog from an evil earl intent on drowning him."

"That was all set up by Lord Thorpe, though?"

"As a distraction, and it worked very well."

"I understand Sir Galahad is the most tremendous dog in England. At least, I've been told so more than once. Perhaps I might do something for him."

"What do you think of?"

"Let me work on it. Ah, here comes your father."

"Well, Verity, guess what? We've been left high and dry by our monarch. Said she had enough amusement for one evening and we could make our own way home. Slipped out the back like a housebreaker to avoid the palaver of leaving in state."

HENRY COULD NOT be more pleased with how the night had unfolded. It had its high mountaintops and low valleys, but it had come right in the end. He was an engaged man. Engaged to the most delightful lady in England.

It was almost hard to believe his luck.

The idea that Lady Verity experienced word spinning had come as a surprise, though he found it did explain quite a lot. It was no matter; they would hire a woman in Somerset to take over the task. In the meantime, he would act as Lady Verity's reader. Why not? Should not a man besotted read to his wife?

As the queen had left her party behind with no conveyance home, Henry had instantly offered his own carriage. They waited for Lady Darlington to name the prizes for the costumes and then they were off. Henry was not surprised that Lady Verity came out victorious for the best costume—she'd been dressed by the queen, nobody else would have stood a chance. Still, she was exceedingly pleased with the India shawl she'd won and would hand it over to Valor to soften the oncoming blow.

The carriage ride had been a bit awkward, as Henry could not leap across the seat to Lady Verity with her father sitting right next to her. Lady Pegatha smoothed it over by rattling on about the various costumes and who had looked charming and who had, perhaps, flattered themselves. According to his aunt, a lady of Mrs. Patton's years had no business dressing as a saucy lady's maid.

The duke had laughed heartily. "I believe the effect was meant to be pert, but her girth rather defied the idea."

As Lady Pegatha and the duke went on, he and Lady Verity simply stared at each other. Just as they had done when he'd gone to the duke's house for dinner.

It seemed he would have the opportunity to stare at the lady all his life.

They'd reached the duke's house and Henry was determined to escort Lady Verity to her door. It was entirely unnecessary, as the duke was there, but Henry hoped His Grace would not mind too much.

The duke was a liberal sort of gentleman so pretended he did not particularly notice. While his back was turned, Henry gave Lady Verity a light kiss on the cheek.

"Oh no!" a cry came from over their heads.

Henry looked up to see Lady Valor hanging out a window. And looking rather irate.

"I'd better go in and smooth things over," Lady Verity said.

"I will come tomorrow," Henry said.

"Yes, but don't miss the lecture at The Royal Society," she said. "I will be quite interested to hear of it."

"Really? The effect of magnesia on uric acid?"

"No, not really. But I should not like to interfere with your studies." Lady Verity paused. "You do not dissect monkeys, do you?"

"No," he said, laughing. "I do not dissect anything."

She looked most relieved to hear it, and Henry supposed she'd picked it up from the correspondence between Carlisle and Symmons regarding the circulatory systems of slow-moving animals.

"Verity?" the duke said.

"Go away!" Lady Valor shouted at him from overhead.

Henry bowed and made his way back to the carriage. He climbed in and then waved to her as she peeked out the drawing room windows.

Lady Pegatha sat back, looking very pleased. "So you've done it."

"I have done it."

"I think you will do very well together."

"I think so too."

CHAPTER NINETEEN

VERITY HAD BEGUN to look upon her youngest sister as a capricious potentate who could only be soothed by offerings laid at her feet. When she'd gone abovestairs after the masque, she'd ignored Valor's glare and handed over the India shawl she'd won from Lady Darlington. Valor had been the littlest bit mollified, or so Verity had thought.

As it happened, what had mollified Valor was a sudden idea that had come into her mind. The following morning, she'd convinced Thomas to deliver a letter to Lord Wembly's house by claiming Verity wrote it and it was a secret love note.

It had been anything but. Valor had gone so far as to compose a letter and sign Verity's name to it.

Fortunately, Lord Wembly had not been at all fooled by it. He brought it along when he came to the house the following day. Handing it to Verity in the drawing room, he remarked upon Lady Valor's suspicious absence. She would later be found hiding in a corner of her bedchamber with Sir Galahad.

Verity had unfolded the note to reveal the most outrageously composed breaking off of an engagement.

Lord Wembly—

It pains me to take this step but I must tell you to go away forever. After thinking about things, I realized that I cannot leave my Papa, or my sisters, or Sir Galahad. What do you really have to offer against all that? Also, I don't want to be stared at while I'm asleep.

My mind is made up. Do not ever come to the house to talk to me about it! This is goodbye forever! Do not come here!

Verity Nicolet

One might imagine a young lady breaking off an engagement that was not her own would be scolded severely. Which she certainly would have, had the duke not found the letter so amusing. At the end of it, Valor had only shrugged and said she must have been sleepwalking when she wrote it. She really could not remember anything about it.

The following day, despite his having his troth broken by her hand, Valor received a rather magnificent gift. Lord Wembly had delivered a bed for Sir Galahad.

Rather than the pile of blankets by the window that he liked to nap on, or Valor's bed when she was around to lift him into it, this was a bed fit for a monarch's canine. It was a four-poster canopy bed in miniature, with silk hangings and an overstuffed mattress. It even came with a brass plaque announcing it belonged to Sir Galahad, the most tremendous dog in England.

Like the capricious potentate she was, Valor was greatly soothed by this offering from one of her acolytes. She took to sitting with Mrs. Right and, under the housekeeper's close direction, sewing little pillows to go on this remarkable new bed. The duke had since been informed that it must travel with them to the Dales.

Winsome predicted her chances of a successful season without Valor throwing a lit torch on the proceedings grew slimmer by the day. At least, if history was anything to go by.

Since then, Lord Wembly had come every day. Sometimes, they sat in the drawing room. Sometimes, they rode to the park with the duke's grooms following for propriety's sake. Verity was insistent that Lord Wembly not miss any special lectures at The Royal Society. He would come and recount what he'd heard, even the effects of magnesia on reducing uric acid. Verity took it all in, every new fact was interesting.

The morning came when she was determined to call on Lady Lilith. She did not know if it were the lady's at-home day, but she had discovered where the lady resided through Felicity. She was on Berwick Street.

Verity had not prior traveled to Berwick Street. It was respectable enough, but she'd somehow assumed that Lady Lilith would live on a square. Despite the very modest appearance of the street and worrying that Felicity might have got it wrong, Verity was determined to proceed. She could not ignore a heartbroken lady and was determined to cheer her up.

She would point out all the admiring glances she'd seen going in Lady Lilith's direction. Verity had not seen any particularly admiring glances, but that had only been because she'd not been looking out for them. Lady Lilith was very pretty and an earl's daughter. Certainly there had been no end of admiring glances.

Her father's groom rapped on the door. He had to rap several times and Verity waited for some minutes before it was answered by a rather surprised young lady in a stained apron. At least, Verity supposed she must be surprised as her mouth was hanging open.

"Lady Verity Nicolet," she said. "I've come to call on Lady Lilith, if it is convenient."

LILITH HAD SPENT the past week attempting to dodge her father over the idea that she must seriously consider Mr. Grantley's suit. It was not that her father was at all admiring of Mr. Grantley, or at all admiring of the idea that his daughter might marry a gentleman in trade. It was just the economy of the thing. They might scrape the money together for another season but what was it all for? Their best chance had been Lord Wembly, and he had engaged himself elsewhere.

Lady Verity had stolen Lord Wembly right from under her nose. She'd taken one of the few single gentlemen who did not need a substantial dowry.

"I'll give you one thing," Clara said, "it's a deal more complicated to be one of the high and mighty than I thought. I got a pa who makes a fine living so I can marry or not and won't find myself in the poor house. Then here is you, having to marry a fellow you don't even like."

"I do not have to marry Mr. Grantley," Lilith said. "I've not agreed to it. At least, not yet."

There had been incessant knocking on the downstairs door. Lilith presumed it was a tradesman dunning for a bill. "Why does not that kitchen maid answer it and tell that person to be gone?" Lilith said.

"She'll be pretendin' she don't hear it, the little minx," Clara said. "I'll go and see to it."

Before Clara could go and see to it, the kitchen maid threw the door open and said, "She's come to see ya. A lady."

The kitchen maid stepped aside, and Lady Verity sailed into the room. Lilith and Clara leapt to their feet.

"Lady Verity?" Lilith asked, hardly believing her own eyes. Why was she here? She must have discovered Lilith was the author of the print. Was she to be denounced? Was everybody to know what she'd done?

Lady Verity crossed the room and took her by the hands. "Lady Lilith, how well you look! I apologize for barging in unexpectedly, but I did not know when your at-home day was and I was determined to see you. You do not mind it?"

Lilith shook her head. It was an extremely odd and exceedingly friendly greeting if it was a prelude to any recriminations about the print.

"I'll arrange tea," Clara said, bobbing a curtsy and running from the room.

"Might I sit?" Lady Verity asked.

"Yes, of course," Lilith said.

They sat on the sofa of the cramped room that was used as a drawing room of sorts. "What a pleasant room," Lady Verity said. "It's sunny, which is always so cheerful."

Lilith looked around. Certainly, for a lady like this, a lady who lived on Grosvenor Square in a fine house, there was nothing particularly pleasant about the room. Was she being mocked? Was it being pointed out to her that the room was small and the furnishings worn?

"I did so long to see you," Lady Verity said, "I found I could not delay longer."

Certainly the lady knew about the print and had come to gloat over her success. Lilith found herself too tired to even fight against it. "You've won, Lady Verity. I freely admit it. Do your worst."

Lady Verity seemed entirely startled by the admission. "If by won," she said slowly, "you mean Lord Wembly. Yes, we are engaged. I have not come to do my worst, whatever that would entail. I came because I know what it is to be heartbroken, and you do not have sisters to commiserate with. You did love him, I imagine?"

Lilith was sent into a tailspin. She'd come as a sister? It was preposterous.

"I can see that you do, or at least did," Lady Verity said, shaking her head sadly. "But I am of the belief that fate has a plan for all of us. Whoever is truly meant for you will appear. I am quite sure of it."

This was too much. Who was she to speak in such a manner? Was she to act the local vicar counseling one of his flock? "Oh yes, fate has a plan for me all right," she said bitterly. "I will be forced to wed a man in trade who is ten years my senior because of my father's reduced circumstances. Lord Wembly might have prevented all that. He is very rich and does not require a dowry, which I do not have. But as you said, fate had something else in store."

Clara came into the room with their sad-looking tea tray.

Lilith wished there had been no tea coming at all. She wished Lady Verity to leave, and she certainly did not wish the lady to note the difference between this paltry service and what she was used to at home.

"Did you love Lord Wembly, though?" Lady Verity asked.

"I liked him well enough," Lilith said, pouring the tea and spilling some of it on the linen that covered the cracked porcelain tray.

"But you see, I love him," Lady Verity said. "I really, really love him and do not give a toss for his money. I would love him if he had nothing at all."

That was the absolute limit. She would love him if he had nothing at all. "Oh yes, why not?" she said. "It is insanely easy to imagine one would not mind doing without funds when one has never experienced it. I can assure you it is not so easy when you *have* experienced it."

Lady Verity took her cup from Lilith's shaking hands. "I see. But will your father really press you to wed a gentleman you do not like?"

"What choice will we have? If I return to Town next year, will there magically be a gentleman turned up who does not give a toss for my lack of funds?"

"It's all to do with the dowry," Lady Verity said, tapping her finger on her chin.

Lilith was really beginning to wonder if Lady Verity were dense or if she were feigning ignorance. Of course it was all to do with the dowry!

"I have an idea," she said. "I will write to the queen. She is imposing, frightening really, but she is very kind. She helped me, I do not see why she would not help you in some fashion. Yes, I will do it."

"Write to the queen?"

"Yes, goodness, I imagine she does not understand your circumstances. How could she? I, myself, did not entirely understand. But I really believe she might be willing to do something. I do not know what, but if you are suddenly called to Buckingham and Lady Pembroke is to escort you and Lord Dartmouth meets the carriage, do not be frightened!"

Lilith did not know quite what to make of it. Lady Verity wished to write the queen on her behalf. Lilith believed she would do it, too. She had expected Lady Verity to swan in and gloat over her victory, but instead she was devising a ridiculous scheme to try to help. It was not a scheme that had a hope of producing anything, but nevertheless.

That print she'd devised about Lady Verity, that print that had begun to haunt her, loomed large in her mind.

"I can see you are dubious over the idea," Lady Verity said. "But just think, the queen summoned me over that mocking print that went round. As you can imagine, I thought the very worst when I walked into the palace. I thought I might be sent back to Yorkshire, or even to prison because The Royal Society was caught up in it. I still don't know if it's a crime to mock an institution with a royal seal. That is not what happened, though. The queen was determined to help me, and she did help me. By the by, she composed that print of Lord Wembly on a fainting couch, she was that on my side of things."

Lilith burst into tears. She could not hold it in longer. She could face anger, but not pity. Not kindness when there should be ridicule.

"You cannot help me," she sobbed. "You should not help me."

Lady Verity handed her a handkerchief. "Do not be ridiculous. I *can* help you and I *will* help you."

"Not when you know why you cannot help me."

The next half hour was spent informing Lady Verity of precisely what had gone on with that very first print. It was perhaps to Lady Verity's credit, and an homage to her character, that she had never once suspected it was another lady at the bottom of it.

When she'd finished, she expected Lady Verity to storm out and inform all and sundry that Lady Lilith was at the bottom of it all. Why not and who cared? After all, Lilith would be forced to accept Mr. Grantley and would have already fallen so far down in the world that an extra push to the bottom of the well would mean little.

"You were that desperate to avoid marrying the older man your father has suggested to you. Well, it cannot be allowed to go forward, it is too cruel. I will write the queen today and we will see what comes of it. In the meantime, tell your father to keep faith. His daughter is not done for yet!"

With that, Lady Verity took her leave. Lilith sat for some minutes feeling frozen where she was. What in the world had just happened?

VERITY HAD BEEN well-pleased with her visit to Lady Lilith. Of course, it was not entirely pleasing to know that Lady Lilith had designed that print that had started all the trouble. But then the trouble had ended wonderfully, and it was well that Verity would not forever wonder who'd done it. That part of it had really weighed on her. Was she to wonder each time she was introduced to someone new? Was it you? Or if not you, do you know who it was?

As well, the lady had found herself in desperate circumstances and had only lashed out. Her tears had told the tale of guilt and so Verity could not be angry with her. How could she possibly be? She had everything and Lady Lilith had nothing. She would be terrified to be in Lady Lilith's shoes. She thought Lady Lilith was right when she pointed out that it was a simple matter to imagine one would not mind lacking funds, and then it was another thing to actually experience it.

Verity was as good as her word and wrote the queen. It was a daring thing to do, but it was the only thing she could think of to help. She'd briefly considered asking her father if he might fund

Lady Lilith, but then she recalled he was already tasked with funding seven daughters. He was ever so cheerful in the face of such a burden but perhaps he would not like to fund eight.

In any case, she thought her letter to the queen just might produce results. She instinctively felt that Queen Charlotte was amused to make herself involved in Verity's own situation. So why not Lady Lilith? Perhaps it took the queen's mind off the poor king. And so between the flurries of activity that went on in preparation for a wedding, she had written the Queen of England.

Verity's father had been convinced by both herself and Lord Wembly that there should be no unnecessary delay to the wedding, considering what had transpired so far. The duke and her intended had gone together to Doctor's Commons to secure a special license and the day was set.

They had intended to have the ceremony in the drawing room and a reception in the dining room, with only close relations attending. That plan was a bit thrown up in the air when Verity unexpectedly received a reply to the letter she'd written to Queen Charlotte regarding Lady Lilith's pitiable circumstances.

Lady Verity—

I am rather astonished at the temerity of your recent letter. I had no inkling that one of my subjects would attempt to coerce me into raising up a lady who is in straightened circumstances. You are, indeed, daring to do it.

On the other hand, it was kindly done and I do not like to think of an earl's daughter being forced to wed under the circumstances you have described. I will consider it.

In the meantime, I understand from the Archbishop that Wembly has obtained a special license. I presume you wed in St. George's. An invitation to myself and Lady Pembroke would not go amiss.

Charlotte R

There was some confusion about what to do next. Finally, the duke sent an invitation to Buckingham House outlining that the wedding would be a small one and held at Grosvenor Square. Verity had almost hoped the queen would decline to come as the day was likely to be fraught enough. But, she'd written that she liked to see the outcomes of her efforts and so she would come. Though, she remained dubious over the idea that a duke's daughter would have such a small ceremony.

Verity supposed she should be deeply honored by the queen's wish to attend, though she felt she could do without the honor. One thing she did do, though, was invite Lady Lilith. She would be introduced to the queen, who now knew her circumstances. Perhaps that might set off ideas in the queen's mind about what might be done.

The rest of the staff took the news of the queen attending rather hard. The duke's household descended into a frenzy. Nobody was more frenzied than Cook, who declared that the original menu must be thrown out entirely and he must start anew. He would also require a large increase in his budget for the celebration.

There were tradesmen of all descriptions that must be hired, and everything must be fit for a queen. He had planned to bake the wedding cake himself, but that was no longer sufficient! Monsieur Bernard must be contracted with at once! Monsieur Bernard was the only man in London to bake a cake worthy of a queen. As well, multiple pineapples must be had, no matter the expense! Furthermore, Lewis & Lewis must be assigned to make the ices!

Mrs. Right did mention, several times, that it was not the queen getting married, but Verity. He ignored that piece of information and informed Mrs. Right that he would never get over it if he failed and the Thames was within walking distance— he would disappear forever!

As no lord with any modicum of sense wished for a cook in the throes of a mental collapse, the duke speedily agreed to all of his demands. As the temperature of feelings in the house rose, Verity had begun to fret over all the details and if they would meet with the queen's approval. However, her father assured her he'd got everything in hand. Then Wembly had pointed out that no matter what went on, they would be married at the end of it. Mrs. Right suggested Verity turn her mind to more personal things, like her dress.

So she did. She had loved the dress from the moment Madame LaFray had sketched it for her. It was the palest yellow chiffon with a matching silk underdress. It was simple but for the intricate embroidery around the hem of flowers growing in a garden. The flowers were all different types and colors, and of different heights—peonies, delphinium, lavender, and hollyhock. It spoke of newness and springtime, precisely what she wished to say in this moment.

It *was* actually the moment, too. She was in her dress while Valor sulked on her bed and Winsome weighed in on what jewelry to wear.

"The dress is so delicate," Winsome said, "wear the simple diamond necklace. Rubies, emeralds, or sapphires will clash with it."

Verity was inclined to agree. "Though, I must wear the sapphire bracelet given to me by Henry."

"Henry!" Valor called from the bed. "You call him *Henry*? I'm so embarrassed and I'm not even doing it."

Verity had some grave concerns over how Valor would conduct herself while the queen was in the house. It was all well and good for her to make boldly ridiculous statements and complaints when it was only family, but not within the queen's hearing.

"Valor, I will remind you that the Queen of England is going to attend the wedding. You must be on your very best behavior and say nothing to offend."

"I never say anything to offend," Valor said sulkily.

Winsome snorted. Verity said, "It is an actual crime to offend the queen. You shall not like Papa to go to prison over it?"

"That's right," Winsome said. "You are too young to be locked up so Papa would have to go in your place."

Valor leapt off the bed as if it had caught fire and raced to the door.

"Where are you going?" Verity asked.

"To tell Thomas I put sugar in the salt cellars on the table so he can fix it!"

Valor disappeared out the door. Verity sighed as Winsome put the delicate diamond necklace around her neck and did the clasp.

"Do not worry about Valor, she'll be all right now that she thinks Papa might have to pay for her crimes," Winsome said. "Are you ready? Really ready to get married?"

"Very ready," Verity said.

Winsome seemed pensive. "I know I let Valor do all the complaining, but it really is sad that we are not all together anymore. Now I'll go home with just Valor."

"But there is always the London season every year, Winsome. That's when we can all be together."

"I know, but will you not miss the Dales?"

"I will, but it's time for me to make my own home now. It will be your turn next year."

"I hardly feel ready."

"But you will, when the time comes."

Mrs. Right bustled into the room. "Everybody but for the queen has arrived, including Lady Lilith. You ought to go down, your fiancé is looking in fine form."

Of course he would do. Wembly always looked in fine form.

Another worry clutched at Verity's heart. She'd been assured nothing could go wrong there, but had that been right? "Mr. Amesbey, the curate from Grosvenor Chapel? Has he come?"

"Oh, aye, he's here," Mrs. Right said with a chuckle. "Though I think he is still on the fence over whether or not I might have sold my soul to the devil, as I hinted to him last year. Further weighing on his mind, the queen will come to hear his delivery. He is upright, but I think he feels it."

Verity nodded. Last season, Mrs. Right had managed to convince another one of Lady Marchfield's butlers, Mr. Cremble, that she was in league with the devil. Mr. Cremble had brought in Mr. Amesby to, well, she was not sure what—get the devil out of Mrs. Right? In the end, Mr. Cremble took himself off, and he was to get Lord Marchfield's living, so everything had worked out rather splendidly for him. However, Verity supposed the whole thing had left Mr. Amesby wondering what went on in the duke's house.

"I wouldn't fret over it," Winsome said. "At least we do not have to contend with that scoldy Bishop Porteus. In any case, once the curate sees that the queen attends us, he will not dare speculate that Mrs. Right has gone to the devil."

Verity nodded. Bishop Porteus had indeed been frightening. At least to everyone but for the duke. She gave herself a little shake. She wished to throw off all worry and fear—she was going to be married. Bishops, queens, curates, none of it mattered. She was going to be married to Henry Foster, Baron Wembly, and he was divine.

CHAPTER TWENTY

HENRY WAS IN the front hall, awaiting Lady Verity's descent. He'd felt compelled to do so. Such was his luck in securing the lady, he would not fully believe in it until they were pronounced married. It was not completely unknown that a bride might change her mind at the last minute. It would cause a scandal, but he did not suppose a scandal would ever put the duke off.

Then, of course, one never knew if Lady Valor would attempt to throw a wrench into the works. He had already seen that young lady cause some sort of ruckus in the dining room. It was to do with the salt cellars, though what specifically, he had no idea.

And then, Lady Lilith was in attendance. Verity had told him all about writing to the queen on Lady Lilith's behalf, which he'd really not thought a good idea. However, she told him after it was already done so there was no point debating it. Now the queen would attend them. His bride had been determined to have Lady Lilith on hand so she might be in front of Her Majesty.

He heard a stir from above and looked up. There she was, accompanied by Mrs. Right and Lady Winsome. She was perfect. Her dress seemed to float in the air around her and it was everything pure and sunshine. His lady really did have very refined taste.

She skipped down the stairs to him. "Verity," he said, "you

look lovely. The loveliest lady in London. You are perfect."

She stood on her tiptoes and kissed his cheek. "Hello, my baron."

Just then, Charlie raced through the front hall. "The queen! Her carriage just arrived."

Henry held his arm out and Verity leaned on it. Though she had met the queen twice already and she'd found the lady very kind, she seemed nervous to find the Queen of England was moments from stepping into her father's house.

"Steady on," he whispered.

She smiled at him. Charlie threw the doors open. The queen and Lady Pembroke stepped into the great hall and both footmen bowed low. Thomas in particular bowed so low that Henry wondered if his forehead had touched his knees. He led Lady Verity forward and they made their obeisance.

"A handsome couple, do not you think, Lady Pembroke?" the queen said.

"Very handsome indeed," Lady Pembroke said.

The duke, hearing of the arrival, came from the drawing room to greet the queen. He led her and Lady Pembroke to places of honor. Henry led Verity in, handed her over to the duke, and approached the curate.

The drawing room was full of people, as the duke had a large family. All of the elder sisters and their husbands had come. It was only Lady Pegatha and Leland Dunmore, the Marquess of Manderbey, for his side. Manderbey, who'd he'd been friends with since his school days, had come in from Hertfordshire for the ceremony. Lady Verity was accompanied by her bridesmaids, Lady Winsome and Lady Lilith. Lady Valor might have been a bridesmaid too, but she was currently sulking in the back row of chairs and whispering, no doubt, insulting things to her dog.

Henry had attended his share of weddings over the years, but he was not certain he'd ever seen one presided over by a curate who appeared minutes from a faint. The poor man's hands shook, his face was pale, and his voice wavering. Henry was not certain if the cause was some prior interactions with the duke, or the queen's attendance. Perhaps it was both.

Nevertheless, the fellow plowed on. The duke gave his daughter to him and Henry said his piece. "With this ring I thee wed, with my body I thee worship, and with all my worldly goods I thee endow. In the Name of the Father, and of the Son, and of the Holy Ghost. Amen."

He slipped the ring onto Lady Verity's finger. He'd had it specially designed as an acrostic spelling out troth: topaz, ruby, onyx, tourmaline, and heliodor. He had pledged his troth, and his lady would know it every day of her life.

What a lucky man he was.

LILITH HARDLY KNEW how she came to be a bridesmaid attending Lady Verity and Lord Wembly's wedding, with the Queen of England just feet away from her. Lady Verity had informed her that she'd written to the queen on Lilith's behalf and that the queen indicated she would consider it.

She did not know what could be done for her, should the queen decide to take an interest. What she did know, though, was that she would be forever grateful to Lady Verity Nicolet, now Baroness Wembly, for her kindness. Even if she was forced to wed Mr. Grantley, she would not forget that somebody had tried to help her, and that particular somebody was the person she had sought to hurt the most.

It had been a powerful lesson, and she was chastened by it. She was also determined to carry forward Lady Verity's example. Should she encounter another lady requiring assistance and should she be in a position to help, she would help. She would take it on as a penance.

As she looked around at the large family gathered round, she wondered...she hoped, that she might have the same someday.

Only time would tell.

VERITY'S MIND, WHICH had been habitually filled with ideas on how she could hide her word swimming, was only filled with one thing now. She was married, she was married, she was married. She was married to Henry Foster, the most wonderful baron to ever take a breath in England.

The ceremony had concluded, and probably in the nick of time for Mr. Amesbey. The poor curate looked vastly relieved to have got through it. The duke, ever liberal, invited him to stay on for the wedding breakfast. Verity was not terribly surprised when he demurred, mentioning prior appointments. He'd hurried out of the house as fast as his legs could carry him.

The party had since moved into the dining room. The footmen had added extra leaves to the table to accommodate the crowd, as on a usual day, they favored smaller parties. Now, not only did they have the queen, Lady Pembroke, and Lord Wembly's friend, the marquess, but when one added in all her sisters and their husbands, it was a proper party.

Since it *was* the queen, the seating arrangements were a bit different than they might have been. That lady took the top of the table with the marquess to her right and the duke took the bottom with Lady Pembroke to his right.

Fortunately, Verity did not give a toss where anybody was sitting. She had been seated next to Henry and he held her hand under the table.

After the wine had gone round, the duke said, "Here we all are. Your Majesty, it has become somewhat of a tradition in this house that my youngest daughter, Lady Valor, starts us off on account of threatening to never leave me and be my hostess forever. Valor?"

Verity was certain her eyes had gone wide. At least, if they were anything like the eyes of her sisters. Valor was wildly unpredictable.

Valor herself was wide-eyed. "Am I allowed?" she said.

"Why not?" the duke said.

"Because you might go to prison, Papa. On account of I'm too young. You'd have to go in my place."

"Oh dear," Verity whispered to Henry, "Winsome and I told her that."

"Prison? What in the world were you planning on saying?" the duke asked.

"Now I am too intrigued, I must hear it," the queen said. "Go on, child, nobody is going to prison."

Valor seemed much encouraged by that assurance. "Well, I will say that just because five of my sisters have made a mistake doesn't mean we all need to make that mistake." She paused and stared meaningfully at Winsome. "It's too late for Verity, but it's not too late for you."

These sage words of advice were met with silence, as nobody quite knew what to say to it. Suddenly, the queen laughed. She said, "Am I to understand that you are firmly against your sisters getting married? Why?"

Valor looked at the queen as if she was perplexed as to why it would need explaining. She said, "The men stare at you while you sleep. Mr. Stratton already admitted it!"

"One time," Mr. Stratton muttered.

"I see," Queen Charlotte said. "I suppose it is hard that you do not have your sisters by your side any longer. I suppose it is hard that they have all gone to other counties."

"It really is!" Valor said.

"Well, young lady, consider this—I was not just sent to another county, I was sent to another country. I did not know the language or the culture very well and I did not meet my king until our wedding day."

This, quite naturally, horrified Valor. "Did you try to run away?"

"Certainly not. I faced it," the queen said. "And over time, the one thing I learned from the English is their ability to chin up and soldier on. As you will do, even if you find the circumstances trying."

"Maybe I could." Then, seeming to consider the idea, Valor said, "Do you want to see my dog? He really is tremendous."

"Perhaps later," the queen said kindly. "I do like a tremendous dog."

And so, they went on very jolly after the hurdle of Valor's speech had been cleared.

It did eventually come time for the couple to depart. Dear Lady Pegatha had given over her house and would stay at the duke's house for the night. In the morning, the couple would set off for the Isle of Wight.

They were waved off by a crowd of people, including the Queen of England. Never had any couple been so blessed.

And then, alone. Finally.

Lady Pegatha's household staff were the souls of discretion. A sideboard in the dining room had been set up with cold meats, cheeses, rolls, and pastries. Bottles of champagne, hock, and lemonade stood on ice blocks in porcelain buckets. Where the people were who had set it all out, Verity could not say. They had seemed to disappear into the walls.

Though it was very considerate of them, she was not at all hungry. Rather, she pointedly glanced at the stairs. Her baron smiled, grabbed a bottle of the hock and two glasses, and took her by the hand. They ran up the stairs laughing all the way.

Henry's room in his aunt's house was far different than what she was used to. She had grown up in a house of seven sisters and their rooms were light and airy and dusted in chiffon and pastels. This was so manly and full of dark wood and the scent of bergamot and oakmoss. It was all man, and it took her breath away.

Then Henry, her all man, took her breath away.

With four older sisters married, Verity had been well informed of all that would take place. She did find, though, that she hardly needed their information. She came to the conclusion that when one was with the right person, no particular instructions or preparations were needed.

Once Henry had removed his shirt and she saw him, the him under his well-pressed linen and perfectly tied neckcloth, she trusted her instincts. As it happened, her instincts were rather good.

Later, they would open the bottle of hock and remove to the window seat overlooking Berkeley Square. The sun had set, and she lay back in Henry's arms as they watched people and carriages going hither and thither. It seemed amazing to them that none of these people seemed to be aware that Lady Verity and Lord Wembly had married that day. These strangers just went about their lives as if nothing at all momentous had happened.

Something momentous had happened, though, and at least they knew it themselves.

They fell asleep in each other's arms, as they would do for the rest of their time together on earth.

THERE WILL ALWAYS be discoveries for the newly married to encounter in those early days. One of the first things that Verity and Henry came upon was that they were both eager to get going in the morning. Henry had been surprised by it, as he'd had the idea that most ladies approached the morning as Lady Pegatha did—a long and slow awakening with breakfast in bed.

As it was, they had bounded out of the house that first morning, both eager to begin their journey to the Isle of Wight.

The further surprise, which Henry had not even thought of, was that his lady did not bring a maid. It was a course in lady's buttons, and it did take some time. It had seemed a deal easier to get them unbuttoned than done up again, but he got the hang of it eventually.

It took them two days in Wembly's carriage to reach Ryde, stopping at The Angel at Guildford that first night. Though really, they hardly noticed the time going by as they were entirely wrapped up in each other, in both their minds and their arms. At Ryde, they spent the night there too and took a wherry in the morning.

Wembly's cottage on the Isle of Wight was charm personified. As Henry had warned, bookshelves lined most of the rooms, but for the bedchambers. The bedchambers had been positioned to look out over the sea with small balconies attached. This allowed the convenience of never needing to close the curtains as there was nothing but water to peek in at them. Considering what a peeper might have seen, that was just as well.

Their days and nights were divided into a pleasing rhythm. At night, they were eyes on each other, and hands on each other. During the day, they lounged on the balcony as Henry read from a book of Verity's choosing. She had wide-ranging interests, no subject was to be discounted, and they had long conversations about what they'd discovered.

Verity's mind had been waiting to be filled, and she took in everything. Over the years, she would become Henry's righthand as he proceeded with his research. She had a remarkable memory for what she'd heard and would often bring up a fact or a point he'd forgotten about. She positively gloried in being able to converse on hundreds of subjects, no longer fearing that she'd invented what she'd just said.

They spent a month in that little cottage and the quiet of it was just what Verity had wanted. There was no better way to begin to deeply understand another person than hours and hours of talking with nobody else listening in.

Verity discovered that Henry had always longed for brothers and sisters and, if not for Lady Pegatha, he would have felt very alone in the world. He did not wish for a quiet house, but one filled with the raucous sounds of life. He even went so far as to say that he would not care if the noise of it interrupted his studies.

As for Henry, he discovered the lengths to which Verity had gone to hide her word swimming. He found out how trying it had been and how she'd always been in terror of being found out.

If she were particularly panicked, she might say something ridiculous. Like inquiring into the eyesight of fish. Despite being surrounded by sisters, it had been lonely hiding a secret.

In their own ways, they had been two lonely people.

Then those two no longer lonely people would retire at night to become better acquainted in other ways. As far as Verity was concerned, intimate relations were a marvel and the sort of thing people did not know they were missing until they experienced it. She wondered that people did not talk about it more.

Wembly Cottage on the Isle of Wight was a place they would return to often. As their family grew, the cottage grew too, until it was a delightfully ramshackle collection of rooms and additions. Eventually, though, they did decide to make their way to Somerset and take up their life as a newly-married couple.

Verity had been pleased as Punch to find her Dales pony already settled into the stables. Riding in Somerset was a bit different but there were still plenty of farmers' fences to jump. Henry did his best to keep up with his bride and manage any complaints from nearby farmers.

Though Verity had been informed of the haphazard nature of her lord's house, some things needed to be seen to be believed. As Henry had described it, the house had begun as a fortress. So many houses in England had but then been torn down and a more modern structure put in its place.

Over the centuries, the Baron Wemblys had not been so inclined. They simply added on to what was there. Henry said his ancestors had never gone in for modern ideas so why go to the expense of a modern house? His own father had gone so far as to say if he ever spied Palladian columns from his grave, he'd come back to haunt the inhabitants who had put them there.

As no famed architect had ever been hired for the various expansions, it was a will-nilly collection. Add rooms over here? Why not? It will only mean that two corridors would now lead to nowhere. What about rooms over there? Why not? We can break through some broom closets to do it.

And then, there had been that one eccentric baron who was convinced the king's soldiers might turn up at any minute to take his estate. That gentleman had devised any number of false walls, fake fireplaces with small doors in the back, and bookshelves that swung open to secret rooms. At one point, Verity began to be certain that there were more secret rooms than regular rooms.

For the first months, Verity had carried one of the maps that were laid all over the house in a pocket to reorient her when she lost her way. She also carried a small bell to indicate her location. Though sometimes, she meant to be lost so Henry could search the house for her. He would be reading in his library and hear the tinkle of a far-off bell and know it was time to put down his books and begin the search for his wife.

Once she was discovered, she would be carried back to their bedchamber to be sure she did not get lost again. They gave up the habit in the years when there seemed to be a child around every corner, but then they took it up again when those children left the house to pursue their own lives. This was much to the chagrin of the household staff, as they thought it was rather unseemly of a middle-aged couple to run around like youths. Henry was a well-built man, though, and he had no trouble throwing his wife over his shoulder despite leaving his prime.

Over the years, they liked to have visitors. For their guests' convenience, Verity suggested to Henry that they ought to add little plaques to the walls that indicated "You are here—drawing room that way" or "You are here—there is nothing but a brick wall that way" and so forth. Verity was certain the signs must help, though Baron Wembly's estate was a popular destination for a house party as couples might disappear and then claim they'd been turned around and lost.

When the first baby came, two years into their marriage, the sprawling nature of the house became even more pronounced in Verity's mind. Young Henry Foster, a red-haired and mischievous sort of boy, was forever wandering away. When he could not be found, all in the house set off with maps to locate him. Of course, in those days he got lost by accident. As Verity and Henry's brood grew to four rambunctious and red-haired boys, they often took themselves off to get lost on purpose.

They even discovered a long-abandoned room high in the ramparts that became the headquarters of The Fearsome Four, as they called themselves.

Verity kept a close eye on all of her boys to catch any signs of word swimming. She would sometimes surprise them with a new book and ask them to read aloud. Somehow, it had skipped a generation. At least, mostly. The youngest of them struggled with reading, though not as severely as Verity had done. Fortunately, he was a farmer at heart and liked nothing more than being atop his horse, surveying his fields, and talking with like-minded men at the tavern about crops. Wembly bought him a small estate not too far from his own where he farmed to his heart's content and let his wife do most of the reading.

All her boys were well-acquainted with the condition so they might look for it in their own children. Verity did not wish for another soul to spend years of their lives in a constant state of fear that somebody would find out about them. Had she and her sisters understood their mother's condition, Verity herself would never have had to keep it a secret. As it was, she'd felt very alone in it.

She did suspect that the condition was more widespread than was generally known. She suspected that people, rich and poor, covered it up in a variety of ways, believing themselves to be the only ones who suffered from it. That, coupled with the fact that she'd wed an exceedingly rich man, prompted her to take steps.

Baroness Wembly arranged for places across England that were manned for a few hours a day with readers. Sometimes nearby a tollhouse, sometimes in the center of a village, some-times attached to a haberdashery or grocer. Any citizen could bring a piece of writing, or a blank paper to be written on, and have a person well-versed help them through it. This gave employment to educated men and women who were not so educated as to become a teacher or had other reasons for not pursuing more formal employment, and it gave a free service to those who had before had to pay for it. As it was not likely to be popular with those who had once charged a fee for such a service, Verity gave those people preference for the job and paid them out of Lord Wembly's pocket. It did come, though, with the caveat that if they were caught charging, they were out.

As for herself, over the years she hired a series of clever girls to read and write her letters. Some of them went on to marry, a few of them took positions as teachers or governesses. As the queen had once enjoyed meddling in her business, Verity greatly enjoyed helping launch those young ladies in whichever direction they chose.

Lilith enjoyed the same. The queen had decided to step in and assist her and had done a rather marvelous job of it. She'd provided a dowry and perhaps most importantly, her public backing. Lilith was wed the very next season to a steady and reliable viscount. She had once had ambitions to rule society, but now she found she enjoyed the peaceful regularity of her viscount. She appreciated having a firm foundation under her feet. Most of all, she appreciated that her children would have just the same. She never forgot Lady Verity's kindness and they would become fast friends over the years. After all, they were practically neighbors and Lilith's influence went a long way to stopping her viscount from firing his gun off at all hours, as had been his habit. Lady Pegatha was often visiting Lilith's house, only to move on to Baron Wembly's house.

Unbeknownst to the people he left behind in England, things worked out rather marvelously for Mr. Klonsume. He was startled, to say the least, to discover that Mrs. Right had cooked up a ruse to get him out of the house. He was not at all surprised that he would have been put forward for a knighthood, but he was gobsmacked that an English housekeeper could fool a clever fellow like himself.

However, the one thing he knew about his American ingenuity was that it never let him down.

Having been sent back on a ship to America, Mr. Klonsume put his American confidence and ingenuity to work. He'd insisted Lady Marchfield fork out the funds for a private berth and a certain amount of money in his possession, and he rubbed shoulders with the other people aboard with deep pockets. It seemed to him that despite Americans being a proud people with every right to be proud, there still was that unspoken regard for nobility and rank. His old employer in New York had been a striver into certain circles and was forever mentioning his pedigree of being descended from one of the passengers of *The Fortune*, the second boat that had arrived after *The Mayflower*. That was nothing compared to Mr. Klonsume's reinvention.

The circles Mr. Klonsume preferred to travel in were not so rarified as to care about *The Mayflower* or any boats that followed, nor would any of the members of those circles have the first idea of whether he'd been actually knighted or not. After all, was it not more pleasant to be a large fish in a small pond than a minnow in the ocean? He was determined to leave the noses-up crowd where they were—it was far more satisfying to be at the top of the hoi polloi.

By the time he docked in New York, he was known as Sir Morus, of the Order of Owen. He'd kept the clothing he'd been given to wear to the knighting ceremony, had there been one, and would wear it on special occasions. As he'd not got hold of a crest, he invented his own and plastered it on every available surface in his household. It was comprised of two lions surrounding a phoenix in flight, carrying his knight's sword to the sky. He had made all sorts of medals to hang on his coats, indicating various braveries done during his time in England. He even invented a Klonsume lineage motto—*We Rise to the Heavens*.

One of the advantages to being seen as rich was that it seemed everybody around one wished for one to be even richer. He was forever being given sage investment advice and did very well using the small pile of money that he'd squeezed out of Lady

Marchfield.

He eventually married the daughter of a rich factory owner from Boston and became even richer. That lady styled herself as Lady Klonsume. It was well he did do so well financially. Now that he was a Sir, he could hardly be expected to hold a job. He often made a great show of writing a letter to Lady Marchfield, an English countess and a great intimate of his, he claimed. He made an even bigger show of it the one time she'd written him back. Of course nobody was privy to the contents of that letter, which instructed Sir Morus in no uncertain terms to stop sending her letters.

Sir Morus and Lady Klonsume were invited everywhere within their strata of society, which was perhaps not at the tippy-top. Being a leader of sorts, he was often able to explain 'how things were done at Buckingham' and what was 'good form.'

American ingenuity had served him all his life, and it continued to do so until the day he died. Though, perhaps his last idea on showing his milieu an example of good form was ill-advised. Well into his seventies, it had not been the most ingenious idea to perish by falling into a lit fire while demonstrating how the English used two fire pokers, elegantly pinched between thumb and forefinger, to rearrange the logs. Especially since it was not even true. But then, one would suppose Mrs. Right would not be surprised to hear that Mr. Klonsume had gone up in flames of his own making.

Lady Marchfield was, if she was anything at all, made of stern stuff. Her brother might wonder when she was going to give up installing butlers into his house in an effort to establish regularity, but she was not such a wilting daisy as that. She found herself very reluctant to admit defeat, as that would mean her brother had prevailed. The duke would likely be happy to know it, as he did enjoy the spectacle of his housekeeper driving those butlers out as fast as they came in. She was already thinking of where she could find the next one.

As a London season had gone once more, a new one would

come again. That would be time for Winsome to take her place in society. In fact, she had already met one gentleman who had sparked interest. The Marquess of Manderbey had attended Verity's wedding, and he was found to be rather divine. Of course, she was doubtful that the marquess had even noticed her.

As for Manderbey, he certainly had noticed. If only the lady were not so suspicious over everything he said. Why did she look at him as if he were some sort of climber or grifter? Why was she always trying to catch him out?

Why would she not? It was not as if any of the duke's daughters would go forward in a rational manner. Where would be the fun in that?

The End

About the Author

By the time I was eleven, my Irish Nana and I had formed a book club of sorts. On a timetable only known to herself, Nana would grab her blackthorn walking stick and steam down to the local Woolworth's. There, she would buy the latest Barbara Cartland romance, hurry home to read it accompanied by viciously strong wine, (Wild Irish Rose, if you're wondering) and then pass the book on to me. Though I was not particularly interested in real boys yet, I was *very* interested in the gentlemen in those stories—daring, bold, and often enraging and unaccountable. After my Barbara Cartland phase, I went on to Georgette Heyer, Jane Austen and so many other gifted authors blessed with the ability to bring the Georgian and Regency eras to life.

I would like nothing more than to time travel back to the Regency (and time travel back to my twenties as long as we're going somewhere) to take my chances at a ball. Who would take the first? Who would escort me into supper? What sort of meaningful looks would be exchanged? I would hope, having made the trip, to encounter a gentleman who would give me a very hard time. He ought to be vexatious in the extreme, and *worth* every vexation, to make the journey worthwhile.

I most likely won't be able to work out the time travel gambit, so I will content myself with writing stories of adventure and romance in my beloved time period. There are lives to be created, marvelous gowns to wear, jewels to don, instant attractions that inevitably come with a difficulty, and hearts to break before putting them back together again. In traditional Regency fashion, my stories are clean—the action happens in a drawing room, rather than a bedroom.

As I muse over what will happen next to my H and h, and

wish I were there with them, I will occasionally remind myself that it's also nice to have a microwave, Netflix, cheese popcorn, and steaming hot showers.

Come see me on Facebook! @KateArcherAuthor